ContRact

Volume One

Brandon Nowakowski

VIC'SLAB

ContRact: Volume One
Distributed by Vic's Lab, LLC

Copyright © 2024 by Brandon Nowakowski

This is a work of fiction. Names, characters, businesses,
places, events and incidents are either the products of the
author's imagination or used in a fictitious manner.

Cover art by Jimmy O.
Cover design by Shoaib Akram.
Artwork copyright © 2024 by Brandon Nowakowski

Printed in the United States of America

First Edition 2024

ISBN-13: 978-1-942178-10-1

Vic's Lab, LLC
P.O. Box 10865
Danville, VA 24543
www.VicsLab.com
A light novel, GameLit, and superhero book community.

Special thanks to all of my patrons at the Fires of Creation Patreon who supported this project and kept me productive. Without all of you, it would not have come to fruition.

Special thanks as well to Vic's Lab for helping me to get this published. You've helped me to live one of my dreams.

CHAPTER ONE
CONTACT

In the bedroom of a non-descript apartment where the only light was provided by the red display of a digital alarm clock reading five fifty-nine A.M., a still figure lay in bed, dead to the world.

The instant the clock changed to read six A.M., before the alarm could let out an entire beep, a hand shot out from underneath the covers and switched it off.

"...That's three days in a row now. Look at me being all responsible." the twenty-year-old man mumbled to himself before swinging his legs over the edge of the bed and planting his feet on the carpeted floor. He made his way to the bathroom, located directly across from the bedroom, and splashed some water on his face to wake himself more thoroughly.

As Issa Aono ran his damp fingers through his brown hair and met his own green-eyed gaze in the mirror, he reflected that things hadn't always been this way. Honestly, he had used to be terrible about getting up in the morning. He had never been overly late during his first year of university, but he had always felt rushed in the mornings.

Eventually though, a couple of weeks after the beginning of his second year, something had just... clicked. He had found himself able to get up in a timely manner and get through his mornings at a leisurely pace. The key had been to settle on a routine.

Really, Issa reflected as he pulled on a button-down shirt, his life as a whole had become a routine. He didn't hate it or anything, but the fact was there.

"What day is it? Oh, yeah, right." Issa idly switched on his CRT television as he went to prepare some manner of breakfast, able to see it clearly thanks to the large cutout in the wall of his kitchen.

"Good morning everyone~ It's Wednesday and you all know what that means: Weird World Wednesday! Some stories are wild, some are wacky and some will just give you the willies! But they're all wonderful and today's story in particular is one that just seems to keep coming back!"

Issa had decided on toast with jam and idly smiled at the upbeat woman who hosted Weird World Wednesdays, whose name was Wendy. The show was, as the name suggested, a weekly segment that ran every Wednesday morning and served as a sort of tabloid program covering topics like the supernatural or particularly juicy criminal activity.

Issa knew better than to take every story on the program seriously, but it had good entertainment value, at least in his opinion. Plus, Wendy's obvious enthusiasm for her segment was infectious.

"That's right! We're talking about those strange and mysterious contracts that supposedly grant wishes! We've gotten all kinds of testimonies about these, but they all say the same thing: Three questions, three answers, one wish. And nobody knows where in the world they come from! In spite of this, they're sure making waves!"

Issa chuckled to himself as he finished off his second piece of toast and listened to Wendy go over some of the more sensational stories that had been passed around on the subject recently. For ongoing stories, she was fond of doing the occasional recap. It was a good way to fill a segment in the event that nothing particularly new or interesting had happened, so Issa assumed that it had just been a slow week.

"You'd better be careful though; whoever or whatever wrote these might be watching you! If you see or hear anything, be sure to give us a call!"

Issa switched off the TV and mused that It was all nonsense, of course, but the bubbly newsgirl had a point: a lot of people were talking about these so-called contracts. It was the sort of thing that made for great urban legend fodder and the younger generations in particular were eating it up.

Still, nonsense or not, there was one part of the show as a whole that resonated with Issa, especially lately:

He just couldn't shake the feeling that he was missing something. That there was something more to the world that was just out of his reach.

This, he reasoned as he shouldered his backpack and exited apartment 203, probably wasn't all that unusual and pretty much anyone could say the same thing. After all, didn't everyone want something more in one way or another?

Issa had been fortunate to find an affordable apartment in relatively close proximity to his university. It only took him about twenty minutes to walk there at a brisk pace. He did as he usually did during his commute and fell into a combination of casual observation and idle thinking.

The sun had begun to rise only recently and the buildings around him threw everything into a dim sort of pseudo-dawn. In spite of the early hour, the streets were already busy with vehicles and pedestrians alike.

Saying something like "already" might be a bit of a misnomer though; I'm not sure if the traffic ever stops completely. The city noise used to bother me, but now I'm completely used to it. I guess people really can adapt to anything.

Issa arrived to class early, as he had started doing a month or so ago. Once or twice, he had been alone in the lecture room, which had been a novel experience the first time it had happened.

"Yo, Issa! Over here!"

Usually, however, there was at least one person there ahead of him. In these cases, nine times out of ten, at least one of those people would be Rao Lassare.

Rao was a sociable young man with dark, reddish-brown shoulder-length hair with bangs that framed his face. He was a year younger than Issa and had only started at the university the previous semester. It would ordinarily be odd for a freshman and a sophomore to have more than one or two classes together, but Rao had apparently done well on some advanced placement tests and earned himself a few credits beforehand.

"Hey, Rao. What did you forget today?"

"Aw, come on. You just *assume* I forgot something?" the young man responded with a cheeky wink that momentarily obscured one of his purple eyes. This was an uncommon color and made him a curiosity, but was not unheard of. If anything, having people stare at his eyes tended to give Rao a bit of a swelled head, especially when it was girls.

Issa responded to his friend's question with a deadpan stare, having indeed automatically assumed that he had forgotten something.

"O-okay, fine. I need to borrow your notes."

The reason for his assumption, quite plainly, was that Rao very nearly always forgot something.

"There, was that so hard?" Issa groused as he leaned over and opened up his pack, only to find that, placed neatly on top of his miscellaneous notebooks, was a rolled-up piece of paper held shut by a red strip of ribbon. It resembled a sort of scroll, save for the fact that it was very obviously regular paper.

Regardless of what it looked like, Issa had absolutely no idea how it had gotten there.

"What's wrong? Did you lose them?" Rao queried as Issa ran through his memories of the previous evening.

I did my homework last night and it definitely wasn't there. Nobody's been in my apartment since then either, so...

...wait, who turned out the lights?

While he had been lost in thought, someone had snuck up behind him and placed their hands over his eyes. There was also the familiar sensation of a pair of firm yet slightly pliable things pressed against his neck.

"So distracted~ What could you be thinking about, hmm? Or maybe it's not some*thing* but some*one?*"

"Good morning, Elsi."

"Wow, no fun." Elsi Thompson pouted before she released Issa and swiped the rolled-up paper from his backpack, waist-length brunette ponytail swaying and hazel eyes glittering with mischief.

Elsi, unlike Rao, was the same age as Issa and they had known each other since they had started at the university the previous year. She was undeniably clever and had a pleasant, playful demeanor, but he had a hard time dealing with her sometimes when she decided to have her fun at his expense. At least, he had at first before he had gotten used to her.

"What's this? A love letter?"

"I'm almost sure it's not." Issa deadpanned as he swiped the paper back from her, "I actually have no idea what it is or where it came from."

"Whoa, seriously? That's super cool, isn't it?"

Issa gave her a confused look, prompting her to explain.

"What if it's, like, one of those magic wish-granting contracts?"

"Oh, come on."

"I'm serious!"

"No way."

"Think about it though."

Issa wasn't having any of it, causing Elsi to pout at him again.

"You at *least* have to open it."

"Fine, fine." Issa rolled his eyes as he tore off the ribbon, resigned to at least humor his friend. He smoothed out the paper and stared dumbly at it while Elsi whirled around, raised her fists and proudly proclaimed, "Called it!"

There, on the page, were three evenly spaced, handwritten lines that divided the page into thirds.

What do you Desire?

What are your Terms?

What is your Payment?

"Looks like I win that bet, huh?" Elsi grinned as she leaned over Issa's shoulder to get a better look at the paper.

"AH-HAH!" Rao's sudden outburst was punctuated with an accusatory finger pointing at Elsi as he leapt up onto his chair.

"I see through your clever deceptions, Elsi Thompson! This was all a *ruse* to make me forget about the *date* you owe me! I won our bet fair and square, so we're still going out tonight!"

Issa and Elsi both stared at Rao uncomprehendingly as he caused the chair to rotate and began laughing maniacally.

"Yes! I will win your heart once and for all! You shall be mine! Muahahaha~"

"...Well, that's Rao for you." Issa decided as he turned back to the paper.

"At least he's happy?" Elsi pondered as she rested herself on Issa's back again, draping her arms over his chest in a half-hearted attempt to get some sort of reaction out of him.

"Anyway, whatcha gonna do with it?" she asked,

gesturing to the paper on the table.

"Probably throw it away." Issa responded after barely a second's thought.

"Really? Seems like a waste."

"Whatever. Class is about to start, so get off me!"

"Right, right."

C-O-N-T-R-A-C-T

Classes that day passed by without any particular incident for Issa, at least externally. He diligently took notes while Elsi alternatively absorbed everything like a sponge or already knew it and Rao practiced various essential life skills such as sketching, staring vacantly at the blackboard and launching paper footballs over Issa's head and trying to land them in Elsi's cleavage.

In actuality, it was just the one football, but Elsi either didn't mind or was bored enough to let it slide because she retaliated by nailing him between the eyes with it. Knowing her, it was probably a little of column A and a little of column B.

Still, even though he was certain that the paper, however the hell it had ended up in his backpack notwithstanding, was just some sort of prank, Issa found himself unable to avoid thinking about it. He had, as he told Elsi, decided to throw it away. Just scrap it and get on with things. He very nearly did too: in-between classes he had held it over a trash can, prepared to let it go.

…But he couldn't. He wasn't able to articulate why, but he kept it.

As he did on days where he didn't have any late classes, Issa used the phone in his apartment to call the local temp agency he worked part-time for doing odd-jobs and asked his boss if there was anything for that evening. He was told that business had been slow that day and there weren't any one-shot tasks that needed doing. He didn't really have any homework to do either.

Thus, Issa found himself with a free evening. Ordinarily, he'd consider hitting up Rao or Elsi, but they were on a date, so that was a no-go.

This was how Issa ended up sitting at his desk in the living room of his apartment, pen in hand and staring at the paper.

"This is crazy…"

What do you Desire?

What are your Terms?

What is your Payment?

Desire, Terms and Payment, huh? So, to put it simply, "What do you want, how do you want it and what will you pay for it?"

Simple. Right. Not.

Issa grasped the bridge of his nose with his thumb and forefinger as he tried to solve the puzzle before him.

It's in short-answer form, so I can put whatever I want. "I want nothing. Go away. Leave me alone."

At that moment, Issa was struck by a sudden memory of a previous episode of Weird World Wednesday.

"Today we're wondering whether who, or what, wrote these weird writs have wonderful wishes they'd like wrought! And wouldn't you know it, one wonderful Weird World Wednesday fan has called in with an idea! Caller, you are on the air!"

"Please, don't talk, just listen. I...I screwed up. I found one, yeah? I made a Contract, but I didn't think. I said I'd give it whatever it wanted if it would grant my wish. Then...then it appeared. They look human, but they're not!"

"I...I don't know what they are, but they're some kind of freaks! This one said it wanted my—AHHHH ***click* *brrrrrrr****"*

"Wow! Well, viewers, that was certainly weird, wasn't it? Let's cut to commercial now, okay?"

Now, there were plenty of call-ins, especially on a show like Weird World Wednesday, that were pranks or dramatizations meant to improve ratings. It was practically expected on a show like that. However, just to be safe, Issa decided that he should take things a bit more seriously.

Right...so no stupid wishes.

Okay, first things first: Desire. What do I want? No, that's not it. The real question isn't "What do I want?" Otherwise that would be the only prompt.

Dots were rapidly being connected and Issa realized the potential ramifications of the mistake he had been about to make by putting down any old thing just for the sake of proving that the paper wasn't real.

"There's not a single damn part of this that's simple!"

Issa sat there, wide-eyed and panting as though he had just run a lap around the apartment building.

Holy...I almost blew it there. Treating this like some easy quiz or something...if this does turn out to be real, I almost screwed myself!

He slumped back in his chair and took deep,

calming breaths, before breaking out into laughter.

Listen to yourself, Issa. You've already nearly convinced yourself that this thing is the real deal. Calm yourself down.

Right. Now the real question: "What do I want badly enough to offer something valuable in return?"

That's right. It has to be something valuable. If I assume that I'm actually bargaining with someone…or something, then I need to make this worth their time as well as mine. So what do I want that badly?

Satisfied that he was at last asking himself the proper question, Issa eagerly gripped his pen, positioned it over the paper and…

…proceeded to write absolutely nothing.

The sheer anticlimax of the moment crashed down on his shoulders like a ton of bricks, causing his pen to clatter to the desk and his elbows to thud onto the wood as he gripped his head in frustration.

After all of that, Issa was stymied by a very simple revelation:

He didn't know what he wanted.

Issa swiveled his chair around, stood up from his desk matter-of-factly, stretched and decided that he was going for a walk. He had nearly reached the door when he turned around, snatched up the paper, rolled it back up and stuffed it into his pocket without any real thought given to what he was doing.

The March evening air was cool and pleasant. Issa inhaled deeply in an effort to cool his head, only then fully realizing that the paper was in his pocket.

Why did I bring this thing with me?

Issa was troubled as much by his own behavior as the mysterious appearance of the paper. He had acted on impulse alone multiple times that day, which was rather unlike him. It wasn't as if he was some cold, emotionless robot or anything, but he still liked to think that he, well, *thought* about what he was doing normally.

Another deep breath, head tilted back to get the most out of it.

There. That was it. Just breathe deep and relax. Crisp air, a gentle breeze, the quiet—

"AHHHHH!!!"

—screams of a woman in danger.

"Oh, come *on!*" Issa complained even as he tore off running towards the direction the scream had come from.

Now, Issa didn't consider himself to be a hero or anything of that nature. Ordinarily, his first reaction would have been to find a payphone or a convenience store and call the cops. He would have done exactly that were it not for two things:

Firstly, he was acting impulsively that day.

Secondly, though he prayed that he was mistaken, he *knew* that voice.

As such, Issa Aono's body moved without him telling it to, racing towards a gap between two buildings, the only thought in his head being a fervent prayer that he wasn't about to find what some part of him already knew he would.

"Oh no…"

Issa skidded to a halt just out of sight of the alleyway and peered around the corner to see six people. Four of them were standing in various confident and/or threatening poses, eyes fixed on the young woman who had her back to the wall and a darkening bruise on her left cheek. The last occupant was a dark-haired young man who sat slumped against a brick wall, blood slowly dripping from his forehead.

Elsi! Rao!

Issa's next pulse was less a heartbeat and more a full-body jolt of electricity. Adrenaline was flooding his veins, slowing down his perception of the scene in front of him as his mind was emptied of all thoughts save for two: fight or flight.

If Issa were to think back on that event, he would have reasonably expected his head to flood with thoughts and noise. A chaotic tide of impulses and emotions. All manner of things. He would have expected to more or less lose his mind, but that wasn't what happened.

He went calm.

Issa knew that if he ran, he was damning Elsi and Rao to whatever fate the other four men had in mind for them. Therefore, "flight" wasn't an option.

That left "fight."

Issa needed something to help even the playing field. He needed a weapon.

There! Leaning against a nearby dumpster was a section of metal pipe a little over two feet long. That, combined with a surprise attack, would most likely allow him to incapacitate one, if he did it right.

Moving as silently as possible, Issa crouched low to the ground and crept to the pipe, feeling the cold metal sap the warmth from his hand as he grasped it tightly.

Issa took a split-second to choose his target from amongst the four men, whom he had mentally named

Vest, Skinhead, Beanie and Prettyboy.

Prettyboy and Beanie were the furthest away from him. Prettyboy was the one actively speaking with Elsi while Beanie leaned against the wall next to her and grinned.

That still left Vest and Skinhead. Skinhead was the one closest to the unconscious Rao, hand planted against the wall above the younger man as he observed Prettyboy's actions. Vest was the most open, standing in the center of the alley with his back completely to Issa.

Vest it was.

Issa sprang into action, the pipe whistling through the air as he bashed Vest in the side of the head, causing him to let out an involuntary grunt as his head jerked to the side and he dropped like a sack of bricks.

Issa stood there, panting.

The alley had gone quiet.

Everything had stopped.

His body had moved almost without his will and now his mouth moved as if on its own.

"Come on you *bastards!* I'll beat you *all* down!"

The words had left Issa's mouth before he had been consciously aware of what he was saying. His blood was burning in his veins, *pounding* in his ears, spurring him on towards...what?

Had he acted in the hopes of intimidating the group? Was he trying to get someone else's attention? Did he actually think that he could defeat all of them by himself?

Elsi was staring at Issa wide-eyed as though she couldn't believe what she was seeing. Prettyboy, on the other hand, had only turned around halfway, hand still planted on the wall next to Elsi's head as he gave Issa a disdainful look that only pretty-boy types could pull off.

"Waste this idiot."

As Beanie pulled out a switchblade and Skinhead cracked his knuckles, Issa had his first conscious thought since the whole ordeal had begun.

This may have been a mistake.

Issa raised his pipe in front of him, attempting to use the extra reach it granted him to his advantage while he frantically tried to think of a plan.

If I'm gonna run, now's the time.

...

Well, it was worth a shot. If I can distract them, maybe Elsi can get Rao out of here?

Issa swung the pipe in a wide arc in front of him as he gradually backed away, doing his best to keep Beanie and Skinhead at a distance.

That's right, keeping them away from me is my best bet. I don't really know how to fight and I'm sure they're stronger than me.

"Come here!" Skinhead was the first to try something, lunging towards Issa to try and grab him. Issa swung his pipe wildly and caught his hand with the jagged end, knocking the limb away and giving him a ragged wound.

Okay, this could work. Play keep-away, be patient, let them come to me and then—

Bonk

—run into a wall because this is an alley. Right.

...Shit.

Issa, now cornered, swung the pipe wildly over

and over in front of him, desperately trying to land a lucky shot of some kind.

I know I can't win.

Beanie backstepped to avoid a blow to the head.

I know that.

Skinhead strafed to avoid a shot to the groin.

I know that, but...

Beanie leapt at him, knife at the ready.

But...

Issa responded with a thrust of his pipe, which Beanie had seemingly anticipated, as he dropped his head low, ducking underneath the blow as he continued his forward momentum, scoring a savage cut along Issa's right forearm. The sudden shock caused him to release the pipe, which rose into the air, rotating slowly.

What choice do I have?!

Without pausing to think about whether it was possible, Issa's left hand shot out and seized the pipe in midair, bringing it crashing down onto Beanie's right shoulder with a sickening crunch.

Now it was Beanie's turn to drop his weapon as he let out a yell of pain and staggered backwards, arm swinging limply. Issa was barely able to raise his pipe in time to block a second knife, this one wielded by Skinhead, who had brought his blade down in an overhead swing.

CLANG

Issa's non-dominant arm trembled with the effort of holding back the larger man's weapon as his right arm fumbled behind him, blood flowing freely from his wound.

There was the crinkling sound of paper as his

fingers brushed against the top of the roll sticking out of his pocket. Seizing onto whatever hope he could, Issa grasped the edge of the paper and removed it from his pocket with a flick of his wrist that caused it to snap open, flecks of blood from his arm hitting the pavement.

Hey, you freaky piece of fairy-tale paper...I still don't know what I want...

Beanie had knelt down and retrieved his knife with his left hand.

...And I know there's no chance of me getting out of this...but...

Beanie snarled in pain and fury as he ran at Issa, knife held in front of him.

But if you could make it so my friends got away, that'd make a believer out of me.

Issa could hear Prettyboy shouting something at Elsi in the background, a finger pointing at him as though he were making some sort of point. He had pinned her arms above her head with his other hand. Issa struggled mightily, shoving Skinhead's knife up and away from him—

Then he felt a deep impact on his lower torso, as though he had been punched, but the fist had gone through him. Glancing down, he saw immediately why.

He had been stabbed.

The shock of the injury delayed Issa's reactions, allowing Skinhead to abandon his knife and seize Issa's pipe from his weakened grip, bashing him over the head with it and sending him crashing to the ground.

Over the sudden ringing in his ears, Issa thought

he heard Elsi screaming. There was the crack of something breaking, a cry of pain from one of the men.

"GET AWAY FROM HIM!!!"

The sound of Elsi's yell was followed by something hitting the ground. Issa managed to raise his head just in time to see Skinhead round on Elsi and send her toppling over backwards with an uppercut to the jaw.

Elsi...damn it...why didn't you run? That was your only chance...

Heh...guess I'm one to talk, huh?

Issa reached his right arm forward; his left having been pinned underneath him.

I guess none of us are making it out of this, huh?

His head impacted the concrete once again as he lost the strength to keep it held up. His hand followed suit shortly thereafter, causing him to feel a combination of rough concrete and smooth paper, now wet with his blood.

Just before he lost consciousness, Issa thought he heard a voice in his head.

<What you Desire is 𝕊⊘𝕞𝕩&@𝖭. This I have heard.>

<Your Terms are 𝔻Λ𝕃𝕊𝔻#𝖵. These I have understood.>

<As Payment, you offer 𝕊𝔸╠𝔻╫@𝓵. This I have accepted.>

<Contact has been made. Our Contract has been forged.>

There was the sensation of something shifting in the air above him, then Issa knew no more.

CHAPTER TWO
CONTRACT

" . . . S ter..."

"...ey...ister..."

"Hey, mister!"

Issa Aono was fairly certain that he was dead. It seemed like a fair assumption, given that his last memory was of lying face-down in a pool of his own blood. The men who had done that to him had still been nearby as well and the odds of them just leaving him be seemed fairly low, if he had even survived long enough for that to be an issue.

Still, there were a few things that struck Issa as odd.

Firstly, while he very clearly remembered being on his front, the feeling of hard ground against his back and cool air on his face told him that he was currently facing upwards.

Secondly, he was actually in quite a large amount of pain. It felt as though he had been beaten all over, which made sense in retrospect.

Thirdly, and this was quite honestly the strangest bit, he felt as though someone was sitting on his stomach.

Issa opened his eyes slowly, blinking a few times to clear his blurred vision.

"Hey, mister, are you awake?"

Issa blinked one more time for good measure before accepting that there was indeed a girl straddling his stomach, propping herself up with her hands on his chest as she leaned in to get a better look at his face. She had long hair of such a bright silver that it was nearly white and seemed to exude a sense of otherworldliness.

She's cute...could she be an angel?

"Phew! That's a relief! It would have *sucked* if you died right after I got here!" the girl beamed at him, clearly pleased.

As she did, Issa noticed that she had a fanged grin and a pair of slit-pupiled, ruby-red eyes.

Okay, definitely not an angel.

...Maybe I got the wrong idea about where I ended up? That's a comforting thought.

Now that he was starting to regain more of his faculties, Issa noticed that there was a particular smell hanging heavily in the air. It was familiar; right on the tip of his tongue.

Oh, that's right. It's...

Issa propped himself up on his elbows in order to get a better look at his surroundings.

...iron.

Some part of Issa's subconscious mind already knew what he would see. That must have been why he was able to observe the scene around him without yelling or retching.

He was indeed still in the same alleyway that he had been in before. There was no sign of Rao or Elsi, which gave him hope that they had gotten away somehow. As for their four assailants, well…

…it was a bit difficult to tell if what remained added up to three bodies or four.

The ground and sections of the brick walls shone eerily in the moonlight, wet with the evidence of the recent carnage. As Issa's gaze shifted from his surroundings to the newcomer sitting on him, he saw that the same red stains ran from the tips of her fingers up to just past her elbows.

She had done this.

"So," the girl was either oblivious or uncaring to the expression of growing realization that was spreading across Issa's face, "are you the one who made a Contract with me?"

As Issa stared into her otherworldly eyes, whose shade was beginning to resemble blood more so than rubies, there was a single thought that dominated his mind:

What have I gotten myself into?

"Hey! I get that you're probably tired, but this isn't exactly the best place for you to pass out again, okay?"

Issa forced his mind back to some semblance of alertness, recognizing the truth of her statement: nothing good would happen if someone found him in the middle of an alley with what looked like the results of throwing multiple people into a gigantic blender and forgetting to put the lid on.

"Who are you?" he asked, needing something else to focus on.

"Zurie. Zurie the Contractor." she replied as she stood up, licked some blood off of one hand and offered it to him, pulling him to his feet with a surprising amount of strength for a slender girl that was at least a head shorter than him.

"Contractor?" Issa slurred the question as he staggered slightly, feeling lightheaded.

"I'm all up for some Q&A, but we should really get out of here." Zurie reminded him, "My ability only lasts so long, especially when it's used on an area like this."

"...My apartment. It's..."

"I'll help you. Just tell me where to turn. Can you do that?"

"...Think so..."

Issa trudged through the strangely empty streets like a drunk as the self-proclaimed Contractor supported his weight without apparent effort, giving the occasional instruction but otherwise just doing his best to put one foot in front of the other.

Eventually, the pair reached the small apartment building that Issa called home. Upon discovering that the stairs to the upper floor were quite frankly beyond him in his current state, Issa found himself momentarily lifted by Zurie as she hopped up the stairs, taking three at a time.

All in all, it was hardly surprising that Issa nearly collapsed as he stepped through the door to his apartment.

"Easy," Zurie said soothingly as she steered Issa into a chair, "I might have been able to patch you up, but you did lose quite a bit of blood. If I wasn't full already, you might not have enough to pay me with."

Issa stared dumbly at her as she retreated to the kitchen to get something to drink, judging by the clinking of glasses. Sure enough, she returned with two glasses. One with water and the other with some of the apple juice that had been in his refrigerator, which she handed to him.

"Payment? Blood?" he asked in-between sips, finding that he was in fact extremely thirsty.

"Well, yeah. You offered your blood as payment, remember?"

"I think I'd remember doing something like that."

"I mean, you got it all over your Contract."

"Contract?"

"Oh boy. I guess I'm starting from the beginning here, huh?" she cleared her throat, taking a moment to gather her thoughts.

"There are three components to a Contract: Desire, Terms and Payment. Any of this sound familiar?"

Issa nodded, remembering the mysterious paper from earlier.

"Well, most people use their words to describe these things. You, on the other hand, decided to just drench the thing in your blood. Most Contractors wouldn't even look twice at a Contract like that, but thankfully for you that's kinda my thing."

"What, so Contractors are vampires or something?" Issa hazarded as he drained his glass and set it down on the table.

"All Contractors? No. Me? Sort of."

"Sort of?"

"Sort of." she chirped as if that alone told him

everything he needed to know, "Anyway, while using your blood leaves your Desire and Terms open to interpretation, as Payment it's pretty straightforward: Since you offered blood as payment and I drink blood, that makes you my personal food source for the duration of our Contract! Make sure to take care of yourself so I don't drain you dry~"

Issa kneaded the bridge of his nose between his thumb and forefinger, getting a headache as his groggy brain attempted to process what would have been too much to deal with on a normal day. It was at this point that he noticed that his clothes were filthy and he felt sticky.

"I'm gonna take a shower." he decided before standing up from the chair far too quickly and blacking out from anemic shock.

C-O-N-T-R-A-C-T

Issa woke up to the familiar sensation of his mattress against his back and his head being propped up slightly by his pillow. He felt slightly fatigued, as though he had slept poorly or overexerted himself the previous day.

That was one hell of a dream I had. Maybe fatigue really can carry over from something like that?

Issa pondered this for a moment before glancing over at his clock to see how much time he had remaining before his alarm went off, offhandedly noticing that his room seemed a bit brighter than it usually did.

Issa sat upright as he took in the fact that the clock read 8:57 AM.

"Well, there goes my perfect streak. Shit."

Thankfully he didn't have any classes on Thursdays. Still, it sucked that he had broken his rhythm. He just *knew* that it was going to be a bitch to get back into it again.

Oh, well. Worse things had happened, Issa mused as he roughly flopped back down on to the bed, causing the mattress to bounce and the lump of blankets to his left to shift and let out a small grunt of protest.

Wait, what?

Issa's head snapped around as a head of white hair emerged from underneath the covers, revealing the same pair of red eyes from his dream that apparently had not been a dream.

"Morning." Zurie yawned at him.

"Whoa!" Issa reflexively leapt out of the bed, rotating in midair to land facing his surprise bedmate, "What are you—" he cut himself off as an unusually breezy feeling caused him to look down, revealing him to be nude.

"Well, you're obviously feeling better." Zurie smirked cheekily at him as she sat up and stretched, causing the covers to fall away and show that she was every bit as nude as he was.

"I...you..." Issa stuttered, his brain firing on all cylinders as myriad possible scenarios coursed through his head regarding their mutual state of undress, "What *happened* last night?!"

"You passed out. I didn't think it'd be a good idea to just leave you on the floor and covered in your own blood, so I stripped you off and cleaned you up." she replied matter-of-factly as she scooched to the edge of the bed, "I didn't feel like rummaging around your room to find fresh clothes, so I tossed you into bed. After that, since I was pretty dirty myself, I took a shower too. I didn't exactly have anything else to change into though and there was only the one bed, so I decided to join you."

Issa merely gaped at her.

"What? Were you planning on making me sleep on the floor or something?"

Issa opened his mouth, closed it, opened it again, then closed it again.

He had quite honestly not given that any thought. Really, he hadn't given *any* of his newfound situation *any* thought, since he had rather quickly gone from near-death experience to having a supernatural roommate.

What did this so-called Contract mean for him? Could he keep Zurie hidden? *Should* he keep Zurie hidden? How would he even do that? She would have to stay *somewhere* and he didn't exactly have the funds for another apartment just for her, so she would have to live with him.

For how long though? She needed clothes and he knew little enough about *that* as it was. She said she drank blood, so maybe food wouldn't be a factor. Or would it? Did she still need to eat? Was she allergic to anything?

What would she do while he was gone all day? He couldn't just enroll her at his school for the sake of keeping an eye on her, again because of money. Maybe he could get more input from his friends, but this didn't seem like the kind of thing he wanted to get them involved in. And what about—

"Hmm...still a bit anemic, I guess? It makes sense, considering."

Issa's train of thought was interrupted by Zurie turning his head from side-to-side, examining him carefully.

In other words, she was less than a foot away from him, in all her glory.

"You need to put something on and so do I!" Issa frantically grabbed a t-shirt from his dresser and threw it at Zurie while he seized the first pair of underwear and pants he saw. Upon dressing himself and turning around, he saw that his shirt was big enough on her to at least preserve *some* degree of modesty.

Why does some part of me feel like I just made the situation worse?

"We need to talk about a few things." he said as he exited the bedroom, followed by his new roommate.

As he prepared breakfast (Zurie, having indicated that she was not hungry, settled for a glass of juice), Issa explained his concerns to Zurie regarding her living arrangements and the subsequent questions this left him with. She did not interrupt him or deign to answer any of his questions as he asked them, simply sipping her juice and giving him a thoughtful look.

"Well," she said after he had finished, "you're being remarkably level-headed about this. I might have underestimated you."

"Are you making fun of me?"

"No, I'm actually impressed. Most people don't take so quickly to this kind of thing, you know. Hmm..."

"What?" Issa asked suspiciously.

"Okay! I've made up my mind! I'm gonna help you!"

"Isn't that why you're here?"

"What, the Contract? No, not really. Honestly, I could have just let you die and left last night."

"What." Issa had to consciously fight off another headache.

"A Contractor is only bound by the wording of their Contract. Desire, Terms, Payment. They have a thing they're supposed to do, a way they're supposed to do it and what they get in return. So, what were those things for you?" she crossed her arms and cocked her head at him.

"...Blood?"

"Exactly. And what does that mean?"

"I have to provide you with blood, right?"

"That's Payment. What about the other two?"

Issa took a moment to think about that.

"...I have no idea."

"Neither do I. That's the problem."

"What? But I thought you said, right before you appeared, that you understood everything?"

"Actually, no. I heard your Desire and accepted your Payment."

"And understood my Terms, right?"

"...Sort of."

"'Sort of?'"

"Look, it's not exactly open and shut, alright?" she frowned at him, "Because of my affinity for blood, I could get a vague sense of who you were and what you wanted, but nothing I can put into words. Not yet anyway."

"You accepted my Contract based on...what? A gut feeling?"

"It's hard to describe for someone who's never felt

it. Just be glad it was *me* you ended up with; most Contractors wouldn't even *consider* such a Contract in the first place…unless you wish I hadn't taken it?"

"No, no." Issa held up his hands in a placating gesture, "I'm just, I just…I just want to understand, that's all. Speaking of, what do you mean by 'not yet?'"

"The more I drink your blood, the better I'll come to understand you. The idea is that once I know you well enough, I might be able to figure out what your Desire is."

"Okay, fine. What's all this about helping me then?" Issa followed up, deciding to accept what she had told him so far.

"Well, I *could* just take however much blood I want from you whenever I feel like it, since you never specified how much you were offering, but I won't do that."

"Ah, well, that's good to know."

"Even with me just feeding when I'm hungry though, you'll definitely notice side-effects. Anemia for one thing."

"So I'll be tired, weak and other not-fun things?"

"Yeah. Not fun. That's why I'm gonna help you with that!"

"How?" this question prompted her to stand up and gesture broadly to the apartment at large.

"Total lifestyle change! You're gonna eat, drink, sleep and exercise to keep yourself in tip-top blood-regenerating shape!"

"Uh…"

"Oh, don't look at me like that. I had the chance to get a good look at your body last night and I gotta say, you've got potential." she gave him a saucy grin.

"I don't need to hear about this."

"Suit yourself."

"So, what about clothes?" Issa threw out, wanting very much to change the topic, "You're going to need those. Plus room and board."

"Well, I'm staying with you, obviously." she immediately responded, confirming what he had suspected, "All I really require in terms of food is blood, though other fluids and the occasional snack are nice too. As for clothes, well, I'm fine with just bumming off you until you figure something out."

"Even if you are, *I'm* not."

"Why not?"

"Because having you walking around in nothing but an oversized shirt is making me feel like a pervert!" Issa nearly shouted in exasperation.

"Well, don't you have a girlfriend or something that you could ask for help?"

"No, I don't have a girlfriend. Although…"

Issa's thoughts turned to Elsi. During the time he had known her, she had always been dependable and she would most definitely be able to help the situation, but would it be a good idea to get her involved in…whatever Issa had inadvertently gotten himself involved in?

He voiced his idea and subsequent concern to Zurie, who gave him a wry smile.

"Then make something up. Tell her I'm a visiting relative or something and I need clothes for whatever reason. You've apparently got a halfway-decent head on your shoulders, so *use* it. I don't care either way, for now at least."

"You'd think you'd put a bit more effort into a situation that involves you so much."

"Hey, I've got a place to stay, a bed to sleep in, a personal food supply and, for the moment, some things to occupy my time with. The clothes thing is on you."

I'm gonna get her back for this. Somehow.

After mentally swearing his revenge, Issa stopped dead in his tracks.

"Oh shit! Rao and Elsi!"

It had not completely clicked with him until that moment that he should *probably* check up on the pair that he had attempted to save the previous night. Issa dashed over to his beige desktop computer, switching it on as he rifled through some papers on his desk.

"I know he wrote down the new password for me...there!"

The instant his computer was operational, Issa opened his web browser and logged into the chatroom that Rao had set up for their private use. He, Elsi and Issa chatted on it throughout the week about various things, especially on days that they didn't have class. If he was lucky...

Sure enough, Issa saw a fresh set of messages and breathed a sigh of relief.

<GAO>: That must have been one hell of a date last night. My head is pounding and I can't remember anything!

<GAO>: How about it, EL? Am I hot stuff or what?

<ELNO>: You were an absolute dream.

<GAO>: (☉ _ ☉) Really?!

<ELNO>: Especially when you tripped into a

wall and knocked yourself out and I had to drag you.

<GAO>:   (ㅁ ´Д `)ㅁ Sarcasm! My one weakness!

<GAO>:   Explains the headache though.

[<SSIA> has joined the chat]

Issa was immediately confused, which was a feeling he was becoming far, far too familiar with.

I can understand Rao not remembering much, seeing as how he took a pretty bad shot to the head. Elsi though? There's no way. Why would she lie about something like this?

"Hmm, yeah, that makes sense. I honestly expected something like that." Zurie said thoughtfully from over his shoulder. Issa rounded on her.

"What do you mean this makes sense?! How could both of them forget something like that?!"

"Issa, how many Contracts do you think there have ever been?"

"What?"

"It's not a small number, let me tell you. In spite of this, nobody believes that Contracts are real apart from a few superstitious sorts. Why do you think that is?"

"Well, because people don't go around talking about them. I mean, who would believe them? *I* hardly believe it and I'm *talking* to a Contractor right now."

"And do you think that nobody has ever summoned a Contractor in public before? Or in front of their family? Or with their friends as a dare?"

"Of course I don—…oh god."

"How can two people keep a secret Issa?"

"If…" Issa gulped, "If one of them is dead."

"What? NO! *What?!*" Zurie recoiled.

"What?"

"It's because the physical Contract is confidential! Anyone but the Signer who was present for the ceremony has their memories rewritten to explain away any lingering effects caused by it!"

"Oh. That's not as bad as I thought."

"Now *I'm* the one who doesn't need to hear about this."

Issa shook his head and turned back to his computer, typing out a message that was quickly responded to.

    <SSIA>:   Are you guys okay?

    <GAO>:   My head will heal, but my male pride may never recover from such a heavy blow.

    <ELNO>:   Oh, shut up. You'll be fine.

    <SSIA>:   What about you, EL?

    <ELNO>:   Eh? Why would I not be okay? WHAT DID YOU DO?!

    <SSIA>:   Nothing! No reason! Nothing!

    <GAO>:   GET HIM ELNO! AVENGE MEEEEE!

Issa was fairly satisfied at this point that his friends were indeed alright. That meant it was time to try and enlist some help.

    [PRIVATE]->[ELNO]

    <SSIA>:   Hey, Elsi, are you free today for a bit?

    <ELNO>:   Ooh, a PM? What are you scheming, Issa?

    <SSIA>:   I need your help with something... girl-related.

    <ELNO>:   Details. I need them. Now.

    <SSIA>:   Only if you promise not to tell anyone.

\<ELNO\>:   Nnnngh…Okay, fine.

\<SSIA\>:   I may or may not have suddenly acquired a roommate, who may or may not be of the female persuasion.

\<ELNO\>:   OHMYGODWHAT

\<SSIA\>:   Due to certain…circumstances… though, she doesn't have any clothes or other things.

\<ELNO\>:   What, is she running around in nothing but a t-shirt or something?

\<SSIA\>:   I don't have to answer that.

\<ELNO\>:   Oh my god, she is.

\<ELNO\>:   How's your neck?

\<SSIA\>:   Uh, fine? Why?

\<ELNO\>:   Because that means you didn't sleep on the floor. And you wouldn't make a girl sleep on the floor. Which means you were IN THE SAME BED ISSA YOU'VE BECOME A MAN!!!

\<SSIA\>:   NO! Nothing like that happened! I checked!

\<ELNO\>:   You CHECKED? So, you weren't sure? What, did you pass out and wake up naked in your bed?

\<SSIA\>:   Stop that.

\<ELNO\>:   Wait. If she's new, as in brand-new, and you fell asleep before her and woke up naked, then she didn't know where your clothes were. That, plus you needing to check if anything happened…

\<SSIA\>:   How are you doing this?!

\<ELNO\>:   I don't know whether to be impressed at your restraint or exasperated at your inability to take a hint.

\<SSIA\>:   Pretty sure she doesn't see me like that.

<ELNO>: Issa, for a girl to sleep naked in your bed she either has a thing for you or doesn't even see you as a man. Women are resourceful. If she really wanted to find something to wear, she would have.

<SSIA>: ...So you'll help?

<ELNO>: I will be at your place later.

<SSIA>: Cool. When?

<ELNO>: When I feel like it. God.

<SSIA>: T.T I'm so glad you're my friend.

<ELNO>: I love you too ;P

Issa switched back to the main chat with a tired exhalation. He really did like Elsi, but sometimes she was too smart and observant for his own good. She could have been a private eye or something if she wanted.

<SSIA>: Anyway, I'll see you guys tomorrow. Get some rest, GAO.

<GAO>: My recuperative abilities cannot be comprehended by you mere mortals! I AM INVINCIBLE!!!

<ELNO>: Pfft~ I got stuff to do so I'll see you guys later!

[<ELNO> has left the chat]

<GAO>: She'll be back.

<SSIA>: Bye.

[<SSIA> has left the chat]

<GAO>: ...He'll be back too.

CHAPTER THREE

SUGGESTION

Contractor Masia let out a long-suffering sigh mixed with cigarette smoke, lamenting the unending stream of headaches that seemed to plague his existence as he stared into the sky.

"When it rains, it pours. Fitting, I suppose." he mumbled in a self-mocking tone.

It wasn't as though most of his growing list of annoyances was his fault and that wasn't just his ego talking either; the majority of them were well and truly beyond his control. Whether that made the situation better, because he was blameless, or worse because he could do nothing about it was something of a toss-up.

The otherworldly man did not *enjoy* being in-control per-se, it was simply that there was far too much chaos in the world for his liking otherwise. Smooth. Methodical. Following a master plan. That was how things ought to be.

And if nobody else was going to orchestrate that, then it was his duty to step up and take the reins for himself. Shepherding. Guiding. Showing others the way to self-betterment with himself as the example.

"What's up?" a familiar voice interrupted his thoughts, as his Signer was so often wont to do.

"There's another one."

"Shit, already? As if the one from last night wasn't already enough to deal with."

The Contractor did not respond, opting instead to take another drag on his cigarette.

"Those things'll kill ya."

"That's almost funny."

"Come on, I'm hilarious."

"Repetition kills any joke."

"I'm not sure you've *got* a sense of humor in the first place."

"Don't confuse its level of sophistication for a lack of it."

"Yeah, yeah. 'See what lies underneath' and all that. So, how many does that make now?"

Redirect, wear down, engage, redirect. As much as his Signer might complain, it was clear that the young man *was* paying attention to his lessons, even if that *was* a pathetically transparent ploy. Still, he was trying and that warranted positive reinforcement.

"Since I arrived in this Realm, at least three others have been summoned within the confines of this city. Possibly more."

"So, if we assume there's been at least one more, that's five summonings in about five months. Do you think they're all still around?"

"Unlikely. Given the variety of forms a Contract can

take, the odds of at least one being short-term is high."

"But you don't know for sure?"

"A Contractor emits a unique energy signature when they travel between Realms. This is something not even the most learned among us can control. For any Contractors in the immediate vicinity, the feeling is unmistakable."

He paused to take one final drag on his nearly spent cigarette before disposing of it in the ashtray he had brought outside with him.

"However, once a Contract has been forged, a Contractor's energy output dwindles to almost nothing unless they are given a reason to exert themselves. For a skilled individual, they could even engage in minor ability usage without alerting others."

"Oh, so that's why nobody ever comes knocking when you cut loose on me?"

"Believe me, if I ever 'cut loose' on you, you'd know it. Or maybe you wouldn't. It would depend on how well you dodged."

"You know, it really chaps my hide that you're able to beat the tar out of me without even trying."

"If you are given an example to aspire to, then you can improve more quickly. That's always been the essence of a master-student relationship."

"A lot of good that did me last night…"

"Your guard was down."

"You weren't even there, how would *you* know?"

"While you aren't anywhere near my level, I'd be much mistaken if I said that you hadn't improved somewhat. Random hooligans shouldn't pose much of a threat at the very least. Plus, whether I was there or not, I'm quite sure you were distracted. Ergo, your guard was down."

"Well, at least you showed up in time to clean up the mess, right?"

"A mess that *your* antics are doing a fine job of recreating."

"Give me a break! I can only deal with these things like I know how to."

"By making a fool of yourself?"

"It works. Sort of."

"It is a *distraction*, not a *solution*. If what you've told me about one of your friends in particular is true, this won't throw them off for long. Thank the heavens for the Confidentiality Clause."

"I still say it's weird that people's memories can just be modified like that."

The Contractor *did* chuckle at that.

"If, in all of your time in this world, *that* is the strangest thing you ever see, you will have led a mundane life indeed."

C-O-N-T-R-A-C-T

Issa Aono collapsed to the floor, panting heavily. Zurie had wasted no time in beginning his training regimen, though she had promised that they would "start things off easy" since she didn't know what he was capable of and he wasn't back to one-hundred percent yet. She had set him to doing some fairly basic calisthenics such as push-ups, sit-ups, squats, jumping jacks and other such things.

In rapid succession.

With no breaks between sets.

Determined not to let her get the better of him, Issa had kept going for as long as he could until his body just gave out and he found himself on the floor.

"Alright, I guess that's enough for me to get the picture. Take five." Zurie sat cross-legged on the floor next to Issa and tapped her chin thoughtfully, "I can't really say I'm impressed, but I guess I shouldn't have expected much better, huh?"

"You really…know how to…motivate a guy…"

"Your motivation is not being exsanguinated, mister, or have you forgotten?" she said sarcastically, "Though, I guess you did keep going for longer than I thought you would, so that's something."

"So, apart from giving me war flashbacks to Phys Ed, what else is there? You said it was a lifestyle change, so what other fun things do I get to look forward to?"

"Nutrition for one thing. Your body regenerates blood plasma pretty quickly as long as you keep up your fluid intake, but red blood cells take a bit longer to replenish. Incidentally, a lack of red blood cells is what causes a lot of the symptoms of anemia."

"What you're saying is I need to work on speeding up my red blood cell generation then? How do I do that?"

"Well, exercise is a big part of it, but there are a few key nutrients that will help you out. Iron, Vitamin B-9, Vitamin B-12, copper and Vitamin A are the big ones, though there are some others."

"Wait, copper?"

"Not a ton of it, but a baseline amount helps with iron absorption."

"No, as in, where am I supposed to get that from?

You don't expect me to start gnawing on electrical wires, do you?"

"As tempting as that thought is, you'll just have to make do with beans, nuts, poultry…liver."

"I'll pass on that last one."

"Hmm, too bad, since it's also a good source of iron along with red meat, beans and dark, leafy greens."

"What are you, a nutritionist?" Issa cocked an eyebrow at her as he sat up.

"No, I'm an interdimensional vampire who came here to grant your wish." she deadpanned.

"…Point taken. What about the rest of those nutrients?"

"B-9, or folic acid, is also in those leafy greens, beans and nuts. B-12 is in red meat just like iron and also fish and dairy products. Vitamin A is in the leafy greens too along with some fruits and carrots."

"I get the sense that I'm going to be eating a lot of steak and spinach. Oh well, it could be worse."

"Plus a few other things I'll be throwing in there."

"Why's that?"

"Well, if I'm going to be molding you into the shape I want anyway, I may as well bulk you up a little. Not a ton, just enough to add some definition. I'm not much of a fan of the big, macho types."

"I feel like we've gotten off-topic."

"You're right. Time for some stretches!"

It took a rather large amount of discipline for Issa to only respond with "…Great."

Zurie set him to doing some assisted stretches, her disproportionate physical strength easily offsetting her small frame and lack of weight. It still hurt, but was far less strenuous than the earlier exercises had been, which left him able to talk with her.

Well, I may as well address the elephant in the room.

"So, when do you need to…eat? Drink? Blood. When do you need that?"

"Ordinarily I'd be pretty hungry right after forging a Contract, but seeing as you were already pretty drained, I decided to get what I needed elsewhere." she punctuated her statement by applying increased pressure to his back.

"Agh! Oh, I get it. You mean the guys that were attacking Elsi and Rao."

"No sense letting all that fresh blood go to waste, even if they didn't taste very good. Try holding that position by yourself for a bit."

It took a considerable amount of focus for Issa to ignore the way his hamstrings were screaming at him, so he was unable to continue their conversation until she had allowed him to relax and shift to the next posture, which saw him lying on his front with Zurie straddling his back. In a desperate bid to distract himself from the sensations of what she was very obviously *not* wearing, Issa asked the first question that popped into his head.

"Blood has a taste? Apart from iron, I mean?"

"Definitely. Taste and nutritional value can vary wildly from person to person. There's a science to it, but you probably don't want to know all that. Suffice to say that those guys not only tasted bad, they weren't very nutritious either. That's why I had to drink from each of them." she wrapped her arms around one of his legs and began hauling back on it, causing his quadriceps to cry out.

"Nnngh! You have some reason to think my blood will be better?"

"Oh, *god* yes."

"...I feel as though I should be concerned."

"Maybe if I was the type who didn't know how to control herself, but don't worry. I already promised I wouldn't drain you dry, didn't I? No matter how good you taste."

"*Why* do you think I'm going to taste so good?"

"I know the quality of your blood, Issa." Zurie released the first leg and grabbed his other one, "You drenched your Contract in it, so I had more than enough to get an idea of the type of person I was dealing with. People like you always taste the best."

"People like what?"

"Oh, come on. You can't expect a lady to reveal all of her secrets at once, can you?"

"Who's revealing what now?" a new female voice joined the conversation as the sound of his door closing reached Issa's ears, "Sorry, I know I said 'later' but I figured that 'earlier' would be better than 'later,' plus I couldn't wait to meet your new roommate and...*hello.*"

Issa craned his neck as much as he could from his position on the ground with Zurie still stretching his leg and caught sight of Elsi with one hand resting on a cocked hip and a very, *very* amused look on her face.

"Issa, you should've been more honest with me. I might've knocked if I knew I could've been *disturbing* something."

"I swe—ARGH—it's not what you think!"

"There!" Zurie released his leg and stood up, turning to face Elsi, "Hello! You must be Elsi, right? Thank you so much for agreeing to help us out!"

"You aren't helping, Zurie." Issa grumbled into the carpet.

"Your name's Zurie? Don't mention it! It's well worth the price of admission, believe me."

"The pleasure's all mine!"

Issa could imagine the look on her face. Big, shit-eating grin showing off those fangs and—

—oh SHIT.

Issa frantically flipped himself over on the ground, scrambling for some sort of excuse as to why his new roommate had fangs, red, slit-pupiled eyes and an extremely uncommon hair color...

...only to find that Elsi and Zurie were looking at him like *he* was the weirdo.

"Huh, guess he got his second wind. Maybe stamina's your strong point, Issa?"

"You hear that, Issa? *Stamina~*"

Issa was so busy trying to process the situation that he didn't have the time to be embarrassed.

Why is she okay with this? How *is she okay with this? Elsi's inquisitive by nature and* nothing *gets past her!*

"Issa, you're being rude. Stop gawking." Zurie chastised him gently.

Issa stood up with a sigh, resigning himself to yet another unexplained situation.

Well, I guess Zurie's not worried about it, so it's probably okay, right?

C-O-N-T-R-A-C-T

All things considered, the talk between the two women was fairly brief. There was plenty of small-talk, but Zurie's answers to questions regarding her history or personal life were brief and vague, practically non-answers all things considered. Issa had fully expected Elsi to pursue the topics and she would seem as though she was about to, but then she would pause and just move on to the next thing.

All told, it weirded Issa out.

Still, the main purpose of the meeting was fulfilled: Elsi had some old clothes that she was willing to let Zurie have until they could organize an outing to get her some proper outfits and other various sundries.

"I'll give them to Issa tomorrow so he can bring them back with him. Ordinarily I'd ask if you just wanted to swing by and grab them but, well…" she indicated Issa's t-shirt that currently comprised the entirety of her wardrobe.

"Oh, I'm fine waiting! I'm really grateful for your help, Elsi!"

"No worries." Elsi waved it off, "Any friend of Issa's is…say, how did you two meet again?"

"Oh, you know." Zurie smiled innocently, eyes fixed on Elsi's. For a few seconds, they stared at each other.

"Yeah…" Elsi nodded absently, "yeah, I see what you mean. Well, I'll see you later! I'll give you guys a call soon to set up that shopping trip!"

Issa walked her to the door, now feeling well and truly suspicious.

"Thanks for coming. I honestly didn't know what to do." he said as she opened the door.

"Don't mention it. See you tomorrow." she made to close the door but Issa caught it.

"Are…are you alright? Is everything okay?"

Elsi gave him a searching look, hazel eyes boring into his in the way only hers could.

"I…" then she shook her head and the look was gone as though it had never been there, "Don't be silly, Issa; I'm fine! Sheesh, you're acting weird today." then he released the door, whereupon she closed it and was gone.

"What did you do?"

Issa rested his fist against the door, pointedly avoiding turning around.

"What was that?"

"What. Did. You. Do?"

"Issa, what are you talking about? And turn around, it's hard to hear you like that."

Issa did not turn around.

"I felt like something was off during your whole conversation with Elsi. You barely answered any of her questions and it didn't seem to bother her at all."

"So? She could tell I wasn't up to talking about that stuff, so she let it go."

"Elsi Thompson does *not* let things go!" Issa's voice was slightly raised now, "She was acting dazed and stilted the whole time, as if she was concussed or something!"

"Issa, turn around." she sounded exasperated at this point.

"Why? So you can do to me whatever you were doing to her?"

There were several seconds of silence.

"I'm not deliberately keeping anything from you, you know; there just wasn't any reason to talk to you about this."

"Convince me."

"Do you remember last night, when I mentioned my ability?"

"My ability only lasts so long, especially when it's used on an area like this."

"...Yes."

"Well, that same thing is what I was using on Elsi. Now, will you please turn around and let me explain myself?"

"...Eye contact." Issa realized, "You kept eye-contact with Elsi when she was about to question you. That's how your ability works. It's like a vampire's charm or mind-control or whatever."

"It's called Suggestion, actually, and it's a fairly rare ability even among vampires, at least where I'm from." she responded coolly, "And eye-contact isn't required, it just makes it more efficient."

"Which is why you want me to turn around: so you can use it on me."

"No, Issa, I want you to turn around because looking at someone when you talk to them is a sign of trust and respect!"

"I just found out that you can mind-control people and you admitted yourself that you weren't planning on telling me about it unless you were forced to. What's more, you're only in this for my blood. I'm a food source. How does any of that add up to me being able to trust you? How do I know you haven't used Suggestion on me *already*?"

The sound of muffled footsteps approached his back. Issa was prepared to be spun around and bitten or mind-controlled or something. What he was *not* expecting was to feel something rest against his back in-between his shoulder blades and a tired sigh to ghost over his spine.

"I didn't tell you because I was afraid that *this* was how you would react. Even where I come from, it's hard for others to trust you when they learn that you can influence their mind. That's why it's considered best practices to build a strong relationship with someone before revealing that little tidbit of information. I've learned that the hard way."

Issa frowned, feeling a surge of sympathy towards Zurie.

"So, if I'm understanding correctly, you mean that it's not an ability that you usually use? Not unless you have to?"

"It consumes energy to use, even if I'm skilled enough to keep it to a minimum. Couple that with the fact that, as you've proven, it tends to arouse suspicion and no, I try not to use it too much."

"Then why?"

"Because it's generally not a good idea to reveal too much to outsiders without reason. If the wrong people become aware of Contractors, it doesn't take a genius to figure out that it would be a complete mess. As for how heavy-handed I was with Elsi...I didn't have a choice. I wasn't expecting her to fight it so hard."

"What do you mean?"

"Originally, I just gave her a subtle Suggestion that there wasn't anything too unusual about my appearance. No fangs, normal eyes basically. Even after that, she started shooting me funny looks every now and then, so I had to re-apply the Suggestion. That was my first sign that something was wrong: Suggestion is supposed to last for a decent amount of time, especially for a simple one like that."

Issa felt the fingertips of one hand lightly brush his back.

"Then the questions started and I panicked a little. I upped the power of my Suggestion gradually and at the end it was nearly four times what a normal person should have taken and it *still* wasn't enough. She nearly broke it altogether when you were saying your goodbyes and I had to hit her with it *again*."

"You said it uses energy. How much?"

"I burned through nearly a quarter of what I drank last night."

"That's a lot?"

"For this kind of thing, yes, it's a lot."

Issa took a deep breath and relaxed the fist against the door.

"Well, I guess I'll need to put my nose to the grindstone with this routine of yours, then." he turned around as he spoke, causing Zurie to let out a small noise of surprise.

"Wait—you mean—really?" she stammered as she stared up at him.

"I mean, I can't just let you starve and it's not like I'm going to have you attack random people." he poked her forehead with his index finger, causing her to stumble backwards a half-step, "Plus, we do have a Contract. I can't exactly ignore that. I'm gonna go finish getting dressed. Could you whip up a shopping list for me so I can go get all this nutritious new food?"

"Sure!" she chirped happily as she snatched a pen off of his desk and skipped to the kitchen where he kept a shopping list on the front of his refrigerator.

Which he had definitely *not* told her about yet.

Oh, well. It makes sense that she might have done some poking around last night and if she's gonna be living here I guess there's no harm in it.

Issa gave a physical shrug to match his mental one and went about selecting a shirt and some socks.

Elsewhere, Elsi was nursing a bitch of a headache and the distinct feeling that she had missed something.

CHAPTER FOUR
INTERROGATING REALITY

Elsi Thompson was having a rough day. It had started out well enough, what with getting Issa's surprising message and getting to meet his new roommate (teasing him mercilessly all the while, of course), but then she had started getting a headache. Not a normal headache either, since this one seemed to just get worse and worse as time went on. She had toughed through it while she was at Issa's, but hadn't stuck around too long either, hoping that some fresh air would do her some good.

If not, there was always the bottle of painkillers she had at home.

The fresh air and painkillers had sort of worked, she supposed. The headache hadn't gotten any worse on the way home and had even subsided somewhat, though it had still been very much present throughout the latter part of her day. It wasn't unbearable or anything, but it was super annoying and made it difficult to focus on what she was doing. It felt like there was television static inside of her brain.

Her mom had noticed that something was wrong and, upon being told that it was a headache, had offered a few well-known solutions and even did some quick research on pressure points to try and help her daughter. Elsi had appreciated the attempt but, in the end, nothing really helped, so she decided to just turn in early and try sleeping it off.

Unfortunately, getting to sleep with such a headache was about as easy as it sounds. In the end, she had resorted to downing a glass of wine in the hopes that it would at least help her GET to sleep even if she might not STAY that way.

After a while, the alcohol finally allowed Elsi to drift into unconsciousness...though it was a far cry from the blissful relief she had hoped for. Images and sounds flashed through her mind, chaotic and nonsensical at first but gradually warping into brief sections of clarity, like a video that had been corrupted so that only snippets of it were still viewable.

She saw Rao, slumped against a wall while she retreated from a group of men. She couldn't hear what was being said until one of them, a pretty boy with rose-red hair, had backed her into a wall.

"Hey there, beautiful. Name's Casanova and I'm pretty well-known around these parts. A fine thing like you's got no reason to be hanging around a loser like that; why don't you come with me and I'll show you a good time?"

Elsi's dream vision shifted and suddenly Issa was there, yelling and brandishing a pipe. Casanova's goons descended on him and her vision shifted again. She saw the moment when one of them plunged a knife into Issa's torso...

...and then suddenly everything was clear and sharp. The dreamy haze was lifted and she saw every detail, heard every sound, felt the cold brick digging into her arms from where Casanova had pinned them above her head.

Her eyes were burning.

She screamed Issa's name and slammed her forehead into Casanova's face with a sickening crack that told her she had broken his nose, causing him to release his grip on her. She dashed past him towards the nearer of the two men who were bearing down on Issa. His back was facing her and she could tell from a glance that he had some sort of injury to his right shoulder.

Her eyes were burning.

With a shout, she leapt forwards and brought her elbow down onto the man's wounded shoulder, causing him to scream and collapse in agony. The sudden lack of resistance made her stagger forward as his companion swore and began to approach. She saw Issa on the ground, blood pooling around him from his stab wound and a nasty-looking cut across his forearm.

Her eyes were burning.

For a brief moment before the pipe that entered her field of vision rendered her unconscious, she saw Issa reaching for a familiar-looking piece of paper that was on the ground in front of him.

Then everything went black.

That wasn't right.

That wasn't what had happened.

She remembered how that night had gone and that *wasn't* it.

...Then why did it feel like a memory?

Her *eyes* were *burning*.

Elsi woke with a start and immediately groaned in pain and clutched at her head. The headache wasn't any worse but now it felt like it was moving forward to the front of her head. Into her face. Into her *eyes*—

Elsi leapt off the bed, nearly crashing into her dresser, and staggered through her door, down the hall, towards the bathroom. She needed to see. She needed to *know* that there was nothing wrong.

Even so, when she flicked on the lights and sagged onto the vanity, using her hands to support herself and looked into the mirror, she was unsurprised to see that there was *absolutely* something wrong. Whether that was due to her instincts and groggy brain or because the sudden flood of sensory input prevented her from actively thinking about anything else was a toss-up.

Elsi saw her own face, mouth slightly parted but for one side that was stuck shut. A sheen of sweat on her brow that caused some of her long brown hair, freed of its usual ponytail, to stick to her skin. Eyes wide and staring...

...and decidedly not her own.

The hazel coloration was still the same, but Elsi was fairly certain that the human iris was incapable of contracting in the necessary way to stretch a pupil into that particular shape. The round, black holes that usually dotted the center of the eyes were dilated and pointed into shapes that resembled eight-pointed stars.

It was eerie. It was uncanny.

And Elsi would have been scared if she had been able to focus on any single thing, but except for that brief instant that she had been able to focus on her face alone, she was being assaulted by a storm of detail regarding everything else within her field of vision.

There were exactly seven smudges on the mirror, two of which were clearly from a recent attempt at cleaning it. There were twenty-seven hairs in the brush and three in the comb. The hand soap was roughly fifty-eight percent full, fifty-nine point-two if she counted the amount in the straw. The faucet was leaking water at a rate of approximately one drop every six minutes and thirteen seconds. The left tap was roughly two degrees off of the alignment of the right. Her toothbrush had rolled onto its side at some point after she had entered the bathroom, likely due to the vibration she had sent through the vanity. Her right hand was slowly slipping off of the vanity and would pass over the edge in forty-three seconds if left alone. How long had she been looking in the mirror? A minute? No. Ten seconds? No. One second? It was too much she couldn't think she needed to turn it off her eyes still hurt her headache was building even more ohgodmakeitstopit'stoomuchpleasepleaseplease please—

Elsi lurched to the side and vomited into the toilet. She closed her eyes and waited for her body to finish purging itself of whatever was causing this. She heaved once, twice, three times more before the proverbial well ran dry and she was momentarily thankful that she hadn't had much of an appetite the previous evening due to her headache.

"Urgh…fuck." she half-groaned with a combination of relief and fatigue as the headache started to recede. Still not wanting to risk opening her eyes, Elsi stood up and felt her way back over to the sink, gathering some water in her cupped hands before tossing it into her mouth, swishing it around and spitting what remained of the sick down the drain.

"Honey? Are you alright?" her mother's voice came from down the hall. It wasn't a surprise that she had been woken up, Elsi supposed. She hadn't exactly been quiet.

"I'm fine, Mom." she called back in as steady a voice as she could manage, "I think I ate something funny. Might have been where the headaches were coming from."

"Do you have a fever?"

Elsi took a moment to check, pressing the back of her hand against her damp, but no warmer than average, forehead.

"No, I'm good. Really. I think I got it all out of my system."

"Alright. I'm going back to bed then."

"'Night, Mom."

Elsi had said what she said in order to prevent her mother from coming in and potentially seeing what was going on, but as she waited to hear the bedroom door closing, she realized that she did actually feel a lot better. The headache was nearly gone and her eyes didn't hurt anymore either. With a moment or two of hesitation, she opened them and sighed with relief when they looked normal again.

She took the opportunity to splash some of the

still-running water onto her face to wash away the sweat and felt rather refreshed afterwards. If nothing else, she was able to think once more and didn't feel like she was going to hurl again. She cleaned up after herself and returned to her room.

As Elsi shut her bedroom door behind her and flopped back down onto her bed, she realized that she could still remember her dream in its entirety. If anything, the images were actually *clearer* than they were before.

And just like before, they felt like memories.

As she sifted through these mental images, she also realized that her visit to Issa's earlier in the day had been stranger than she had given it credit for. Really, while Zurie had seemed nice enough and had seemingly shared her enjoyment of picking on Issa, what the girl *hadn't* said could fill a much bigger page than what she *had*.

It was odd, thinking about it after the fact, that Elsi had been so accepting of the white-haired girl's silence and redirections. She was sure as hell *not* satisfied with the non-answers she had been given and wanted very much to grill Zurie until she gave her something better than, well, *nothing*.

…So why hadn't she?

At the time she had simply felt, in a strangely passive way, that it was the best thing to do. She had reasoned that she had only just met the girl and that it would be rude to pry.

Screw that. *She* had only just met *Issa* as far as Elsi knew and she was *shacking up with him!* It wasn't as though Elsi was jealous or anything; she liked Issa well enough, but was plenty content with just being his friend. They had even talked about it once. It had started as a joke, but then he had gone quiet and gotten a thoughtful look on his face.

"Wait, for real? Are you…I mean, I wasn't serious…*"*

"Well, I'd be lying if I said I hadn't thought about it once or twice, just offhandedly. It…could work.*"*

"I…guess?"

"Well, think about it: We get along pretty well and I don't know what you think, but I find you plenty attractive."

"You're not bad yourself, but that's not…it just feels weird, you know?"

"Yeah, it kinda does. I wouldn't want to be second-guessing it the whole time. We're probably better off as-is."

"Cool, glad we can agree on that. Don't think I'm going to stop teasing you though."

No, what had Elsi Thompson all hot and bothered was the fact that *Issa wasn't that kind of guy.* He wouldn't just meet some girl on the street and invite her to come live with him then and there. There was something else going on and for some reason Elsi had allowed herself to be shuttled out of the apartment without finding out what it was.

Although…it couldn't have anything to do with the paper from earlier, could it? She had needled Issa about considering the possibility that it was one of the rumored magical contracts, but she hadn't actually *believed* it. She *still* didn't! That sort of thing…it just didn't *happen.*

…No matter how much it would explain about the situation at-hand, assuming that her dreams/memories were accurate.

How else could they have gotten out of that situation? If she assumed for a moment that it *had* happened, why was she at home, in bed, without so much as a scratch on her? For that matter, why didn't Issa and Rao remember anything? Why hadn't *she* remembered anything? Why was she remembering *now?*

In that hypothetical situation, the only explanation that made any form of sense was that Issa's contract had been the real deal and that he had somehow used it to save them. After all, in a situation like that, it was pretty clear what someone's "Desire" would have been, as the paper had put it.

Of course, that still begged the question as to what the hell Issa was doing there *in the first place*, but Elsi didn't feel like looking that particular hypothetical gift horse in the mouth. Either it had happened, in which case she probably owed her life to Issa having been there, or it hadn't, in which case all this speculation was pointless.

...But that would be boring, so she decided to follow the rabbit hole a bit further.

Elsi began to experience a familiar feeling, as though a dull current of electricity was running through her entire body. Her fatigue melted away and she sat bolt upright in bed, swung her legs over the edge, stood up and headed for her desk.

This feeling of restless energy only ever meant one thing for Elsi Thompson: she had found something *interesting*. Her brain was spinning into high gear and she wouldn't be able to rest until she had delved into the object of her focus. Her current "record" was something along the lines of ten hours of sleep over the course of a week. It had happened when she was in high school and she had made damned sure that it was a one-time thing afterwards.

Instead of flipping the light switch located next to her bedroom door, Elsi headed in the opposite direction and grasped a pull string that hovered above her desk. When she pulled it, a single suspended bulb lit up with a satisfying click, creating a spherical zone of slightly dim yellow light.

Elsi's room, much like the young woman herself, could be vaguely described as "half-normal, half-quirky, half-bizarre."

Elsi didn't feel as though her self-image should be restricted by such things as "conventional wisdom," so the fact that this description resulted in one-and-a-half people didn't really bother her. If anything, it meant she could swap out the spare half for one of the others when she needed to. It was convenient, especially in cases like this where it was time to throw normalcy out the window.

That was where the light came in. When she combined it with her slab of a desk and various tools she tinkered around with, it reminded her of an interrogation scene from the movies. It was cool.

Fitting too, since she was about to interrogate *reality itself.*

Okay. What I'm dealing with here is basically impossible, so I can't really rule anything out. I'll just have to go off of the evidence I already have and let my gut handle the rest.

Elsi sat down on a stool in front of the desk and idly twirled a screwdriver between her fingers.

Item A: The paper. This is where everything starts.

Since this whole thing relies on the assumption that it actually was *some sort of magical contract, I have to allow for that.*

Item B: Issa's new roommate, Zurie. I won't say that the guy can't keep a secret when he has to, but I feel like a new roommate would've come up in conversation. That and her sudden appearance corresponds a little too perfectly with that of the so-called contract. She's most likely related to it in some way.

Item C: The situation in the alley and the fact that everything not only turned out fine, but that everyone somehow forgot about it. Or at least, Rao and I did.

The screwdriver fell onto the desk with a clunk.

Wait a minute. The first thing Issa did was to ask if Rao and I were okay. Rao mentioned his head hurting, but I didn't say anything other than I had to drag him around! Why would he ask if we were both *okay?*

...Unless he had some reason to be concerned because he knows what happened.

Elsi blinked at the map on her wall and chuckled in spite of herself.

Well, I guess that pretty heavily reinforces the idea that the scene in the alley was real, meaning the part about Issa charging in to save the day happened too, even if it didn't turn out so well before the end.

I'll have to give him a hug the next time I see him.

Anyway, even if he is *responsible, the question still remains as to exactly what happened. The contract didn't just...poof reality into some sort of different orientation to make it so the situation never happened, did it? That seems like a stretch, especially considering the fact that there's no way Issa's contract was the only one. If people were running around rewriting reality...I can't help but think the world would be a bit different.*

...Come on, Elsi. At times like this, just go with your instincts. They're usually right anyway; just say what you've been thinking from the beginning.

It has to have been Zurie. She's contracted to Issa or something and that's why she's living with him. If I assume the reason I was acting weird earlier to be that she can screw with people's minds or something, then that might also explain why Rao and I forgot about what happened. Hell, if that's not an ability that's unique to her, it could explain why knowledge of these contracts isn't more widely known.

...What's to say she isn't screwing with Issa's head too? There might be a clause that says she can't or something, but I don't have any evidence to support that. For the time being I have to assume she's dangerous. I should keep playing dumb, too. No need to give her any more reasons to screw with my head.

When I have the opportunity to get Issa alone, then I'll put the screws to him and find out what he knows.

Elsi nodded firmly. She had a working theory and she had a plan of action. All of this still begged the question of what was going on with her eyes, but she wasn't really in the mood to push her luck with more headaches at the moment.

There would be time for that later.

CHAPTER FIVE
CASA DE RAO

I f Issa Aono had harbored any doubts about being a creature of habit, they were dashed when he woke up and realized that in the week since he had unwittingly summoned Zurie, he had integrated her seamlessly into his routine. Meals, exercises, leisure time, he was even starting to become slightly less uncomfortable with her sharing his bed (her acquisition of regular clothing courtesy of Elsi definitely helped in that regard).

He still nearly had a heart attack when he had woken up that one time to find her cuddled into his side for warmth, but progress was progress.

"Welcome my wonderful watchers to today's episode of Weird World Wednesday!"

Issa was momentarily taken aback at the fact that Zurie had tuned in to that exact channel before remembering that she had expressed interest in the program upon learning that they had discussed

Contracts. He had advised her not to expect too much, since they covered a variety of topics based on current events, but she insisted.

Well, it wasn't as though he hadn't planned on watching it anyway, so it didn't really change anything.

At least, that was what he had thought at the time. Later, when he had the time to look back on the events that were set in motion that day, Issa would ask himself whether his fortune had been good or bad. It was, in fact, a question that he would ask himself multiple times over the course of his life.

...The answer was rarely as simple as it should have been.

"Urban wanderers, be wary! Heed Wendy's warning or you might end up painting a wall! We're making a public service announcement today at the request of our local law enforcement, so please pay attention! You know things are looking woeful if they come to us of all people!"

"The situation is this: some whacked-out weirdo has been going around murdering folks! There's really no way to sweeten this up, so I'm just gonna read straight from the report they gave me."

"With twelve confirmed kills and another seven suspected, it was originally estimated that this serial killer has been active for around three months, but new evidence suggests that it may in fact be closer to five. There does not appear to be any connection between the victims, either confirmed or suspected, apart from the fact that they appear to have been in public places late at night. Earlier victims show evidence of claw-like slashing and puncture wounds

with accompanying evidence that they were attacked and killed on-the-spot, but more recent victims show evidence of being accosted and relocated prior to their murders before being deposited elsewhere, where they are subsequently found."

"Additionally, the rate of the murders has shown a noticeable increase coinciding with the revised modus operandi. Members of the public are advised to return to their homes prior to nine o'clock PM whenever possible. If this is not possible, take a vehicle whenever possible and try to refrain from travelling alone. Members of the public are also encouraged to contact local law enforcement with any and all relevant information. Information directly contributing to the capture of the killer will be rewarded. There is a dedicated line for such information, the number for which is being displayed on-screen now."

"At the moment, we do not have a sketch of the killer available and while it is suspected that the killer is male, this has yet to be confirmed. It should go without saying, but whoever this individual may be, they are to be considered armed and highly dangerous."

Issa had known about a few of the recent disappearances courtesy of the news/local grapevine, but this was the first public declaration that it was a serial killer insofar as he was aware.

Well, he wasn't much of a night owl anyway, so hopefully this wouldn't impact his life too much. It was only a matter of time before this psycho got caught now that they had offered up a reward for good info.

"Does the show usually cover this sort of thing?"

Zurie spared him a glance as he shouldered his backpack.

"Well, yeah, but it's not usually quite so...credible. At least, that was what I thought before, you know," he waved a hand vaguely in her direction, "you. Who knows if that was a one-off or if I've been missing out the whole time?"

"Well, I've got nothing else going on; maybe I'll watch the rest of it and see what I can find?"

"Do what you want. See you later."

C-O-N-T-R-A-C-T

"And that's more or less it: You all are going to group yourselves up and choose an interesting and/or pivotal current event to report on. Your group may turn in a single report credited to all of you, but each member must personally cite at least three sources of information. No groups larger than four, due in a week. Have at it."

Current Events projects were both the most and least straightforward types of assignments in Issa's opinion. They could be a breeze if you found something well-documented and interesting or if it was an eventful time, but if there wasn't really anything going on, then you might have to do some digging.

"So, what do you guys wanna do?" Rao sat himself on the table and looked to his friends expectantly.

"You know, if we decided to just do a two-person project, you'd be pretty screwed." Issa pointed out.

"Yeah, but you wouldn't do that."

"Why not?" Elsi raised an eyebrow.

"Because I'm the lovable idiot that brings balance to our trio by providing the everyman's perspective and a healthy dose of comic relief?" he waited a moment, evaluating their deadpan stares, "No? Not buying it?"

"I don't think you're an idiot, Rao." Issa clarified, "My grades aren't *that* much better than yours and using a freak of nature like Elsi as a barometer of intelligence really wouldn't be fair." this earned him a punch on the arm from his female friend, "I just kinda wish you'd show some initiative, that's all."

"I agree with Mr. Backhanded Compliments: We'll work with you, but *you* need to pick the topic." Elsi crossed her arms expectantly.

Rao scratched his jaw for a few dozen seconds as he thought about it before nodding to himself, apparently having made a decision.

"Alright. If I'm in charge, then I guess I'll be setting up the base of operations this time. You two don't have anything going on tonight, do you? What say you come home with me today?"

"I can be free." Elsi shrugged.

"Sure, I worked the past couple of nights, so I should be…" Issa trailed off as he remembered Zurie, "Actually, I might need to make a pit stop first."

"Why not just bring her with you?" Elsi suggested, clearly reading his train of thought.

"What, to help with school work?"

"To hang out. From what you've told me, she doesn't really have much to do. If I was her, I'd be going stir-crazy."

"I guess I could ask if she wants to…I wouldn't want to impose on Rao though."

"I'm sure he'd be fine with it."

"Yeah, I'm sure I would be *if I knew who the hell you two were TALKING about!*" Rao clearly didn't appreciate being kept out of the loop.

"Wait, you haven't told him?" Elsi shot Issa an accusing look, causing him to raise his hands defensively.

"It never came up! It'd be awkward to just drop something like that; I feel like I'd come off as self-centered."

"You're a moron."

"For the love of god, *what are you talking about?!*"

"Issa got a roommate about a week ago. It's a girl."

"DUDE, WHAT?!"

"Wanna react a little louder, Rao? I think there are some people on the other side of campus who didn't hear you." Issa tapped an ear, having been the primary target of Rao's enthusiasm and wondering if the ringing meant his eardrums had been damaged.

"You need to bring her with you. Hundred percent. This is non-negotiable."

"What if she doesn't want to?"

"Elsi, go with him. Make sure she wants to. This is a priority one mission. Rendezvous at my place afterwards. Do not fail me."

"Yes, sir." Elsi gave a mock salute, "Except I don't know where you live."

"Good point. I'll send a car. How long does it take you to walk to your apartment again, Issa?"

"Twenty minutes, few more if I take my time. What do you mean you'll 'send a car?'"

But Rao had already grabbed his bag, hopped off of the desk in a surprisingly fluid movement and headed out the door, leaving Issa staring after him.

"What the hell is he going to do?"

"Come on, let's just get to your place." Elsi patted him on the shoulder, "Odds are he just got too into the role of commander and didn't realize what he was saying. He's probably going to phone the apartment once he realizes what he did."

"I...guess?" Issa allowed himself to be shepherded out of the classroom and fell into step beside Elsi, all the while thinking that Rao had seemed unusually focused.

Maybe he just took what we said to him seriously? He's always been a pretty genuine type of guy. I'm probably reading too much into this.

C-O-N-T-R-A-C-T

"Yes! I totally want to go!"

Suffice to say that Zurie had required no convincing whatsoever. No sooner had Issa finished explaining the situation than she had sprung off of the couch and agreed to go. After her initial outburst, she blushed slightly and gave a dignified cough.

"I mean, it's not like it's a huge deal or anything, I just wouldn't want to be rude; refusing an invitation like that and all."

Elsi apparently thought the whole thing was hysterical. When Zurie pouted at her she actually needed to grab a nearby chair for support.

"I'm sorry! I just didn't peg you as the type to have an adorable side!"

"What are you talking about? I'm plenty adorable!"

"Only until you start ordering people around and

giving them workout routines." Issa grumbled.

"What was that?"

"Uh—"

BEEP

Issa was spared having to come up with a defense when the buzzer to his unit rang. Grateful for the distraction, he hurried over and pressed the button to answer.

"Hello?"

"Issa Aono?" the voice of an unfamiliar man inquired in a clipped tone.

"Uh, yes?"

"I am here to collect you, Ms. Thompson and your quote unquote 'lady friend.' Please gather whatever you require and meet me outside."

Issa gaped at the intercom and turned his head to an equally shocked Elsi and a bemused Zurie. He attempted to speak but only ended up mouthing "what the fuck?" at Elsi, as though some part of him were afraid the man on the other end of the intercom would hear him. She made a helplessly confused gesture and jabbed a finger at the intercom.

"Right. Thank you. We'll be right down."

"Very good."

"Elsi."

"Yeah?"

"What just happened?"

"I think we underestimated Rao."

"Wow."

"Yeah."

"Good for him."

"Right?"

"We should go."

So it was that Issa, Elsi and Zurie exited apartment 203, descended the stairs, exited the building and found themselves face-to-face with a man who stood slightly taller than Issa with piercing green eyes behind rectangular glasses and brown hair that was pulled back into a bun. He was well-dressed, but practically so in slacks, a button-up shirt and a waistcoat.

Issa, who was a fan of the dress-casual look himself, approved. Not for the first time, he wished he had a bit more cash to burn, thinking he might enjoy classing up his look a bit.

"Vemris Masia, at your service." he said, inclining his head and placing his right hand over his heart as he did so. He then straightened and swept his gaze over the three standing before him, "Follow me, if you would."

Almost immediately upon meeting the man, Issa decided that he was the sort of person you were better off just listening to. Elsi and Zurie apparently agreed, judging by how they followed in equal silence.

As it turned out, they didn't have to follow Vemris for long, as he had a car waiting for them in the parking lot. Issa felt mildly relieved when he saw that it wasn't a limo, as if that made the whole situation somehow more approachable. Vemris directed Issa to the passenger seat and opened a door to the back for the ladies.

"Our trip will not take long, but make yourselves comfortable." the driver intoned as he took his place and started the car.

None of them said very much during the trip,

which left Issa with little to do other than pay attention to the route and consider the man sitting to his left.

Vemris Masia… "efficient" is the word that comes to mind, I think. He doesn't say any more than he needs to, but he's not rude about it. He dresses well, but not so much so as to draw attention. And there's something about the way he moves…I can't quite describe it, but it feels familiar for some reason.

As Vemris had stated, they arrived before long. In fact, only about twelve minutes had passed. Having paid attention, Issa understood: Rao lived in almost exactly the opposite direction from the college as himself. No wonder he had decided to send a car!

Of course, that still left the question of why Rao had the car to send in the first place, let alone a driver to send along with it. The house they pulled up to was nice enough, but it wasn't "in-house chauffer and spare car" nice.

Vemris led the trio to the door and opened it without knocking, holding it open and gesturing them inside.

"Rao is most likely in the kitchen. This way."

They followed him through the entry and mudroom and into a hallway that angled off to the left. They passed an entrance to what looked like a sitting room and Issa caught a brief glimpse of the hallway proper lined with doorways before they took the first one on the right into a rather sizeable kitchen.

"Oh, hey guys! I was starting to wonder if you'd changed your minds." Rao was indeed seated at a small circular table, eating chips and looking over four different newspapers spread out on said table, "Sorry I didn't wait for you to bust out the snacks; I was kinda hungry after running most of the way back. Even had to stop to grab these papers."

He cleaned his hands off with a piece of paper towel and extended one to Zurie.

"It's the first time we've met, but you've probably already heard about me. Rao Lassare."

"Zurie." she shook his hand and smiled at him, "I have indeed heard some things about you."

"Good, I hope?"

"Let's go with 'entertaining.'"

"Hey, better than 'boring.' So," here he got a glint in his eye and Issa wasn't fast enough to stop him, "how long have you been dating my boy, Issa? How far have you gone? Any embarrassing secrets that I can use as blackmail material?"

"We aren't, we haven't and none!" Issa steered Rao back over to the table by his shoulders and sat him back down by giving him a small shove into the chair, "And we're here to work, so I'll thank you to stay on-topic."

"Indeed." Vemris nodded approvingly, "I'll bring refreshments. You all should get started with your assignment and hopefully you'll have something figured out by dinnertime."

As Elsi and Issa raised eyebrows at Rao, Vemris looked at him and frowned slightly.

"You didn't tell them?"

"I...kinda forgot." Rao gave his friends a guilty look, "I mean, you don't mind, do you? It's not like we don't have enough to go around or anything, so I thought it'd be nice."

"I don't have a problem with it." Issa confirmed

and Zurie nodded her assent. Elsi took a moment to think about it.

"Yeah, it should be fine. I'll have to use your phone to call my mom and let her know though; don't want her making too much and end up having to throw something away."

"Sure, no problem." Rao confirmed.

"Speaking of parents, where're yours, Rao? Working still?" Issa wondered.

"No. Well, probably. They don't live here, see." Rao explained, "This place is kind of...just mine. I mean, they *own* it, of course, but they only bought it so I'd have a place to stay while I'm going to school, so..." he trailed off, clearly feeling awkward. To his credit, the stunned stares he was receiving probably had something to do with that.

"Dude," Elsi broke the silence, "are you rich or something?"

"My folks are, I'm not." Rao corrected her.

"What's the deal with Vemris then?" Issa followed up, "Is he your butler or something?"

"Tutor, actually." the man in question answered for himself as he returned with a small tray holding glasses and a pitcher of iced tea, "Although given the miscellaneous duties I perform, the title of caretaker would also be accurate. In either case, 'Vemris' will suffice."

He served the tea as he spoke, not spilling a single drop in spite of the fullness of the pitcher. Issa was about to question the absence of any ice when he touched his glass and found that it had apparently been chilled.

"So as not to dilute the tea." Vemris answered his

question before he could ask it, "Also, young miss, it is rather impolite to stare."

Zurie gave a start and put a hand to her head.

"Sorry! It's just, your movements are so graceful. I guess I was mesmerized." she gave a disarming grin and Issa wondered if she was attempting to use Suggestion to smooth things over. Whether this was the case or not, Vemris held her gaze for a moment before giving a "hmm" and setting the pitcher back on the tray on a part of the table not covered by newspapers.

"Call for me if you need anything." he said before walking out of sight.

"He's kind of intense, huh?" Elsi remarked, sipping her tea, "Well, anyway, have you come up with any ideas yet, Mr. Moneybags?"

"As a matter of fact, I *have*." the man of the house responded proudly before indicating one newspaper in particular, "We're going after a serial killer."

"We're going after what now?" Elsi queried as Issa choked on his iced tea, "What's your deal, Issa?"

"I think I know who you're talking about." Issa responded when he could breathe again, "Weird World Wednesday featured a story on them today. More of a public service announcement, really. Anyway, what do you mean we're going *after* the killer?"

"Well, not *after* after. It just sounded better that way."

"What sounds *better* is us not getting killed."

"Relax. This'll all be done during the day. The first thing I figured we'd need is some info about past killings, so that's what we'll be working on tonight.

I've got a bunch more where these came from," he indicated the newspapers, "and if I needed to, I could ask Vem to go over and get some info out of the police. You've seen what he's like; they'll probably give him whatever he asks for before he's halfway through his request."

"If you got me that," Elsi spoke slowly, not seeming to look at anything in particular, "I might be able to map out the previous victims and predict where they'll strike next. No promises though."

"It'd be cool if you could." Issa grinned, "They were offering a reward for any info that helps catch the guy. Or girl."

"Guy. Probably."

"What makes you think that?" Zurie gave Elsi an intrigued look.

"I'll know for sure once we get those police records, but the method of killing is really forceful and violent. Add to that the fact that recent victims were dragged off while still alive and it just seems more likely that any killer who's physically able to do that would be a man."

"Alright." Issa nodded, accepting her reasoning, "So, Rao's getting the info, you're mapping it out, what does that leave for me?"

"You're going to help me sort through it and get the data organized. I tend to be pretty chaotic when I'm in the zone, so I'll need you to keep things manageable and record my findings. Besides, you've got neat handwriting."

"Don't you do odd jobs for a temp agency too?" Rao chimed in, "You probably know the local areas pretty well then."

"I mean, I'm not a walking map or anything, but I can find my way around, sure."

"Maybe you can add some insight to the locations we find?"

They continued bouncing ideas off of each other, making note of the ones that felt the most promising. When Vemris reappeared and began preparing dinner, Rao told him about their idea and subsequent request regarding the police.

"I'm afraid you may be overestimating me," Vemris warned, "but I will do what I can. You should try and find alternative sources of information just in case. Either way, I cannot promise anything for at least two or three days. Any request will need to go through the proper channels and be approved beforehand. Ordinarily, I imagine it would take quite a bit longer, but given the urgency of this case and their request for help from the public, I imagine they will be inclined to accommodate."

And so it was that a group of college students decided to investigate an active serial killer. Little did they know that along the way they would discover something far more dangerous.

Chapter Six
First Blood

The man sat with his knees hugged to his chest, trying to replace the warmth that was steadily being sapped by the wall against his back and the holes in the rusted piece of metal that could only charitably be called a roof. Most people might consider scooting forwards a few inches in a bid to get more comfortable, but to this man, such a thought was blasphemously foolish.

After all, if he kept his back to the wall, *he* couldn't sneak up on him.

"Gotta see him coming. Gotta make sure I always see him coming."

"You could run, you know."

The other one was speaking in a low voice from where he sat on top of a shipping crate. His slouching posture and downcast gaze caused the upper half of his face to be obscured by his unkempt hair.

The man didn't respond.

"You could run." the other one said again after a few more minutes of silence only interrupted by the muffled sounds of vehicles and machinery, "He should be asleep for a while yet, I think."

Yes. *Him.* Violent, unpredictable and undoubtedly the single most terrifying one the man had ever met. His life had ended already, it was only a matter of when *he* decided to make it official.

The hell of the situation was that the man had only gotten himself into all this by accident.

It was true: he never should have been in that place at that time. He had gone there on a whim, nothing more. In so doing, he had made the single biggest mistake of his life.

One which was likely to be his last.

"What would be the point in trying?"

The other one apparently didn't have an answer ready for that, since he remained silent for at least ten minutes after the man's question. Indeed, he remained so still that the man wondered if he had simply fallen asleep.

"There's a chance you could escape."

Even through the other one's flat tone, devoid of all inflection, the man could tell that these were empty words. Escape was absolutely impossible.

"Why are you even bothering?"

"I remember hearing that a bit of hope can be good for a person's health. You might not believe me, but I really am on your side."

"Whatever good that does in a situation like this…"

Really, it was more than a little ironic when the man took the time to think about it: His head was clearer than it had been in a long time, but now all he could comprehend was his own impending doom.

"If you're worried that I'll try and stop you, don't be. My fate is the same regardless of what you do, so I have no reason to stand in your way."

"Suppose for a moment that I *did* run. When he woke up, he'd come after me, right?"

"Yes."

"And even if I managed to make it out of the city, he'd catch me."

"Most likely."

"I wouldn't survive that."

"No."

"That's why I'm staying: If he's going to get rid of me one way or the other, I want to see him coming."

"…As you wish."

C-O-N-T-R-A-C-T

After a dinner that was really quite good, the meeting at Rao's residence continued for another few hours that was split between planning, work and just chatting, the lion's share of which was divided between Elsi interviewing Vemris and Rao trying to get juicy tidbits out of Zurie.

Now that he knew to watch for it, Issa thought he saw the occasional sign of Zurie using Suggestion to deflect or redirect a particularly probing question, though thankfully this seemed to be a simpler matter with more people present and, thus, less attention directly focused on his Contractor. It also helped that Vemris was currently new and interesting, causing Elsi's questioning of Zurie to be half-hearted at most.

They really needed to figure out what to do about

that because once she had gotten over the intrigue of the new face, Issa knew she'd be back at Zurie again.

Why not just tell her the truth? a part of him suggested, *What harm could it do?*

As Issa considered this, he found that he actually had a few different answers. Part of him said that it wasn't his place to tell her anything that Zurie didn't want her to know. Part of him was afraid that she would laugh him off or, worse yet, get angry because she thought he was lying to her. Yet another part of him just wanted to jealously hold onto the one thing he knew that Elsi didn't.

The biggest part of him, however, didn't respond with words, but an image. An image that would be burned into his mind forever. The image of an alleyway splattered with gore while a girl looked down at him, arms red to the elbow as if she were wearing gloves.

Because it's dangerous.

Otherworldly beings with superhuman abilities who functioned by making deal-with-the-devil type pacts that could easily result in someone losing their soul? Yeah, Issa was pretty sure that qualified as "dangerous."

It was also the sort of thing that someone like Elsi would probably dive into headfirst for the sake of sating their own curiosity. Issa would readily admit to anyone who asked that she was smarter than him, but she also had a tendency to develop tunnel vision when she got excited about something and Issa was scared that she would make the kind of mistake that he himself had nearly made when he was contemplating his own Contract back when he didn't believe it was real.

In the end, he supposed that was what it came down to: Fear. Not for himself so much as for those around him, but the fact that they were both impulsive in different ways didn't help.

Eventually, it got to the point where there wasn't much else they could do that night and Vemris offered to take them home. The ride to Elsi's place, since she lived closer to Rao than Issa did, was mostly silent. It didn't feel *awkward* per-se, it was just that Vemris didn't seem to be one for small talk, Elsi was resting her chin on her hand and staring out the window, clearly lost in thought, Issa simply didn't feel inclined to break the silence and Zurie...he couldn't see her very well, since she was seated directly behind him, but when he caught a brief glimpse of her thanks to the reflections in the sideview mirror, she looked oddly fatigued.

At first, Issa had thought that perhaps it was just a trick of the light, but as Vemris was letting Elsi out of the car and Issa turned to say goodbye, he took the chance to get a better look at the white-haired girl and nearly did a double-take when he saw that she was practically sagging against the door, sweat beading her brow.

"Are you—" he began only for her to cut him off with a raised hand and a mouthed "later."

As Vemris re-entered the car and began the relatively short drive to Issa's apartment, he took it upon himself to break the long-held silence.

"Where are you from, Vemris?"

It was the first non-loaded question he could think to ask and some instinct told him that he needed to draw the man's attention to himself, even for a moment.

"A city similar to this one, though different in its own ways."

"Where about? Any place I might've heard of?"

"I doubt it; it's rather far away."

"If you don't mind my asking, how did you end up here?"

"Work. In my field, you go where you're needed."

"Tutoring, you mean?"

"Indeed."

Issa knew he wasn't getting anywhere, even in terms of keeping Vemris talking. The man really didn't waste words.

"What about the young woman in the back?" Vemris asked his own question before Issa could think of something else, "Her looks are fairly exotic, even for a place as cosmopolitan as this. Where might she be from?"

Issa's first thought was to respond with "ask her yourself," but he was somehow convinced that Vemris had something to do with Zurie's condition. It was the only explanation he could think of for why she wouldn't tell him what was wrong.

"I'm not sure. Never really bothered to ask her." he responded with a shrug, "Maybe she's from the same place as you?"

"Maybe. Ah, here we are."

Vemris pulled up in front of the main entrance and made to exit the car, but Issa held up a hand as he exited the passenger side.

"I've got it; we've imposed upon you enough already."

I don't trust him with Zurie. Not when she's like this. Not when I don't understand the situation.

"It's hardly an imposition, but I'll accept your kindness."

"I'll see you later. Good luck with the police."

"Thank you."

Issa closed the door behind him and fetched Zurie from the back, trying to be subtle about offering her physical support. To his surprise, she shook her head and led the way into the building, seeming as steady on her feet as ever. She unlocked apartment 203 with the spare key he had given her and made her way to the couch before collapsing onto it.

"He's a Contractor." she said as Issa closed the door and locked it.

"Vemris?"

"That's right."

Issa wished that he was surprised by this, but somehow he wasn't. Something about Vemris had struck him as off from the moment he had first seen him. Even so, that still begged a question.

"How do you know?"

"He had near-complete immunity to my low-level Suggestion. Every moment we were in his presence I had to keep re-applying it at a constant rate to stop him from realizing what I am."

Issa's eyes widened at that.

"If it was that bad, why not use a stronger one?"

"Too risky. Beyond a certain point, I can't hide when I'm using my abilities from other Contractors. The effectiveness varies from person to person, but at a certain point all Contractors are able to sense when others are nearby by picking up on their energy output. I'm usually able to keep my presence suppressed even with some use of Suggestion, but if I used any more power at once, someone like him would probably sense it."

"Does…" Issa steeled himself, "Does that mean Rao is a Signer?"

"Not necessarily. There's no rule stating that a Contractor needs to stay by their Signer's side, though most do anyway because it makes fulfilling their Contract easier."

"It's likely though."

"Yeah."

Issa wasn't sure how to feel about that, but there was a more pressing issue at hand.

"I think I know what's wrong with you then: You're thirsty, aren't you?"

She nodded in response; eyes downcast.

"Guess it's time for me to pay up then."

"I'm sorry. I didn't intend to need any this soon, but —" she cut herself off when she saw that he was undoing the top few buttons of his shirt, "What are you doing?"

"You're going to bite my neck, right? You're a vampire, after all."

"Well, it doesn't have to be the neck, but…yes."

Was that a blush, or was it a side-effect of her thirst? Issa decided that it didn't matter as he tugged his collar to the side, exposing his neck.

"Well…I'm ready, I guess."

Zurie turned a bit redder and looked away, mumbling something unintelligible.

"What?"

"I said I can't reach! You're too tall. Sit down or something."

"Oh, right." Issa took a chair from the table and turned it around, seating himself, "How's this?"

She nodded again and stood up, striding purposefully towards him.

"This isn't going to, uh, turn me, is it?" Issa tried and failed to keep his nervousness out of his voice.

"No." Zurie assured him as she hopped onto his lap, "It takes more than just a bite to change someone into one of us, so don't worry about that."

Issa drew an involuntary breath as she ran her fingers along his jaw, as though feeling his pulse, before tracing his neck and adjusting his collar to allow for easier access. The entire time the Signer found himself unable to look away from her eyes. They were half-lidded, as though she were in a trance. Her lips were slightly parted and as she drew closer, he could see that her fangs were more prominent than usual. She placed her other hand against his chest with a gentle motion, but he felt the chair press into his back.

It was then that Issa realized how much his Contractor must have been restraining herself. She was deliberately holding back to avoid injuring him or scaring him, even though he could see the hunger in her eyes.

"Go on."

That was apparently all she needed as, in a single motion, she closed the remaining distance and sunk her fangs into his neck.

Issa had expected to feel pain, but instead all he felt was a sort of...pressure...from the initial bite. As she began to drink, however, the bizarre feeling of his blood being sucked from his veins sent a shiver down his spine and caused him to take a sharp, involuntary breath. Upon hearing this, he felt Zurie stiffen and the feeling abruptly subsided.

Damn, she thinks she's hurting me! There's no way she's had enough yet.

Without further thought, Issa brought his hand to the back of her head and held her to him. Her fingers dug into his chest and shoulder as she resumed drinking with renewed voracity. As she did, Issa gradually began to feel a faint chill creeping through his body.

…It's because I'm losing blood. I did a bit of research because I wanted to know which warning signs to look for. Increased heart rate, rapid breathing and cool, clammy skin are symptoms of stage two hypovolemic shock. It's still manageable, but if I start sweating or feeling woozy, I'll need to stop her.

Even as these thoughts passed through his mind, Issa found that he was reluctant to follow through on them. As he held Zurie close, the feeling of the petite girl in his arms warred with his firsthand knowledge of what she was and what she was truly capable of.

…The greatest predator will have its prey approach it willingly. Vampires might be more terrifying than I gave them credit for.

…But even knowing that, I can't help wanting to stay like this.

Before long, the feeling of being drained subsided once again and a satisfied sigh came from below Issa's ear.

"Sorry, I took a bit more than I meant to. Give me a moment and I'll get you some juice." Zurie sat up, allowing air to chill the space between them. Issa found that he was taken aback by just how brisk it felt. As he got a better look at her, he saw that she had a sort of glow to her that certainly hadn't been present before. With a pang of guilt, he realized just how much paler than usual she had been when they had gotten back.

"You look like you're feeling better."

"Yeah. I was totally right about the quality of your blood!" she flashed him a dazzling grin and Issa wondered if his increased heart rate was due entirely to blood loss or not, "The headache of dealing with Vemris was worth it after getting to drink that!"

She hopped off of his lap, full of vitality and started heading for the kitchen before she stopped and looked over her shoulder at him.

"Oh, and Issa? I sort of suspected this already, but after tasting your blood, I'm sure of it."

"Uh…what do you mean?"

"You're a good guy, aren't you?"

More than anything else that happened that day, those words made Issa blush.

C-O-N-T-R-A-C-T

Thursday was fairly uneventful. Issa was still slightly drained, but he had recovered enough that he was able to make a bit of cash at the temp agency, doing his homework while he waited for the call. Friday was similarly spent, though there were classes to attend. It was early Saturday morning that Issa got the call he had been waiting for.

"Hey man, how's it hanging?"

"Tell me something good, Rao."

"I value our friendship."

"Still waiting."

"Heh, harsh. It took a bit, but Vemris came through. He convinced the cops to give us copies of the information they have on the killings so far. Elsi's chomping at the bit to go through it all, so I'm gonna send Vemris to get you, alright?"

"Sounds good."

Issa hung up the phone and turned to Zurie, who was sitting on the couch watching TV.

"Vemris is coming by to take me to Rao's. Given what happened last time, I'm thinking you should stay behind."

"I can't say I like it, given that we don't know what his deal is yet, but I guess there's not much choice."

Soon enough, Issa's buzzer rang to signal Vemris' arrival and he exited the building, seeing that the car was pulled up to the front entrance this time as opposed to waiting in the parking lot.

"Will the young lady not be joining us this time?" the suspected Contractor inquired as he and Issa seated themselves and fastened their seatbelts.

"She's not feeling up to it."

"I see. Is it the same malady that she was dealing with last time?" at Issa's surprised look, he gave a wry smile, "I could hardly fail to notice; she was barely able to sit up straight."

"Yeah. It's something that she has to deal with every now and then. She's fine, but not quite back to a hundred percent yet, so I made her stay behind and get some rest."

"Should we pick up some medicine on the way back?"

"We have what we need at the apartment, but thank you."

The remainder of the trip was spent in silence, though this was swiftly broken when Issa entered Rao's house and was more or less dragged into the kitchen by an impatient Elsi.

"What took you so long?! I've been looking at this stuff and it's good! Well, no, it's terrible, but it's good for the assignment!"

Eleven manila folders were arranged in a cardboard box, their tabs labeled with numbers and dates, with a twelfth one lying open on the table. Issa caught a brief glimpse of a photograph and what might have been an autopsy report before Elsi shoved a notebook and pencil into his hands and pointed him to a chair.

"Sit down and start writing. We're going over each one a few times, focusing on different points. The autopsy reports are up first."

Issa suppressed a smirk at her obvious excitement before dutifully sitting and assuming the position, pencil poised over the first page.

"December 13th, 1989. Cause of death: exsanguination due to severe trauma to the head and multiple lacerations whose grouping suggests the use of a claw-like implement, though use of a gag along with the urban location precludes the possibility of an animal attack. The decisively fatal wound was one delivered to the throat, which severed the carotid artery in addition to tearing open the windpipe." there was a brief pause as Elsi rifled through the copied photographs, "Ew, I think that would've been fatal with or without the blood loss. Anyway, next victim.

Huh, looks like he took the holidays off. January 3rd, 1990. Cause of death—"

C-O-N-T-R-A-C-T

It was nearly two hours later that Issa finally set down his considerably shortened pencil and flexed his fingers. To say that Elsi had been thorough would have been an understatement. She had scanned each folder no fewer than four times, having him create separate sections in the notebook for autopsy reports (with the locations circled and approximate times of death underlined), victim details, site details and other notes.

Issa had to admit that there was an undeniable method to Elsi's madness, though he had more than once been forced to interject with a clearing of his throat or handful of words to get her back on-topic when her interest had been snagged by something she came across, which was more often than not a picture or side note of some kind.

"Holy crap, my throat is killing me." Elsi seemed to suddenly realize, resting a hand against her throat before Vemris handed her a steaming cup of tea.

"Once you passed the one-hour mark, I began to suspect that such would be the case." he offered by way of explanation.

Rao, who had spent the intervening time supplying Elsi with new folders and re-organizing the ones she had already gone through, flipped through the notes Issa had taken and gave an appreciative whistle.

"So, uh, what next?"

"Did you get that map I asked for?"

"I sure did. Here we go." Rao unfolded a map of the city and smoothed it out onto the table while Elsi took out a red pen.

"This is where you come in, Issa. Based on the pictures and the information regarding where the bodies were found, we're going to mark the locations on this map and label them by date. A few of these are pretty easy to pin down, but the rest are a bit more obscure, at least to me."

Issa obliged, managing to place a handful of dots fairly confidently and having an educated guess as to a couple more before one well and truly stumped him. To his and Elsi's surprise, it was Rao who saw it and offhandedly pointed them to the spot while he was helping Vemris prepare lunch.

"Oh, that's right here. In front of that warehouse."

"How the do you know that?" Elsi stared incredulously.

"It says so right there, see? 'Warehouse MG 03.' MG is shorthand for the Moreno Group and the warehouses are organized in rows and columns by number. The Moreno Group happens to use this section over here, so all we have to do is count over one, two, three and there you go."

When his friends still looked unsatisfied, Rao shrugged.

"My parents taught me to always make sure to understand how the local big businesses function, at least on a surface level. I don't enjoy it, but it's become such a habit that I sometimes skim business articles when I'm bored. Like, *really* bored. Plus, the Moreno Group is huge. This sort of info is something anyone could find out."

Elsi drew lines connecting the dots in chronological order and stared at the map, chewing on her lip and muttering to herself.

"This is weird."

"Did you find something?" Issa encouraged.

"Pay close attention to how the location of the victims changes over time. At first it's pretty spread out and fairly random, but the latter half of the killings, which took place in less than a third of the time frame of the originals, mind you, are all closer together. It's not unusual for a serial killer to ramp up their rate as they go on and get more confident, deranged or whatever, but the thing that really strikes me as odd is that these victims are also more well-hidden."

"So what?" Rao raised an eyebrow, "Like you said, he's getting better at it. Why's that weird to you?"

"Because at first *he didn't care.*" she pointed to earlier dots as she continued, "Found slumped over a park bench. Found in the middle of an alleyway. Found *in the middle of the fucking road.* This psycho has quite clearly never cared about hiding the bodies...until now. And I have no idea why."

"Something must have happened to cause the killer to change his modus operandi." Vemris opined as he served soup and sandwiches, "Perhaps something scared him enough that he felt the need to start hiding the bodies?"

"Like the police's investigation into him, for example?" Issa hazarded.

"Unless he's got ties to the police somehow, or he's the world's most skittish serial killer, I don't think so." Elsi said in an offhanded way as she bit into a sandwich.

Issa was about to ask what she meant before a wave of realization hit him.

"The first time I heard anything about it on TV was this week."

"Yeah, and seeing as how it hasn't made the front page until recently either, I'm guessing the media had specific instructions to keep the investigation on the down-low, at least in terms of specifics." Rao added.

"So, unless he's the sort who's meticulous enough to read the paper all the way through, which I doubt given the fact that he didn't even bother to hide the bodies of his victims, there's a decent chance that he didn't know anyone was after him. Or didn't care." Elsi concluded.

"In other words, what you're saying is the unpredictable, murderous psychopath is acting out-of-character?" Rao said with more than a hint of sarcasm.

"As a matter of fact, Mr. Lassare, that's exactly what I'm saying."

"And I agree." Vemris said, giving the map a thoughtful look, "It's almost as if he became a different person."

"Well, speculating is great and all but we need more than just that." Elsi said with a note of finality, "Since it looks like the killings mostly take place at night and they've been concentrated around the warehouse district lately, I say we hit the streets and see for ourselves. Conduct on-site interviews, that sort of thing. Even if we don't find anything out, it'll look good for the assignment."

"When do you want to head out?" Issa asked.

"Tomorrow morning. We'll start at one end and work our way to the other, breaking partway through to get lunch somewhere. More people means more ground covered, so if you'd come with us, Vemris, and if you can get Zurie in on this, Issa, then we can split into groups."

"Pairs." Vemris corrected, "I should be fine on my own."

Yeah, I bet you would be. Issa thought, *I'll be fine with Zurie around too, but...*

"Maybe you should stick with Rao and Elsi." Issa suggested.

"Maybe *nothing*. I've got a plan so just leave it to the team leader!" Rao grinned.

Oh, boy...

CHAPTER SEVEN
STRIKE THREE

"**N**o."

"Rao—"

"I said 'no,' okay? You're reading too much into this."

Vemris Masia sighed, exhaling a plume of cigarette smoke as he did so. For someone who was generally easygoing, the boy could be stubborn at times. He had a bad habit of allowing his emotions to cloud his judgment, something Vemris had tried time and again to rid him of.

"Whether you want to accept it or not, it is the only explanation that makes logical sense."

"There has to be another explanation."

"Why? Because you would prefer it that way? That isn't how the world works."

"And just because *you* come to a specific answer doesn't make it the right one!"

"Ah yes, the time-honored argument of 'you *could*

be mistaken, therefore you *must* be.'"

"It's better than blindly accepting everything without question."

"Choosing to ignore the evidence is not the same as being blind to it."

Rao's mouth opened and closed several times, but he said nothing.

"Let's go over it point-by-point, shall we? Firstly, when Issa came to class that day, he was in possession of a blank Contract. Correct?"

"Yeah, he had what looked like a Contract. I might ordinarily have thought he was trying to pull something, since he's into that Weird World Whatever show, but it seemed like he actually didn't know where it came from. If you look at it like that...it was probably real." Rao grudgingly admitted before backtracking, "But it could've been a prank! That sort of thing is going around lately too."

"Secondly," Vemris continued after taking another drag on his cigarette, "when I arrived in that alley, having sensed that something was wrong, I found no fewer than three unconscious people, you and Elsi among them, as well as the remains of two others. I'll spare you the details, but the rather spectacularly violent means of their deaths could not have been achieved with human strength. Not in such a short time. I must therefore conclude that a Contractor was involved. Do you disagree?"

"No, I'll take your word for it. Besides, you yourself have said that there are multiple Contractors currently active in the general area, so it's not impossible."

"And I may well have suspected one of them, were

it not for my next point: Thirdly, when I was rushing to your aid, I detected an unmistakable surge of power. The sort that only occurs when a new Contract is forged and a Contractor is summoned. While I won't pretend to have the ability to pinpoint the location of such events, would you care to guess which direction it came from?"

"I would, but I have a feeling it's the old clichй."

"The same direction I was heading, quite right." Vemris nodded, "This means that it was most likely *not* one of the pre-existing Contractors. Do you have any inkling of what my final point might be?"

"Issa's new roommate, who coincidentally moved in with him pretty much right after this all happened."

"Indeed."

"This still doesn't prove anything, or haven't you realized that all of your evidence is circumstantial? Just because a Contractor was summoned doesn't mean that it was Issa who summoned them. Do you have any idea how many people live in this city? Because I really don't, but I know it's a *lot*. Any one of them could've been the one who did it."

"Only one who had a blank Contract at hand which, speaking of my so-called 'circumstantial evidence,' Issa *did*, by your own admission. He would have had ample motivation as well, wouldn't he, with the lives of his two closest friends presumably at stake? Perhaps his own as well?"

"Issa wasn't going to use the Contract. He told Elsi he was getting rid of it."

"Because we both know how simple a matter that is." Vemris observed the way Rao's mouth thinned and his gaze drifted downwards, "Yes, the Contract is designed to tempt and infused with a lure all its own. Only one who is completely free of desire could throw it away without a second thought. If, as you say, Issa is the sort who has a penchant for the supernatural, it would be nearly impossible for him to get rid of the Contract without at least attempting to verify if it was real or not, to say nothing of what his Desire might have been."

"Okay." Rao said through gritted teeth, "There's still one thing that you can't explain though: *Why the hell would Issa have been in that alley?!*"

Vemris shrugged, which only seemed to infuriate Rao further.

"Does it matter? Perhaps it was fate? Perhaps it was the power of the Contract? Perhaps he simply fancied a walk? In the end, all that matters is that he was there. Accept it, Rao: Issa Aono is a Signer. Not only that, but he suspects that *I* am a Contractor."

"What?" Rao was so surprised that he had apparently forgotten that he was angry, "What the hell did you *do*, Vem?! Why would he think that?!"

"I have done nothing, thank you very much. It is entirely possible that Zurie picked up on something, but without knowing what her ability is, I cannot say for certain. The fact remains that he has been unusually on-guard around me and he seemed rather eager to have me watch you and Elsi tomorrow, while he himself was perfectly content searching for evidence of an extremely dangerous man with only Zurie for company. Either he is incredibly overconfident in his own capabilities, or he has some reason to believe that they will be fine on their own."

"For instance, that Zurie is a Contractor. Okay.

Fine. I get it." Rao grumbled, "Speaking of tomorrow, I think I've got everything ready. Here, take this one around back so we can test it."

C-O-N-T-R-A-C-T

Issa Aono was staring out of his apartment window as he and Zurie waited for Vemris to arrive and take them to their so-called "research site" as Rao had excitedly put it.

"There's one question I have regarding Contractors, now that I think about it."

"Hmm? Go ahead." she responded, seemingly only half-listening as she flipped through channels, though Issa suspected she wasn't really watching anything.

"I kind of just went along with it, since you seemed so tense, but why does it matter if Vemris finds out you're a Contractor? Are you enemies or something?"

Zurie was quiet for a moment before she sighed and the noise of the TV died.

"It's nothing like that. Or maybe it is. We don't have any way of knowing and *that's* why it's dangerous."

"I'm not sure I follow."

"A Contractor can be summoned to fulfill pretty much any sort of Contract. As long as they accept the Desire, Terms and Payment of their prospective Signer, that's really all that matters. Until we know for sure what he's here to do, we can't be sure that he won't attack us."

"What if he does?" Issa proffered, remembering the scene of carnage from the alleyway again, "I have a hard time imagining anyone that could be a threat to you."

"I appreciate the vote of confidence, but when you look at the big picture, I'm really nothing special when it comes to a full-on fight. I wouldn't say that I'm weak, but compared to other Contractors, I'm not especially strong either. And even then, that's only scratching the surface of what happens when two Contractors fight each other."

"Wait, you mean this happens often? Two Contractors fighting, I mean." Issa turned around and gave Zurie an incredulous look, only for her to shrug in response.

"I wouldn't say it happens all the time, but Contracts are distributed in places where people are willing to pay a price to obtain what they want. Places such as a battlefield or in front of the leaders of two opposing political or criminal factions would be pretty normal places to see them popping up. It doesn't take a genius to figure out what's likely to happen if multiple Contractors are summoned in those sorts of conditions."

She chuckled mirthlessly to herself.

"Of course, sometimes you'll just find two or more Contractors that don't get along and decide to settle things with violence. We might be separate from your world, but there are some things that all societies have in common. Who knows, maybe Vemris just hates vampires? We're not exactly the most popular sorts, at least where I come from. Like I said, we can't be sure."

"So, the idea is to play it close to the chest until you know for sure that the other one isn't your enemy? I get it, but it seems like it'd be hard to find out one way or the other if you're not able to talk about it." he was rewarded with another shrug.

"Call me cynical if you want, but I don't feel like taking that chance. At least not until I'm sure I could get away from him if things went bad and, until we know what he can do, I can't be sure of that."

BEEP

"Well, someone's ears must be burning." Issa joked in spite of the fact that he felt a little unsettled by Vemris' timing.

The two exited the apartment and found the car waiting for them just like before, only this time Rao and Elsi were already inside, with Elsi in the back and Rao riding shotgun. This saw Issa seated between the two women, which Elsi wasted no time in pointing out. Once they had gotten back onto the main road, Rao cleared his throat.

"Alright, here's the plan: We're splitting up into three pairs. I'm with Elsi, Issa's with Zurie and Vemris is with himself. Look for anything suspicious, chat up anyone you see who doesn't look like a serial killer and report anything you find with these babies." he held up a trio of walkie talkies with wired earpieces, "I've already got these dialed in to the same frequency and I made sure it's not one that's generally used by the police or security guards or whoever. Just don't fiddle with the buttons or lose 'em! They weren't cheap."

"You're pretty invested in this, huh?" Zurie said, examining one of the handsets, "I get it, since it's potentially dangerous and everything, but still."

"Not just that," Rao grinned widely, "have you *seen*

how much they're offering for info on this guy?!"

"No, I haven't." Issa raised an eyebrow, "And I'm wondering how *you* did, since they've kept that deliberately quiet to avoid getting a tidal wave of faulty information."

"Thirty. Grand."

"Get the fuck out of here!" Elsi squawked, "The police would never throw out a number like that, even if it's a pot for them to divide between everyone who gives them good info!"

"That's because it's not their money." Vemris said with the barest hint of a smirk in his voice, "They received a donation from a private benefactor to support their search, with the stipulation that a percentage of the amount would be added to the pot."

"In other words, this guy *seriously* pissed someone off." Rao concluded before sobering up somewhat, "I mean, yeah, it's terrible and everything, seeing as how this probably relates to someone he killed, but let's try and stay positive, yeah? If we do good work here, not only will we get a good grade, but a sweet payday too!"

Issa maintained his reservations, but even so, he'd be lying if he said that he couldn't use a bit of extra money, thanks in no small part to his Zurie-approved diet noticeably raising his grocery bill.

He felt pretty good though, so at least there was that.

Eventually, they parked themselves in a vacant lot near the edge of the industrial park where some of the more recent victims had been found and split up, deciding they would start with the surrounding streets and hit the warehouse district proper after lunch. They split up and began their investigation.

C-O-N-T-R-A-C-T

"Well, glad to know we weren't the only ones who turned up nothing." Rao groused as he tossed a few fries into his mouth and took a gulp of soda.

"I wouldn't say 'nothing,' Vemris chided over his BLT, "just nothing that we didn't already know. We aren't starting from zero, after all."

"Yeah, but we're young and our attention spans are hurting." Elsi pouted before aggressively attacking her burger as though it was the one at fault.

Issa said nothing, preferring to savor his own burger, though privately he understood Elsi's frustration. After all, three hours of rehashing more or less the same conversation with different people and learning nothing new aside from the occasional bit of absurd trivia could try anyone's patience.

His favorite so far had been one couple's theory that the killer was an escaped government detainee who was actually a mutant that would serve to start a worldwide conversion into specially powered individuals, wherein superheroes would not only become real, but an everyday occupation.

"Might make a halfway-decent show." he murmured to himself.

"Wuzzat?" Zurie asked through yet another mouthful of his fries, causing him to shove the basket at her.

"I said if you wanted something, you should have said so while we were at the counter!"

"I'm sorry! I thought I was fine but once I started, I couldn't stop!"

"Yep, those things are evil." Elsi deadpanned, "Don't worry; with all the running around we're doing today, you'll work them off in no time."

Not for the first time, Issa found himself wondering if Zurie *needed* to eat, strictly speaking, or if she just did it out of habit. Maybe it helped to extend the necessary amount of time between feedings?

Or, given how she was devouring his fries, maybe she just enjoyed the taste of food, even if she didn't need it?

I guess there's still a lot I don't know about her. Kind of a weird feeling, seeing as how she's completely integrated herself into my life.

"I am certain that this goes without saying," Vemris warned as they cleared up the remains of their lunch, "but the industrial park, while open to the public, is primarily a place of business. Try not to make nuisances of yourselves."

With that, the group split up again and entered the field of buildings.

For about an hour, nothing noteworthy happened. They had seen several people, all of whom appeared busy, so they didn't interrupt. After this, Issa had the idea of searching the far end of the Moreno Group's warehouses.

"I'm sure Rao and Elsi made a beeline for the one that was in the picture, but it might not have occurred to them to search the opposite end." he reasoned. Zurie had no objections, so that was where they went.

This decision bore immediate fruit when they saw

two men having a smoke break outside of one of the warehouses, each of whom had a stylized "M.G." clearly visible on their uniforms.

"Well, now or never I guess." Issa straightened his collar and approached the men with a friendly wave, "Excuse me, I was wondering if you gentlemen might have a moment to answer one or two questions? We're doing some research for a class of ours and since the Moreno Group is involved, we were hoping to get a statement from some of their employees."

"Well, technically I don't think we're supposed to..." the taller man rubbed the back of his neck, looking genuinely apologetic.

"Oh, go on." the shorter man, who looked a fair bit older, gestured genially to Issa and Zurie, "We're not allowed to talk to the media, but they're just a couple 'o kids trying to do good in school. Isn't that right, you two?"

"Yes. Absolutely." Issa immediately nodded, patting his clothes and even flipping up his collar, "See? No microphones, cameras or anything like that. We'll even keep you anonymous when we cite our sources, if you'd like."

"Can't do fairer than that, eh?" the shorter man turned to his coworker, who still seemed unsure, "What's the harm? And they came all the way out here too. Be a shame to send them away empty-handed, you know?"

"I guess so. It's not like they could do much damage without any recordings, seeing as how we could just deny everything if we had to."

With the men willing to talk, Issa broached the

topic of the killer, citing that one of the bodies had been found near one of the Moreno Group's warehouses and asking if anything had been going on internally since then or if they had heard anything else.

"Well, it just so happens that I was at the main office when the news broke." the taller man recalled.

"We both were; it was a company-wide meeting!" the shorter man confirmed.

"Right. We have quarterly company-wide meetings designed to go over our statistics and to give the higher-ups an excuse to show face to the everymen. Build solidarity and all that. Well, during the meeting, Mr. Moreno was on the stage saying his piece when someone, might've been a secretary of some sort, comes power-walking over to him from off-stage and whispers something in his ear."

"Now, what you've got to understand is this sort of thing *never* happens during a presentation." the shorter man emphasized, "*Especially* when the big man himself is on-stage. To be frank, I think the only reason he handled it as well as he did was he was too surprised to be angry. Word has it the man has a temper, you see."

"Yeah, and everyone in the front quarter of the auditorium got a firsthand earful of it." the taller man nodded, "He apologized and said something urgent had come up but that he'd be right back. He walked off-stage, half-dragging the poor sap who'd interrupted him by the arm, then we heard this muffled shouting coming from the back. Something along the lines of 'what the hell do you think you're doing' and 'if someone isn't dead or dying, I swear to god you're through.'"

"Well, got what he asked for, didn't he?" the shorter man shook his head, "Next thing we all hear is him shouting at the top of his lungs for his son and for a moment I thought something had happened to him, but it turned out he was summoning him. Absolutely *massive* man by the way, his son. No mistaking him, even in a darkened auditorium. I swear he leapt right up onto the stage without even taking the stairs!"

"That was when we all knew that something big had happened." the taller man said gravely, "It's an open secret that Maxwell serves as a sort of enforcer for his father. Whenever there's a security breach or someone tries to sell off company secrets, things like that, it's more or less guaranteed you'll find him there. Hell, I heard someone saw him delivering a briefcase to the chief of police not too long ago."

"Ah, looks like we've got to get back to it. Our break ended about five minutes ago." the shorter man said apologetically, "And here all we did was ramble on! I hope we gave you something you can use."

"No worries at all." Issa assured him, "A candid look into the situation is exactly what we needed. Thank you for taking the time to speak with us."

After the men had returned to work and he and Zurie were out of earshot, Issa turned to her.

"Talk about opening the floodgates."

"Most people actually enjoy talking about things like that, especially if they have a receptive audience. It's nice to know someone's interested." Zurie winked, "Sometimes all it takes is a little push."

"You didn't."

"Of course I did. All I really had to do though was give the older guy the notion that we were harmless and that talking to us was the right thing to do. The rest took care of itself with the occasional nudge to keep talking. Barely took any energy at all."

"Huh."

"What?"

"I was just imagining what would've happened if I was a lawyer. You'd be terrifying in a courtroom."

"Am I not terrifying enough for you as it is? I could dial it up a bit."

"No, no. You're fine."

As the pair headed towards the next row of buildings, seeking out more workers, Issa remembered to radio in their findings.

"This is Issa. We found a couple of Moreno Group workers that were willing to talk. They gave us some interesting stuff, over." Rao's voice almost immediately crackled to life in Issa's earpiece.

"Hey, nice work! We're hunting down our own lead over here; Elsi thinks she's onto something. Keep you posted, over."

"This is Vemris. Nothing to report, over."

"Hey, Issa, someone's coming."

Issa looked in the direction Zurie was pointing and sure enough, a figure was walking towards them from the shadow of a building. As it got closer, Issa saw that it was a man wearing a dull grey hoodie which obscured the upper portion of his face, though bits and pieces of jet-black, unkempt hair were visible.

"Excuse me," the man said to them in a low voice, "but you should leave. Before you get noticed."

"If you're talking about the killer that's rumored to be around here, that's what we're here for." Issa replied, "Any information you have would be appreciated. We can keep you anonymous if you want."

"I'm not worried. I doubt anyone would know my name anyway. Still, I probably can't tell you what you want to hear. You're better off leaving."

"Hey, we've got others here with us. If there's something going on, you should tell us what it is. They won't just leave because we said so." Zurie tried.

"...I want to help you, but—" the man's head suddenly snapped to the side, as though he had heard something, "It looks like I need to go. As do you." he rounded a corner and vanished from sight. Issa and Zurie ran to the intersection, but he was gone.

"What the hell was that all about?" Issa wondered, though he soon had something else occupying his attention as his earpiece crackled to life, Elsi's panicked voice emanating from it in spastic crackles.

"...we need...Rao is...we're..." then the signal went dead.

"Elsi, where are you? Over."

Nothing.

"Repeat, where are you? Over."

A burst of static, followed by a snippet of audible dialogue.

"...rehouse...lead...signal...can't get...Repeat, warehouse...seven..."

Seven? There was a whole column of warehouses that ended in seven! Which one was it?!

"Come on, we don't have time to figure it out! We just need to hit each one until we find them!" Zurie brought him back to his senses, yanking on his hand and forcing him to follow her.

C-O-N-T-R-A-C-T

A mere handful of minutes earlier, Rao Lassare had been filled with excitement at his and Elsi's discovery. She had *somehow* (he had asked but she had nearly melted his brain with her explanation, so he let it be) managed to pick up a trail that seemed to lead away from the site of the body they had known about. This eventually led them to a *brand spanking new body* which had been hidden underneath an overturned oil drum and evidently hadn't decomposed enough to start attracting flies or other critters yet.

Rao had been all set to call it a day right then and there. Get to a payphone, call the cops, show them where the body was, make an official statement, cite that in their essay, get graded and get paid. All-in-all what he would call a successful day.

And then Elsi had a minor freak-out and started going on about how this was new enough that they might be able to track it back to where the victim was actually killed. She had stopped Rao from radioing in their find on the grounds that the rest of the group would probably want to call it a day too, but she wanted to see if she could find anything else first.

In retrospect, Rao would admit that denying her request would have been the smart thing to do.

This, being Elsi and with Rao having dollar signs in his eyes, was the exact opposite of what he ended up doing.

This was strike one.

After all, he reasoned, what was the chance that Elsi would actually *find* something? The fact that she had already found the new body was unlikely enough, but sometimes things like this just *happened.* It wasn't outside the realm of possibility, but her divine intervention for the day was most likely used up at that point. If anything, she might find a clue that would be helpful to the police's investigation and they would get a nice little bump in their collective reward.

When she had started wandering off, muttering to herself and forcing him to follow her, Rao's instincts had warned him that this was a bad idea. That they were in over their heads as it was, especially without Vemris there to pull their asses out of the fire if anything went wrong. He had suggested to Elsi that they hold up for a moment until the rest of the group could join them, but she didn't look like she had heard him.

In retrospect, he should have made the call at that point anyway, but fear of Elsi's wrath had stayed his hand.

This was strike two.

Elsi had eventually led him to a warehouse labeled F-7. That it still bore its generic label led Rao to believe that it wasn't currently in-use by any particular business or organization, meaning that security for it would be minimal, if there was any at all. Furthermore, from the burned-out look of it, it was likely that this was one of the buildings that had been hit by the fire a few years ago, but had not yet been repaired, most likely due to nobody having any vested interest in it.

The ideal place, in other words, to conduct

business of an unsavory nature.

Elsi tried the door and found that it was unlocked. She and Rao entered and found that, as they had expected, the burned-out warehouse was largely empty except for the occasional crate, pallet or tarp.

In fact, it almost looked like that section over there was arranged such that it could protect someone from the elements.

It could've been a hobo. In fact, it most likely *was* a hobo. But something in the back of Rao's mind was telling him to *get out*.

In retrospect, he really, *really* should have listened.

This was strike three.

Elsi had darted around, examining things that caught her eye and keeping up a nearly constant stream of words that seemed to be directed mostly at herself. It almost looked like she was trying to keep up with herself, as strange as that sounded.

"Hey, is everything—" Rao had then placed a hand over her mouth suddenly and dragged her over behind a crate, having heard the metallic protest of the door's hinges. As she made to remove his hand, he shook his head and raised a finger to his lips. She nodded in understanding and he removed his hand.

"Are you here?" an unknown, slightly muffled male voice spoke, coinciding with the sound of footsteps, "And if you are, which one of you is it?"

There was a pause as the owner of the voice waited for a response before sighing in apparent relief.

"It's just me, then."

The footsteps resumed, making for the pile of crates and boxes that formed the wall of the makeshift shelter. Unfortunately, this would also give the man a clear view of Rao and Elsi behind their crate.

"Move." Rao said in barely a whisper as he shifted around to another side of the crate, Elsi following him. Thankfully, there was no debris on the floor to make unintentional noise with.

"On my mark, door." Rao mouthed, getting a determined nod from Elsi.

I need to choose a moment when his back is to us. For that, I need to look.

This would be the critical moment: Rao needed to gauge the man's position without revealing his own. He took a breath and prepared to peek around the corner of the crate.

"No!" Elsi suddenly shouted and dived away from the crate, an arm across Rao's chest as the thunk of metal striking wood emanated from where his head had just been.

"I don't remember bringing you two here." the creak of protesting wood followed by the sound of something being ripped free told Rao where to look as he frantically regained his feet and made sure Elsi was behind him.

"Did he bring you here? No, he wouldn't have. That means you came here on your own." the man's boots thudded to the concrete floor and he straightened up, giving Rao a full view of him.

He was wearing a mask that covered most of his face and pieces of armor that appeared to be homemade, with strips of leather connecting pieces of darkly painted material that Rao couldn't identify. His green hair was wild and untamed, but what drew the student's attention the most was the sharpened pieces of metal attached to his gloves. There were three on each hand, located between his knuckles.

Exactly like the wounds the police reports had repeatedly mentioned.

"It's you, isn't it?" Rao said, as much to keep the man talking while he rushed to find an escape route as anything else, "You're the one who killed those people."

"Me." the man said in a curious tone, "How much the meaning of that word has changed since then. I would have had a hard time using it."

"What do you mean?" Rao shifted so he was standing directly in front of Elsi and turned his body so the walkie talkie at his hip was hidden from the killer's sight.

"You don't need to know." the man sounded almost sad, "Honestly, it would be better if you didn't know any of this, but it's too late for that now. I need to stop you. You understand that, right? I can't just let you go. If he found out that I had, he'd kill *me* instead."

"You aren't making sense!" Rao felt Elsi's hands slowly removing the walkie talkie as she made a show of clinging to him out of fear, "You're the one killing people, aren't you? You're making it sound like it's someone else!"

"What would be the point in telling you? As soon as he gets back, you're dead one way or the other. If you want to live longer, then go sit in the corner. I'll wait for him to notice you on his own if you do, but if you try and leave, I'll have to stop you. You might last an extra ten or fifteen minutes that way."

"Elsi, do as he says." Rao instructed as he felt the

weight of the walkie talkie leave his hip. He turned to look at her, in the process hiding the side of his head that the earpiece was attached to, "You go over there. I'll keep him occupied."

She made a show of caressing the side of his face, snatching the earpiece as she did so before turning around with a theatrical sob and running to the corner, where she knelt hunched over, hiding what she was doing.

"Occupied, you say?" the killer tilted his head slightly, "And how exactly do you plan on doing that? I'm afraid we don't have much to talk about and you need to get in that corner too if you don't want to start bleeding."

As Rao began to turn, he remembered the sudden pain on the back of his head that had knocked him unconscious that night nearly two weeks ago. Once Vemris had explained to him what had happened, he had beaten himself up something fierce over it. He had thrown himself at Vemris' training with a conviction that he had never felt before, all for one simple purpose:

He refused to let something like that happen again.

"HA!" Rao suddenly snapped around, delivering a spin-kick to the head of the unsuspecting and unguarded killer. The man staggered to the side with a yell, but did not fall, catching himself in time.

"Elsi, NOW!" Rao ran at the killer again, desperate to keep his attention while Elsi radioed for help.

"We need help! Warehouse F-7! Rao is holding off the killer, but we're cornered!"

"Oh no you don't!" the killer made for Elsi, but Rao tackled him, doing everything he could to hold him back. His enemy was bigger and stronger than him though, managing to throw him off after a brief struggle and delivering a three-clawed cut to his chest as Rao successfully placed himself between Elsi and the killer.

Damn! At least it's shallower than it would've been if I wasn't on the retreat, but I can't stay that way or he'll get Elsi!

"You're dealing with me!" Rao shifted into the combat stance that Vemris had first taught him all those months ago, "I'm faster than you with all that gear weighing you down, so the only way you're getting past me is to put me down!"

CHAPTER EIGHT
TRAPPED

"*Y*ou want me to instruct you in the ways of combat?"

"Teach me how to fight, yeah. You know, don't you?"

"I am no master, but I can take care of myself, yes. I suppose that I could find a way to work it into your lessons, but before I go through the trouble, I would ask why."

"Well, it's all part of my, uh, 'Desire,' right?"

"...Indeed."

"Plus, getting trained by some otherwordly badass would be really, really cool. I'll be all like 'Yah! Hiyah! Uwaaah~'"

"There will be none of that for a good long while. What you learn shall be the basics of the basics, progressing only when I am convinced that you are ready."

"Do I at least get to pick a style?"

"What use is form without substance? You will build a core of orthodox techniques and, when I am convinced you have developed a strong base, then we can discuss molding that base into something specific."

"How long will that take?"

"It won't happen overnight. You will likely begin to wonder at times if you are making any progress at all but, should the situation arise where you must use what you have learned, you will come to understand its true value."

Rao Lassare was beginning to gain an unconscious understanding of what his Contractor had said to him when he had first asked to be taught how to fight. When he found the time to reflect on the day's events, he would begin to realize how the reactions that had been drilled into his body had made his movements just a little sharper, his reflexes just a little faster. It wasn't by much, but it was the difference between barely avoiding the killer's metallic claws or getting his face ripped off.

To be fair, he was rather fond of his face, so he was extremely grateful for this fact.

At first glance, the masked man seemed to be lashing out wildly with little rhyme or reason to his attacks, but Rao noticed that while his arms were a blur of motion, his footwork was careful to the point of being hesitant. It didn't make sense. He had the reach advantage and was clearly on the offensive, but he was hardly doing anything to press the advantage.

Could it be? Was it possible?

Does this guy actually have no idea what he's doing?

"Remember, Rao: advance while on offense, retreat while on defense. If you manage to shift the range just a little in one direction or the other, you can seize the initiative. Press every advantage you have available to you and end the fight as quickly as possible. The longer it drags on, the more chances there will be for the situation to deteriorate."

Right. Stay calm. Don't make any big moves. Just shift a little at a time. Make him follow me.

Rao shifted a little further away each time he avoided a swipe. He wasn't perfect about it and he took some shallow cuts across his forearms and one near-miss left a trio of painful cuts across his shoulder to match the ones on his chest, but Vemris had made sure to teach him that as soon as he lost his head in a fight that he would lose. Painfully.

And, to be realistic about his current situation, *permanently*.

Followed shortly thereafter by Elsi if he couldn't buy enough time for her to get away.

No pressure.

He had to make a move. His opponent was going to adjust to his movements before long and he didn't have time to come up with a backup plan.

Dear god, how long can he keep flailing around like that for?! Does he ever get tired?! I've barely done anything except dodge and I'm already breathing hard!

Wait, Vemris had told him about this! It was practically guaranteed that you'd lose stamina faster in a real fight than simple sparring because of the stress involved!

In other words, there was no way that the killer

could keep going apeshit for much longer. He'd start slowing down and when he did...

Rao closed the gap in an instant, kicking off with his back leg as hard as he could and keeping his head low. His sudden lunge took his opponent by surprise, leaving his armored torso otherwise unguarded.

Grip the ground with your toes and channel your energy up your legs and into your back. Wait until the last possible moment and release it all at once!

"HAH!!!"

Rao's arms shot forward, palm-out and slammed into the killer's armor right above his solar plexus, sending the man sprawling onto the ground with more strength than he had expected himself to be capable of. His sense of triumph was short-lived, however, as the killer regained his feet and Rao found his limbs refusing to move properly, suddenly feeling as though they had weights hanging off of them.

How did I build up fatigue so quickly?!

In a desperate bid to buy whatever time he could, Rao shouted at the killer with the first question that came to mind:

"Who the hell are you anyway?!"

"Who? Such a thing to ask!" the man made a noise that Rao thought sounded like someone forcing air through their teeth in a bizarre parody of laughter, "Shishishi. Can't you see? Who else could I be but me!" he trudged towards Rao with his shoulders hunched, head jutting forwards and fingers flexing randomly, "Yes, I'm me. Me and no one else! You take it for granted, you judge me for doing what I must, for paying the price that I must pay but it's WORTH IT! DO YOU HEAR ME?!"

As he got closer, becoming more and more animated as his voice rose in volume, Rao noticed something odd. Well, besides everything else about the situation, that is.

He saw that the man's breath was beginning to become visible in the form of small streams of condensation issuing from beneath his mask. Under the guise of taking a steadying breath, Rao exhaled a visible stream of air from his own mouth, grinning as he realized what it meant.

"You lose."

"What are you—"

WHAM

An impact that put Rao's earlier attack to shame sent the killer careening into a stack of crates with the sound of splintering wood. Standing there, arm outstretched, was Vemris. To anyone else, his expression might have made him appear bored or unruffled, but Rao saw the slightly narrowed gaze and the downturned corners of his mouth and recognized the steely glare for what it meant:

Vemris Masia was angry.

"We will have words about this later." he warned Rao before turning and walking towards the broken crates that the killer was attempting to extricate himself from, the air seeming to grow slightly colder with every step he took.

"Where are they?"

"Raah!" the masked man launched himself out of the crates with heretofore-unseen agility and lashed out at Vemris' head, claws whistling through the air—

CRUNCH

—until Vemris caught the offending arm by the

wrist and, in a single fluid motion, repositioned himself behind his attacker, planted his free hand at the shoulder joint and slammed him into the concrete floor, arm twisted at an unnatural angle.

"AUGH!!!"

"Don't make me repeat myself. Where. Are. They?"

"Here, there and everywhere! I never hid two of them in the same—AUUGH!!!"

"Do you expect me to believe that someone as incompetent as you was able to evade capture for this long by yourself? I know you have allies, now tell me where they are before I ruin your arm beyond fixing!"

"Shishishi. 'Allies?' You think he's a *friend?* I'm as trapped as you are!"

"You think me trapped?"

"As a matter of fact, we do."

It wasn't the killer who responded, but a new voice emanating from the heavy metal door as it swung closed on protesting hinges.

The bits of light shining though the deteriorating ceiling gradually revealed a man wearing a dull-grey hoodie and black pants. His face was mostly concealed by his hood, but bits of unkempt jet-black hair stuck out beneath it. His movements were matter-of-fact, neither purposeful nor lazy.

"We are unskilled with such things, so let us explain: We know that you yourself could escape easily if you wanted to, provided that we had no reason to try and stop you, which we do not. However, you will not abandon your Signer or his friend and you are incapable of both fighting us and defending them at the same time. While we cannot confidently say anything to the nature of 'you cannot defeat us,' *I* will say that you cannot do so quickly. Therefore, you are trapped."

What did he just say?

"Tch. I knew something was off, but to think this was the case all along. I was right to keep an eye open."

"To do otherwise would go against who you have always been."

At that moment, Rao saw something he had never seen before: Vemris was well and truly taken aback.

"You speak as though you know me. *Knew* me."

"Have you not always prided yourself on the strength of your mind, Masia?"

"Would someone explain to me just what the hell is going on here?!" Rao couldn't contain himself anymore, "This is making even less sense than usual!"

"Wait, you mean you know what this is all about?!" Elsi spluttered from the edge of the building where she had apparently been slowly edging towards the door before the new guy had shown up, "What the fuck, Rao?!"

"We don't have time for this right now!" Rao groaned, "The important thing is that guy that just came in is seriously bad news if I'm reading this right. Vemris should be able to handle him, but we'd just get in the way."

"You're talking like they aren't human or something!"

"They're *not!*"

"If you are both *quite* finished?" Vemris cut in, a smirk tugging at the corner of his mouth as he took off his glasses and stowed them in his vest pocket, "I have business to attend to, meaning you'll have to deal with *this* degenerate." he stood, eliciting a cry of pain from the masked man as he was dragged to his feet by his mangled arm, "Hopefully now that I've taken one of his arms, you'll have an easier time of it, but don't let your guard down. A cornered beast is more apt to show his teeth."

"Why not just knock him out?" Elsi suggested, "Then Rao and I can get the hell away from here and leave you to do your thing."

"Dealing a decisive blow requires a certain level of focus. If I avert my eyes from him for even a moment, the Contractor will strike. The only reason he hasn't already is because I've had eyes on him since he opened the door."

"Actually, that's only part of the reason. You don't need to know the rest." the hooded man supplied, having stopped roughly ten feet away from Vemris, hands in the front pocket of his hoodie, "Now, if you'll let my Signer go, we can get on with this; I'd rather not take his head off by accident."

Then he *grinned* and Rao felt as though his feet had been nailed to the floor, every nerve in his body shot through with a bolt of frigid lightning brought on by the sheer oppressive *wrongness* in the air.

Killing intent? No, this is something different. Something worse. He'll kill all of us! What can I do?! I'm not ready for something like this! No human can ever be ready for something like this! He's a monster! A MONSTER!!!

"Breathe deeply, Rao. The fear will remain, but you'll be able to move your body."

"Shuuu...haaah..."

Nothing was different.

Nothing had changed.

But he could move.

And that would have to be enough.

Not waiting for any indication that he was prepared, Vemris shoved the masked man away harshly, eliciting one final grunt of pain as he staggered to catch his balance.

"Shiku. If you mess this up for me, it won't be an accident. Got that?"

The killer, apparently named Shiku, did not respond with words, but the eyes behind his mask widened with a maddening fear before narrowing in determination.

"You know, feel free to stay put if you want." Rao said, forcing his mouth into the shape of a confident smirk, "I don't have any reason to come to you, after all, and I'm sure that arm hurts like a bitch."

C-O-N-T-R-A-C-T

Vemris Masia shifted his stance slightly to be better oriented in relation to his opponent, vision perfectly clear without his glasses, which he wore more out of habit than anything else. As another item he wore out of habit, he pulled a pocket watch of a dull silver out of his pocket and clicked it open, giving it a half-glance before closing it and putting it back.

This was something he had always done before an uncertain battle, not that he remembered how the habit had begun. Was it before or after he had...but that was unimportant right now.

"If you know me as well as you claim to, then

you'll be fully aware that I'm not in the habit of making the first move."

"Right."

In the blink of an eye, the Contractor had closed the gap between them and had a thrust kick shooting towards Vemris' center of mass, a cloud of dust shooting into the air from where he had been. Any ordinary man would have been sent flying, perhaps with a ruptured organ or two.

Vemris Masia was anything *but* a normal man.

A clockwise block with his left arm caused the kick to miss while he leaned in with his forward arm, delivering a corkscrewing blow to his opponent that by all accounts should have been avoided with the swaying of his head, but nevertheless delivered an impact that sent him skidding backwards.

"Chi? I thought you weren't the type to make the first move?"

Indeed, Vemris had focused his chi into his fist, forcing it outward at the last moment to strike the Contractor with his life energy. It wasn't a particularly special technique, since anyone with a sufficiently strong soul could learn to utilize it. Still, it was effective in its simplicity.

"You left an opening without expecting me to take it? You are both mad *and* a fool."

"I just thought it might be fun to pretend to be ordinary fighters for a little bit and let our skill do the talking. If you want to bring power into it, though, who am I to refuse?"

Crick

The sound of the small cracks forming beneath the Contractor's feet were all the warning Vemris had before a leg slammed into his hastily constructed guard with enough force to take him off his feet, the chi in his arms being the only thing preventing his bones from shattering as he lashed out with a kick of his own, relying on his experience and his opponent's energy to tell him where he was. He was rewarded with a solid impact and a grunt of disappointment as his opponent's follow-up attack was thwarted.

"Even among Contractors, few can move with such speed. The way it was done may even be unique to you."

"Oh? Think you've figured out my ability already?"

"I'm not so naïve as to think that." Vemris began to channel the energy of the world around him, binding and shaping it with his chi, "However, if I am to match you, I'm afraid I'll have to take things up a notch."

The temperature around Vemris plummeted as mist condensed out of the air around him and coalesced around his arms and legs, forming shells of ice that creaked as his joints shifted.

I can't use my full power in a place like this unless I want to attract attention and put Rao in danger and if I were to transform, every Contractor in the entire city would be made aware of my presence! Even in this respect, he has me trapped! How much does he truly know?

"You look frustrated, Masia."

"And *you* talk too much."

"So you've always said. To *me*, at least."

And then there was that maddening way of speaking! It was as though the man couldn't decide whether he was of one mind or multiple, unless he meant it to be the royal "we," which didn't seem to fit.

And yet, as Vemris clashed with his opponent again, matching raw speed and viciousness with skill and control, he couldn't help but feel that the Contractor truly did know him. He attacked and reacted with the confidence of someone who had not only seen his style of fighting before, but was familiar with it. The real shock came when Vemris, based on instinct alone, stopped a kick before it had moved more than a few inches and swept the man's other leg, slamming him into the ground with a downwards fist, the impact being absorbed by his frozen gauntlet.

"GAH!" the man made an involuntary noise as his lungs were forcibly emptied. Vemris attempted to capitalize on the opportunity by sending another punch at the man's head, but he rolled away, causing only his hood to be torn away from what was now just a thick shirt with a pocket.

He flexed his legs and shot away, flipping over in the air to land on his feet, teeth bared in a feral grin as Vemris saw his face completely for the first time. Unkempt spikes of shoulder-length hair jutted from his head and his crimson eyes danced madly in their sockets.

Vemris knew those eyes. Visions of battle, comradery, confidence, pain, betrayal and understanding flashed through his mind, stunning him long enough for the man to recover. Words both spoken and heard. Lessons both given and received. Life shared and stolen and he *knew* those *eyes!*

"Jensen."

The name spilled from his lips seemingly of its own volition.

"Jensen Kuro."

CHAPTER NINE
OLD FRIEND

Control over one's mind was every bit as critical as control over one's body when it came to combat, if not more so. Indeed, this statement could apply to a wide variety of situations. This was a truth that Vemris Masia understood very well and, over the course of his life, had become quite adept at implementing. This practice was what had allowed him to maintain a level head and adapt to the unexpected, even in situations such as the high-stakes battle he currently found himself in.

But it was failing him.

The feeling of Rao's chi spiking had alerted him to the situation with the man known as Shiku and allowed him to arrive in time to stop his Signer from getting himself maimed or killed. Actually *finding* the killer had been an unlikely scenario, but one that Vemris had been prepared for nonetheless.

Discovering that the killer was a Signer with an

apparently bloodthirsty Contractor was even more unlikely, but even so, it had made a certain amount of sense. As such, Vemris had planned for that possibility as well and had not only been able to keep pace with his opponent, but had actually been gaining the upper hand slowly but surely, in spite of the fact that he was being forced to hold back.

Strategy, discipline, precision and adaptability.

None of these things were sufficient to prepare him for the wave of images, sounds and sensations that flooded into his mind upon seeing the man's face, nor the name that spilled from his lips upon realizing that not only did the man know him, but *he* knew the man.

"Jensen. Jensen Kuro."

The initial surge of memories had stunned him for long enough for Jensen to recover and take the offensive with rapid strikes and a wild grin which sharply contrasted the images that Vemris now had of him.

A blank expression, curiosity only expressed by the slight tilting of his head.

His young ward showing him the stranger he had found standing in the rain.

A group in his living room who thought it would be fun to try and teach him how to smile.

These same images were also proving to be incredibly distracting and were contributing heavily to Vemris' loss of momentum. It was all he could do to defend himself and make the occasional move to keep Jensen in check, but he was beginning to accumulate minor injuries.

"What's the matter? Having a hard time fighting

against your old friend? It never stopped you before!"

Staring at the man as though he were a stranger; seeing something in his gaze that he didn't recognize.

No. It had been a lack of something.

A thrusting kick made its way past his guard and sent him flying as he struggled to breathe. Vemris righted himself in midair with a practiced maneuver and channeled his chi downwards, causing the floor to become slick and allowing him to slide further away, buying a precious extra second to recover even as the other Contractor bore down upon him.

"It must be such a pain with abilities like yours! Come on, cut loose and to hell with the consequences!"

"I must always be careful not to lose myself. If I did..."

"You're not yourself!" Vemris found himself shouting.

He had to ignore the fact that it should have been impossible, that there shouldn't have been any way for a Contractor to remember the things that he did.

It wasn't right. None of it was right.

This wasn't who the man called Jensen Kuro was supposed to be.

Red eyes, equal parts familiar and foreign. It was as though he were staring at a twisted shadow of the man. A dark spirit drenched in blood and screams.

A ghost.

CRASH

He had been shoulder tackled through a pile of old, empty crates. Splinters pierced his skin and larger pieces bruised his back as his opponent laughed and mocked him.

"I don't remember you being this pathetic!"

"Look who's talking." Vemris spat as he rose up, the other man suddenly finding himself unable to advance as the ice from the floor crept up his legs, "Finding yourself in the service of a madman, being reduced to hiding yourself in back alleys and abandoned buildings and allowing yourself to be *controlled* like this? I don't remember you being this *weak*, Kuro!" Vemris punctuated his statement with a heavy blow to Jensen's face from his ice-encased fist that sent the black-haired man to the floor with a grunt, skidding clear of the patch of ice.

"You're wrong…about one thing…" the Contractor coughed as he staggered to his feet, one hand on his head, "He didn't just roll over and hand me the keys; he fought like hell the whole time. Even now—" a lopsided grimace and a muffled exclamation of discomfort "Even now, he's raising all kinds of hell in here. Why'd you have to go and say his name, huh? Here I had him right where I wanted him and you had to go and give him his second wind! It's alright though; all I have to do is take your head off and start over. This sort of thing…it's a once-in-a-lifetime freak occurrence."

Crick

Damn!

Vemris only had time for that single thought as his body reflexively moved to defend against the attack that he knew was coming, though he would be an instant too slow to prevent it. He had allowed himself to become distracted and he was about to pay the price—

But the hit never came.

"Nngh! Son of a bitch!"

Jensen was reeling, both hands on his head, veins bulging and fingers digging into his skull.

"No...I *won't*...you can't..."

"Vemris!" those red eyes locked with Vemris', pleading with him, "Freeze me in place...knock me out...kill me if you have to! Just do it before—"

"RAAAAH!!!"

Vemris had been on the move already, knowing that he wouldn't be getting a better chance. After seeing that his former friend was capable of resisting, he had resolved himself to using solely non-lethal means, but it turned out not to matter as Jensen's body surged with energy which blasted outwards in all directions and forced Vemris to protect himself.

"Hah...hah...Mine..." the man who was and wasn't Jensen Kuro stood slumped over, arms dangling in front of him as he panted and mumbled to himself. Foul, dark energy was coming off of him in palpable waves, "Mine...mine mine *mine* **mine** **_MINE!!!_**" his head snapped upwards, eyes rolling madly and veins clearly visible on his forehead, "This body belongs to *me*. Not him. Not *us*. Me."

He began to approach, purple-black chi enveloping his left arm from the elbow down, looking like an oversized claw.

He's abandoned any premise of concealment. If he keeps releasing energy at this rate, we're sure to be noticed. I can only hope that there aren't any others in the area that would make things problematic.

"I can't use our techniques as effectively with him

fighting me like this. Sorry, but that doesn't leave a whole lot of room for subtlety!"

C-O-N-T-R-A-C-T

"Oh come *on,* this is going beyond just 'weird' at this point! What am I supposed to make of this?" Elsi Thompson muttered to herself as she struggled to keep eyes on both Rao and Vemris' fights, trying to absorb as much information as possible.

She wasn't helpless, far from it. It was just that a normal, if highly intelligent, person could only do so much in a battle like this. Even Rao was showing heretofore-unexpected depths to himself as he stood toe-to-toe with a crazed murderer and managed not to get himself killed.

She needed an edge. Something she could use to even the playing field, even a little.

She was trying to do the eye thing again. If she was right about how it worked, she would be able to perceive everything that was happening. Even if her body couldn't keep up, maybe she could look for an opening or an opportunity to help one of them.

"Super Eyes! Activate! True Sight! Hocus Pocus! Sh*ringan! Go Planet!"

The problem was that she had absolutely no idea how to make it work.

"What the hell are you doing?!" Rao shouted as he and Shiku passed close enough for him to hear her attempts.

"My best, okay?! Also, *duck!*"

Fortunately, Rao didn't think to question her and dropped into a crouch just in time to avoid a three-clawed swipe at his head from Shiku's good arm. He took advantage of the opening to drive an elbow into the killer's gut and slam a knee into his masked face as he doubled over, causing him to stagger away.

"Ow! What the hell is that thing *made* of?!" Rao was prevented from capitalizing on his advantage by the pain in his knee from the impact with Shiku's mask, "While we're on the subject, what is your *deal,* because it's starting to look like your Contractor is the mastermind in all this!"

"My 'deal?' On-the-nose way to put it, don't you think?" Shiku shook his head to clear his senses and then charged Rao again, "You're a Signer, aren't you? So you should already know, right?!" Rao avoided a wide, telegraphed slash by stepping back only for Shiku to plow forward and kick him in the chest. It was sloppy and imprecise, but his greater bulk and heavy boots made it effective nonetheless and Rao tumbled away, rolling to gain distance as the killer bore down upon him, "Not everyone wants to *gain* something! Some people would risk anything just to be *rid* of it!"

His opponent clearly expected Rao to either keep retreating or try to stand up. His long stride and the large arc of his swing said as much; he was maximizing his power and reach.

"Legs!" Elsi shouted, wishing she had enough time for more than single-word instructions. After all, if she didn't choose the correct one then eventually Rao was going to misunderstand her.

"YAH!!!"

Fortunately, that didn't seem to be the case just yet

as Rao, displaying an impressive amount of core strength and coordination, whipped his legs around and swept Shiku's feet out from underneath him, causing him to flail wildly as he pitched forwards, claws catching on Rao's arm and adding three more cuts to his growing collection. Fortunately, none of these appeared to be particularly deep so far, though the fact that he was wearing a red shirt made it difficult to tell just how bad they were.

"Thanks for that." he panted, "I was almost out of ideas. Dealing with that armor is a bitch-and-a-half."

"Whatever you did before with that shove seemed to work. Any chance you could—VEMRIS, UP!"

She shouldn't have been able to see it in time to react. It had been in her periphery, behind Rao and off to the side.

The reasoning for this was quite simple: the human eye is theoretically capable of sending huge amounts of visual data to the brain at once, but in practice only a small portion is ever "rendered" at full detail. This is why, for instance, when one focuses on a single word on a page, while they can "see" most of the page perfectly fine, they cannot "read" it. The ability to perceive detail is a case of literal tunnel vision, while the ability to perceive motion applies to one's entire field of view. Hence, while Elsi was able to perceive motion coming from Vemris and the other Contractor, she should not have been able to discern the fine details while she was still focused on Rao.

The reality of the situation was, though she was in too much of a rush to fully appreciate it at the time, that Elsi Thompson was able to fully perceive the details of everything within her field of vision at maximum visual acuity.

This was how she had seen the moment when the other Contractor had taken Vemris' back and leapt into the air, leaving a cloud of purple-black something-or-other on the ground. Vemris was whirling around, arms raising to defend himself from the attack that was obviously coming, but the trajectory of his movements suggested that he didn't know his opponent was currently airborne, leg raised in preparation for a gravity-assisted axe kick that would crack Vemris' skull at the very least.

In spite of not having known Vemris for very long and having just learned that he wasn't human, Elsi knew that she would rather deal with him than whatever the other one had in store for her.

So she had shouted.

One word hadn't been enough. He wouldn't have had any way of knowing she was talking to him and her warning would have been useless. She had to bank on his physical abilities that, by this point, were obviously beyond those of any normal person.

A sharp crack pierced the air as the descending foot connected, heel-first, with Vemris' upraised arm, sending shards of ice exploding outwards from the point of impact and causing him to grit his teeth with pain even as he seized the offending leg and slammed its owner into the concrete full-force.

"Get him, Vem!"

Oh, no.

Her warning had gotten Vemris' attention and possibly saved his life which, by extension, had possibly saved Rao and herself as well. To that end, it had been completely successful.

It had also, however, gotten *Rao's* attention, causing his focus to drift over to the other fight in time to see Vemris' comeback maneuver. This had prevented him from realizing that Shiku had risen into a crouching position and, upon recognizing the opening, had leapt forward with an overhand strike that had his metallic claws streaking towards the back of Rao's neck.

Elsi saw it happening as her head snapped around. It was almost in slow-motion. She felt her mouth opening to deliver a warning that would have been too late to matter. She felt her body preparing to move, though it was too late to shove him out of the way, even if she had intended to take the hit in a less-vital area.

There was nothing she could do. Nothing he could do. Nothing anyone could do.

Nothing but watch…

…as Rao spun, deflecting Shiku's arm with a high block to the inside of his wrist as his back foot came forward and, in a single motion, he dropped into a deep horse stance and his right arm snapped forward, delivering a vertical fist to his opponent's armor over his solar plexus.

THOOM

With a thunderous report, Shiku flew backwards nearly ten feet until he collided with the wall of the warehouse and impacted with enough force to dent the aged metal before he bounced off and collapsed to the floor, unmoving.

"Fwoo…" Rao exhaled, a curiously blank expression on his face before shaking his head and looking very confused, "I'm sorry, what?"

"Rao! Elsi! Are you guys okay?"

Elsi's eyes widened as she saw Issa approaching at a run while Zurie was turning her attention to the fight between the two Contractors, eyes narrowed.

It was her. She did something. Wait...

"Oh my god, she's one of them too, isn't she?"

"Probably." Rao sighed, watching Shiku warily. He obviously wasn't about to make the same mistake twice, "Vemris thinks she is, anyway."

Elsi felt a sudden surge of jealously, of all things.

"Why am I the only one who doesn't get an uber-powerful magic buddy?"

"Probably because you'd take over the world if you had one."

Issa had reached them at that point and was breathing heavily, having apparently run all the way to the warehouse with Zurie.

"Holy shit, Rao, you're covered in cuts! Do I need to shred up a shirt or—"

"Keep your shirt on, it looks worse than it is. Besides, we should be more concerned about those two going at it over there."

"Zurie went to help Vemris. It should be fine."

"Yeah, don't think we won't be talking about *that* later."

Elsi wanted to point out that *both* of them had been hiding things from her, but she saw something that warranted her undivided attention.

"Guys, talk later. The other guy, Contractor, whatever, he's on his feet again."

Also, my head is really starting to hurt again and I should probably figure out how to turn this off. Wait, off? When did I turn it on? How did I turn it on?! Damn it!

C-O-N-T-R-A-C-T

Vemris had just about had enough for one day. Fortunately for him, the elevated level of Contractor energy coming from Jensen had led Issa and, more importantly, Zurie, right to them. Though his opponent had been steadily gaining an edge as he allowed his power to run wild, his overall condition wasn't much better than Vemris', even after he had broken his arm with that kick.

Now that a fresh addition in the form of Zurie had given them the numbers advantage, however, the battle was as good as won. The enemy seemed to know it too as he backed up slowly, eyes darting from person to person and talking to himself as he weighed his options.

"If only you would stop getting in my way, I could still…yes. Yes, alright, you've got a point. Time to go." the man's aura vanished and the veins on his face receded as he straightened up and raised his voice, "It looks like Shiku went and got himself knocked out and I don't exactly fancy my odds right now anyway, at least with the stubborn bastard doing everything he can to hold me back. As such, we're getting the hell out of here."

"As if we'd let you!" Zurie rebuked, baring her fangs at Jensen.

"The girl has a point, Kuro. While I don't intend to kill you, what makes you think I'll simply stand aside and let you leave? As you said, you're hardly in any condition to defeat the both of us."

"My apologies, Vemris," in that moment, Vemris knew that it was the real Jensen speaking to him, "my Contract compels me, so as much as I would like to surrender, I'm afraid I must resist. Thankfully, I've managed to convince the other one that the least-violent option is the best one right now."

Vssh

To the untrained eye, it would have appeared as though he had simply teleported to the other side of the room, appearing next to the unconscious Shiku and leaving a cloud of dust in his wake. Thanks to his memories and recent firsthand experience, Vemris knew the technique for what it truly was.

Flash Step was what he had coined it in the past. Jensen focused his chi in his legs and used it to cover large distances with a single step. He was far from the only one to have ever utilized this technique, but it came to him almost naturally to the point where it had become something of a signature technique for him.

It had been used against him in their fight, but the difference between that and the version of the technique that he had just witnessed was like night and day.

"Let him leave." he said in a carrying voice, drawing a sharp look from Zurie and a noise of protest from Rao, "I'll explain it to you later, but what you've just seen is what Jensen Kuro is truly capable of. How he was when he fought me doesn't even compare. Let him leave."

There was no further protest as Jensen lifted Shiku and put him over his shoulders in a fireman's carry.

He straightened up to his full height and took a moment to survey the three people before him.

"My apologies." he nodded to Issa and Elsi before looking at Rao and giving him a curious look, "Take care."

Vssh

And he was gone.

"Did I miss something?" Issa was asking the other two as Vemris and Zurie approached.

"Dude, I've been here the whole time and I *still* have no idea what's going on."

Vemris held back a sigh, knowing that he was going to have some explaining to do on a topic that he himself still didn't completely understand.

"Might I recommend that we return home first and treat those injuries? None of them look terribly deep, but they should be disinfected and bandaged at the very least. After that...I shall tell you what I can."

There was general assent, though Rao held up a hand.

"We still need to call the police and tell them about the bodies we found and this place too. We can't exactly tell them the rest, but it should still be enough to net some of that reward money, right?"

"Yes, we should try and get something out of this other than more questions and the best report in the entire class." Elsi concurred.

"Right." Vemris rummaged around in his pockets and produced a handful of coins, handing them to Elsi, "You, Issa and Zurie find a payphone and make the call. I believe there was one just outside the main gate. I'll take Rao back to the house, administer first aid and then return to pick you up."

"With a busted arm? Nice try; Issa's driving." Elsi shoved the man in question forward, "Zurie and I can handle talking to the cops, can't we?" she put a hand on the shorter girl's shoulder and gave her a smile promising that every second not spent on that phone would be spent interrogating her. Zurie gave Issa a "save me" look, but when he answered with an apologetic shrug, she gave in.

"Just try and go easy on her, okay?" he said with a sympathetic expression.

"Only because you asked nicely."

CHAPTER TEN
QUESTIONS

A figure clad in baggy clothing stood in front of a window that could more accurately be called a wall of glass, staring out at the city and sky. Though she stood much taller than the average man, the view afforded to her from the forty-fourth floor was still a novel experience. More than once she had found herself standing there for uncounted minutes, simply drinking in the cityscape before her as it was changed by time and weather. It brought a simple sort of peace to her mind that was sharply juxtaposed by the endless stream of activity down below.

At the moment, though she stared, she saw none of it. She was focused intently on the sensation of the energy that had jolted through her like a spark of electricity mere moments before. It had been one of her kind, that much was clear. One who had certainly not cared whether or not they attracted any attention.

That made them dangerous which, given her

current status as a bodyguard of sorts, made them a concern. It would be in her best interest to turn around and inform her employer, who was seated at his desk and speaking with someone on the phone as he took the occasional puff of one of his seemingly ever-present cigars.

And yet she remained where she was, unmoving and taciturn.

Why? What was it that prevented her from speaking? Why were her veins thrumming with energy as her heart pounded in her chest, leaving her unsure of whether she was frightened or exhilarated? Why did she suddenly want nothing more than to take to the streets and seek out that energy signature? How could she be so certain that whoever she had sensed was someone that she absolutely needed to see, no matter the consequences?

She was not accustomed to such conflicting feelings. She didn't know how to react to them.

So she did nothing. She would remain silent and contemplative until her usual state of mind returned or she was issued an order.

Yes, an order. Something clear and direct that she could simply *act* on without any unneeded complexities getting in the way.

It all just felt so...foreign. As though she were never meant to deal with such things.

"Fiona," her employer's voice, deep and slightly raspy, coincided with the click of his phone being placed back into its receiver, "something's come up that requires my personal attention away from the office. You're coming with me."

"Yes, Mr. Moreno." she responded automatically as

she fell into step behind him and slightly to the side, slowing her longer strides to match his pace as they entered the hall and approached one of the elevators.

"The police are involved, so make sure you behave yourself. I'd send Maxxie, but for whatever reason they're insisting that it be me. Waste of my damn time most likely, but what can you do?"

"Do you anticipate any threats to your person, sir?"

"Most likely not, but image is as important as fact. Between you, Maxxie and the rest of my security detail, I'm more or less untouchable, but it's important that everyone *sees* that, you understand?"

"Yes, Mr. Moreno."

"Well, whether you do or not doesn't really matter as long as you do as I say. I'm the head here, so all the rest of the body needs to do is follow me."

"Yes, Mr. Moreno."

"Good."

As they exited the building and got into her employers' personal limo, which was already waiting for them, Fiona found herself speaking out of turn.

"Sir, I have a request."

"Really? What might that be?" he eyed her warily as a layer of cigar smoke began to build along the roof of the limo.

"I would like to request an afternoon off. In particular, I believe you have a rather long meeting coming up later in the week where you will be unlikely to require my services."

"What, is that all?" he took a moment to think, most likely verifying what she had said, "Yes, I remember something like that. Alright then; as per our agreement, you have all of the benefits I'd offer any other employee in your position, which certainly includes some time off here and there. We'll formalize the request when we get back and I'll have Shirley mark it down. It's less notice than I technically require, but I'll overlook that."

"Thank you, sir."

"Never let it be said I don't reward the ones that do a good job. Keep doing a good job for me, Fiona, I'll keep rewarding you. Nice and simple."

Miguel Moreno was an unusual one as far as Fiona was aware. When she had first met him, he had scarcely seemed surprised at all. Indeed, he had started what most would recognize as a fairly standard job interview, albeit tailored to their unique situation and being conducted by the head of the company himself. He treated her exactly as he would any other employee and while most would consider him to be arrogant, temperamental, domineering or some combination thereof, Fiona was unbothered by his mannerisms.

Then again, Fiona was unbothered by most things.

This made her state of agitation regarding what she had felt earlier all the more unusual. She would make use of her time off in order to find the one who had done this to her. What happened after that...would happen after that.

C-O-N-T-R-A-C-T

"Like this, right?"

"More. You want to make sure it really gets in there. Be firm."

"Ow! Seriously, why does the treatment have to

hurt more than the actual wound did?!" Rao squawked as Issa proceeded to clean his wounds under Vemris' supervision, "And why can't I do this myself?!"

"Because your adrenaline prevented you from feeling the full extent of it at the time and because you lack the discipline to suffer though the pain without backing off. There's no telling what might have been on those claws, even if it doesn't seem as though they were poisoned; that place was filthy."

"I guess. Honestly, I don't even know what those—ow—things were made of. Same deal with the armor; that stuff was *strong.*"

"That actually begs the question:" Issa remembered as he wiped some excess disinfectant off of Rao's arm, "what exactly did you do to that guy? You punched him into a *wall.*"

"Well, I used my chi. Vemris has been trying to show me how for a while, but I've never—ow—really been able to do it on-command. Definitely not *that* much of it at once."

"Chi? You mean that kung-fu power from martial arts flicks?"

"Has anyone ever told you you're kinda blasй about this stuff? Like, weirdly so?"

"Zurie said something like that. I think I might just be so weirded out by all this that I've come full-circle. Besides, compared to some of the other things that've happened, that's downright normal." Vemris chuckled as he finished adjusting the sling he was supporting his injured left arm with, causing Issa and Rao to give him odd looks.

"Oh, it's just that your phrasing was oddly appropriate. You see, chi can be thought of as the energy that flows through all living things. With sufficient training, anyone can harness it to a lesser or greater extent. In that way, you were quite right to see it as normal."

"That's how you Contractors are able to do the things you do then? You're just really good at using your chi?"

"Yes and no. You see—" Vemris was interrupted by the phone ringing, "Excuse me." as he went to answer it, Rao took over his explanation.

"What you have to understand, Issa, is that in a lot of ways Contractors are just...beyond us. There's not any single thing that sets them apart; it's more like... everything. I don't mean they're all the same or anything, but in terms of raw ability, the average Contractor can't even be compared to the average human. Stronger, faster, better reflexes, longer-lived, more durable...you name it. That applies to chi too. It's not that they're all masters at using it like Vem is, but when their capacity is so much higher, it doesn't tend to matter much."

"So, different people have different amounts of chi and Contractors tend to have a lot more than a normal person."

"...Sort of. Your capacity for chi is more than just how much you have. It's more like...something really technical that you'll have to get Vemris to tell you about because I still don't really get it."

"Well, it seems as though we'll have the time." Vemris announced as he re-entered the room, "That was Elsi on the phone. One of the policemen she and Zurie were explaining things to offered to give them a ride back here instead of us having to go collect them."

Issa wondered if Zurie had something to do with that decision, but decided against saying anything as he finished cleaning the last of Rao's wounds and focused on Vemris' explanation of how to properly bandage his arm, after which Rao would bandage the rest by himself.

"You're fortunate that none of these are deep enough to require stitches. I could certainly do it but with my dominant arm unusable, it would be a challenge."

"Why not go to a hospital? Too many questions?"

"Indeed. They wouldn't refuse treatment, of course, but any investigation worth anything would be problematic. You must remember that confidentiality is an important part of the Contracts. Only in the gravest of circumstances can we risk any information about them being leaked to outside parties."

"What exactly constitutes 'grave circumstances' if a serial killer doesn't?"

"Any potentially world-altering scenario including but not limited to apocalyptic scenarios of Class Zero or higher."

"...What?"

"Trust me, dude, don't think about it." Rao advised.

"What about Elsi?"

"It couldn't be helped; she was in the wrong place at the wrong time." Vemris grimaced, "Besides, she seemed as though she would have figured it out on her own. Uncannily intelligent, that one."

"Plus, she saved both our asses."

"That too. Anyhow, you wanted to know more about chi, Issa? We don't have enough time to go in-depth, but I suppose I can give you a quick primer. Rao could probably use a refresher anyway."

C-O-N-T-R-A-C-T

The next half hour or so was spent with Vemris re-iterating everything Rao had already told Issa, only in a much more technical manner. He had insisted that if anyone was to learn about a topic like that, they should be properly instructed from the very first step. As such, by the time Elsi returned with a harassed-looking Zurie in-tow, he had learned nothing new.

I wonder if he did that on purpose? Maybe he still has reservations about me?

"Right, you two have some explaining to do...is what I should be saying, but Zurie was really accommodating, so you can thank her for sparing you an interrogation." Elsi gave Issa and Rao a look that said she still had half a mind to grill them anyway.

"What did you tell her exactly?" Vemris raised an eyebrow at his fellow Contractor.

"The basics. It took a little time for the police to show up and she had already guessed most of the key points, so I only really needed to fill in some gaps."

"Speaking of, what happened with the police? We getting anything out of it?" Rao inquired hopefully.

"We sure are!" Elsi gave a victorious fist-pump, "Not as much as if we'd contributed to a direct arrest and the exact amount still needs to be determined, but the fact that we were able to show them his hideout and a fresh body should help them out a lot. Couldn't really tell them the whole story of course, but it's better than nothing."

"While we're on the topic of stories, and since we're all here, I'd like to hear one from you, Vemris." Zurie crossed her arms, "The one about you and that other Contractor that you decided to let go. It seemed like you knew him, and not just from work either; like you knew him *before*."

Vemris gave her a steady look, seemingly weighing his options before sighing in resignation.

"That's because I did."

"Why is this such a shocker? Between all of you, however many there are, there's bound to be some that know each other, right?" Elsi looked to her friends, clearly wondering if, not for the first time that day, she had missed something.

"I agree. Sure, it's probably not something that happens every day, but it does happen, right?" Issa concurred.

"You know that Contractors are from another Realm, right? Another world?" Zurie prompted, getting a round of nods, "Well, let me tell you, there are more Realms than just ours and this one. A *lot* more. Contractors are selected from a pool of everyone, and I do mean *everyone*."

"Are we getting into multiverse theory? I feel like we're getting into multiverse theory." Elsi half-asked.

"That would probably be the simplest way to understand it." Vemris nodded, "You see, any being with a certain baseline level of intelligence can become a Contractor Candidate. The exact process by which this selection occurs is unknown, not the least of which is because Contractors seldom retain all of their memories. Thus, finding two or more who not only knew each other in life, but are *aware* of this fact, is exceedingly rare."

"What do you mean 'in life?'" Issa asked in a steady tone that belied his inner shock.

"A slip of the tongue."

"Nice try." Rao crossed his arms, "I know you too well to believe that you'd say something like that by accident. Spill it, Vem."

"It really doesn't pertain to—"

"I'm not dropping this. Spill it."

"If you won't tell us, I'll just get it out of Zurie later." Issa pointed out. "And if I don't, you can bet Elsi will."

"Damn straight."

"Please, no. I've been interrogated enough for one day."

"Fine." Vemris relented, though he was clearly displeased, "How do you suppose one travels between Realms to become a Contractor? Interdimensional travel is certainly not a simple thing to achieve and the amount of raw energy involved in such a thing would be incredible. This cost would be considerably reduced in the event that there was no actual matter to transport, no? Given this, the clear solution is to transport the souls of the candidates and then construct physical forms for the ones who are chosen. When do you suppose that one's soul is most receptive to such a thing?"

"At the time of their death, when it's about to leave the body anyway." Zurie supplied, "It's actually really hard to separate a soul from a living body. There are all sorts of conditions that have to be met if you're doing it against someone's will, especially seeing as how a soul is more or less the essence of someone's will."

"Wait a minute." Rao protested, "Vem, you're saying you're dead? How can that be possible? You're right here, in the flesh!"

"I have died once, been deemed worthy of rebirth as a Contractor and, thus, been granted a second life. Perhaps you see this as an over-simplification of the process, but that is more or less what happened. Given that this is the most common method, I can only surmise that the same is true for Jensen."

"Right, let's get back on-topic here: What's the deal with him?" Elsi pressed.

"The Jensen Kuro I knew is...*was* a good man. Sometimes cold, usually aloof and at times, as you saw, a terror on the battlefield, but at his core he was a good man. I can only surmise that the deeds he has been involved in and likely instrumental to are in some way conditional to his Contract with Shiku. He is clearly compelled to defend his Signer at the very least."

"But weren't you fighting evenly enough with him on your own? It should've been easy for you to overpower him with Zurie on your side, right?"

"With nearly anyone else, yes, that should have been the case. However, as my memories of Jensen resurfaced throughout my battle with him, I began to feel that something was off. He wasn't fighting like the man I remembered. It was as though his abilities were being somehow restrained, like he was holding back without wanting to. This was essentially confirmed when he started talking to himself, but if I had any remaining doubts, they were dispelled at the end."

"You mean when he freaking *teleported?*"

"Not at all. He did the exact same thing he was doing up until then."

"How the hell was that the same?!" Elsi argued, "I saw some of what was going on and he was moving pretty fast for short spurts, but I couldn't follow what happened then at all!"

"What you saw then was the true version of that technique, the Flash Step, so named because one who has mastered it can move from one place to another nigh-instantaneously within the span of a single step. I can only surmise that he was continuously at war with himself internally, doing all he could to hold back the entity that was controlling his body until then."

"What you're saying is he's batshit insane." Rao opined.

"That is...a complicated situation and not one that it is my place to delve into. Suffice to say that it is one that I had thought he had gotten a handle on. Something about his Contract must have exacerbated it."

"Contracts can do that? They can...*change* people like that?" Elsi looked mildly disturbed at the notion, which was no small feat.

"If Zurie told you the essentials, then you already know that the simple act of forging one affects the memories of those in close proximity to it. Should both parties agree, and should the Contractor be powerful enough, nearly anything is possible."

"In other words, without knowing exactly what Shiku's Contract with Jensen entails, we can't be sure of anything." Issa summarized.

"Correct. All we can do for now is recover and prepare ourselves for some form of retaliation.

Vengeance isn't in-character for the Jensen I knew, but this one seems unlikely to take such a defeat lying down."

C-O-N-T-R-A-C-T

"Reduced? 'Reduced' he says. I'll damn well say I've been reduced! What the hell would he call *this?!*"

Chunks of earth and concrete splashed into the foul waters of the sewer system as the man who looked like Jensen Kuro but had no name of his own excavated an impromptu hiding spot using brief spurts of energy so as to attract as little attention as possible. Shiku, who had regained consciousness only a little while ago, was doing his best to stay silent, out of the way and beneath his notice.

"Weak! He called me *weak!* He was speaking to you, but he said it to *me!* He should be dead! We should have killed him! How could you have let that stand?! Why did you keep getting in my way?!"

He wanted to rage, thrashing about and bringing wrack and ruin to everything around him.

But that would also bring destruction to his Signer and, pathetic wretch though he may have been, he was bound by his nature to honor the Contract until it was completed, breached or rendered null and void. To go against that would result in... undesirable consequences.

So it was that he found himself digging a new shelter for himself and Shiku, the pervasive stench of sewage, earth and concrete dust seeping into him while he seethed over his recent humiliation.

After an indeterminate period of time, once he had

deemed the area large enough and could no longer use the mindless labor as an outlet for his anger and bloodlust, he could only stand there, teeth gritted, fingers spasming, blood burning his veins as his breathing became more and more uneven.

It couldn't continue like that. Eventually it would build to the point where he couldn't control himself anymore, consequences be damned! He needed another kill, but after what had happened, not just anyone would do. Oh, no.

"Humiliated...I've been humiliated! That's why...yes...I need something big, something *loud*, something that'll make *everyone* fear me!" he rounded on Shiku, who had found the closest thing to a corner he could and was sitting with his back to the wall, "Any ideas for something like that, my Signer?"

Chapter Eleven

Motivation

It was a silent pair that entered Issa's apartment that evening. After all, both Zurie and her Signer had a fair amount to think about regarding both the day's events and what was yet to come. Given this, she was thankful that she had something to distract herself with as she entered the kitchen and started making dinner.

It was the agreement they had arrived at: Issa made breakfast and Zurie made dinner. She had offered to do all the cooking, arguing that it was the least she could do given that she was living with him rent-free, but Issa insisted that he should "do his share" when it came to cooking meals for them. She was prepared to argue, but when he pointed out that he tended to wake up earlier than she did and was typically on a schedule due to his classes, she gave in.

She glanced at him while she was tossing the fixings for beef stew into a pot, seeing that he had sat himself on the couch and was flipping through channels, though he didn't seem to be paying much attention to what was on. She considered trying to get him to talk to her about it, but her gut told her that he would broach the topic soon enough.

Sure enough, when the stew was about halfway done, she heard a telltale sigh.

"What if it had been us?"

Zurie knew what he meant. Truth be told, she had considered the same question earlier that day. Even so, she gave him a questioning look as she stirred.

"If we had been the ones who found those guys instead of Vemris, Rao and Elsi, what do you think would have happened?"

"Probably a similar situation to what we found when we arrived." she shrugged, "I'd confront Jensen while you would have to deal with Shiku. Vemris would've felt it when things started to get out of hand, made a beeline for us and, hopefully, he'd show up in time to help."

Issa abandoned any pretense of watching TV as he turned his head, a grim expression on his face.

"Do you think I'd have been able to hold out as long as Rao did? What he and Elsi told us happened is one thing, but what I saw him do...I'd never have suspected he was capable of something like that, Elsi's help aside."

"What're you saying?" she gave him her undivided attention as she set the wooden spoon aside.

"I'm a liability in situations like that. I'm not arrogant enough to think that I can stand equal to a Contractor, or that I can protect everyone from whack jobs like Shiku, but getting strong enough to defend *myself* should be possible. Vemris did say that anyone can learn to use chi, right? Can you teach me?"

"I could try, but it's mostly instinct for me. Vemris would be better suited for helping you get a handle on it, if he's willing."

A part of Zurie rankled at having to admit that, but it was the truth. As a vampire, her powers had always been directly linked to blood. The more of it she had, the more effectively she could use them. It wasn't as though she could simply *teach* that sort of thing to someone who wasn't like her.

And whatever plans she might have had for Issa, turning him wasn't one of them.

"Yeah, I suppose that makes sense." Issa nodded thoughtfully, "I wonder if he'd agree to it? I'm sure taking on a total greenhorn would be a pain in the ass. He'd have to whip me into shape from square one, not to mention I don't even know if I have any aptitude for using chi in the first place." he rubbed the back of his neck, "I'd hate to think I was wasting his time."

Zurie turned back to the stew so he wouldn't see her rolling her eyes. He was trying to become stronger in order to deal with the very real possibility that a Contractor and a criminal would be coming after him or his friends and he was worried about *inconveniencing* someone.

"You aren't as far behind as you think." she said as she adjusted the heat of the stove, "I can't say much regarding your chi or your skills, but you can take my word for it that your body is nothing to sneeze at. Blood always tells when it comes to that sort of thing and I'm giving it my all to cultivate yours."

"I'm not sure I'll ever get used to being talked about as a food supply." he groused. In spite of his complaints, his mood seemed to have improved some now that he had a plan of action. Or maybe it had been the compliment she had given him?

I mean, what I said is true, she reflected as she added her final ingredient to the stew, *I knew that my training was effective as soon as I tasted his blood before. If anything, he's progressing more quickly than he should be, even with my methods.*

She sipped a spoonful of the broth and considered it for a moment before adding a bit of pepper.

"If only it had been a bit longer before anything like this happened, then I could be surer..." she murmured.

"Did you say something?"

"I said you should probably wait a bit before asking Vemris to train you. Give him and Rao a day or two to rest and start to recover from their injuries."

"Good call." he paused, "That smells good. How's it looking?"

"It's done. Just letting it cool a bit."

"You're a better cook than I'd expect, given your primary diet."

"What can I say? It's a hobby. Just 'cause normal food doesn't give me all I need doesn't mean I can't enjoy it."

"I'm worried I'll start getting spoiled. What'll I do when the Contract is over?" he said in a joking tone.

"Well, uh..." Zurie fumbled, "it'll probably be a while before that happens. After all, I still don't exactly know what your Desire or Terms were." she started to ladle the stew into a pair of bowls.

"We haven't really talked about that, have we?" Issa turned off the TV and took a seat at the table, giving her a curious look as she sat across from him.

"Why the sudden interest?"

"I mean, that's why you're here, isn't it?" he looked taken aback, "It's not bothering you, is it? Not really knowing what you're supposed to do?" he took a bite and chewed as he waited for her to respond before adding, "I dunno, I guess I'm asking if you feel...trapped?"

After a day filled with excitement and surprises, maybe she was just worn out. Maybe she was caught off-guard because she was winding down. Maybe she just hadn't expected that sort of thing from her Signer.

Whatever the reason was, Zurie found herself more deeply affected by that question than she should have been. Not because she didn't know the answer, but because, for whatever reason, she was unable to say it.

Why can't I do it? Why can't I just say "no?" It's the truth. It's the honest truth! Why?!

Then it hit her. A possible reason for his question that made her freeze in place.

"...Do you?"

He blinked.

"No, not really. I was a bit apprehensive at first, but I've gotten used to having you around and the blood thing really isn't as bad as it sounds."

She let out a breath she hadn't realized she'd been holding.

"Well, good, 'cause you're stuck with me for the foreseeable future. It's like I said when we first met: I'll figure it out over time as I learn more about you and drink more of your blood. Now stop asking weird questions and eat your stew. I'm going to be stepping up your training regardless of what Vemris says, so you'd better keep your strength up!"

"Are you angry?"

"Stew. Eat."

C-O-N-T-R-A-C-T

It was difficult for Fiona to say which was more congested as she made her way around the city that Thursday afternoon: regular traffic or foot traffic. It was one thing to see it from hundreds of feet above, but quite another to be in the thick of it as she attempted to find the source of the energy she had felt earlier.

She had an easier time making her way through the crowds than most on account of her imposing stature and stoic expression encouraging most people to give her a wide berth. The exceptions to this were the occasional curious child or sightseer with a camera who insisted on taking a picture of anything out of the ordinary, which a towering woman with violet hair certainly qualified as. She allowed the former due to their harmless, innocent nature and the latter because the shirt she wore had the Moreno Group logo on it and her employer encouraged free publicity.

Indeed, as she had been summoned with nothing but the clothes on her back, Mr. Moreno had given her full access to a wide selection of company apparel, stating that her stature practically made her a walking billboard. The clothes weren't bad and they fit her well, so Fiona didn't mind.

Under other circumstances, her walk through the city would probably have been enjoyable. The early spring weather was pleasant and there was no shortage of things to see, but her search was thus far proving to be fruitless, which put a slight damper on things.

Well, she still had about half of the day remaining. Plenty of time to learn something useful. Where should she look next?

"Excuse me, ma'am?" a voice interrupted her train of thought. Fiona looked down to see a woman she assumed to be a reporter of some kind on account of the microphone in her hand and the cameraman following her around. She did not respond, but the reporter took her attention as license to continue.

"Forgive me if I'm wrong, but weren't you with Miguel Moreno when he was giving a statement to the police the other day regarding the bodies that were found around his company's warehouses?"

Fiona nodded.

"Would it be alright if I asked you some questions?"

"Yes," she agreed, having been given instructions regarding this possibility, "though I am somewhat limited in the information I am permitted to disclose."

"That's perfectly alright! Whatever answers you can give are very much appreciated." the reporter assured her as she positioned herself so that the cameraman could see both of them easily, "Are we good? Good. Alright, ma'am, if you could please state your name?"

"Fiona."

"Fiona, you were present when Miguel Moreno,

the head of the Moreno Group, made a statement to the police this past Monday regarding some bodies that were located near some company-owned warehouses. Could you describe for me the nature of your relationship with Mr. Moreno?"

"I am an employee of the Moreno Group." Fiona responded as she had been told to, "I work directly under Mr. Moreno as a member of his personal security detail."

"So, it would be accurate to say that you work closely with him?"

"Yes."

"As someone in your position, what can you tell me about this most recent incident, which many believe can be credited to the serial killer that the police have been working to track down?"

"Mr. Moreno is taking the situation very seriously. He has taken it upon himself to assist the police in their investigation of any and all Moreno Group property and personnel, provided that they can demonstrate adequate cause. The day after the incident, he sent his son, Maxwell Moreno, along with several trusted members of his personal security team, to conduct a full sweep of the area in the warehouse district occupied by the Moreno Group alongside the police. This was completed last night."

"Did they find anything noteworthy?"

"I am unable to comment on that at this time."

"I understand. How would you say that Mr. Moreno feels about all this on a personal level?"

Fiona took a moment to answer, not having been given a quote for this question.

"It upsets him. He dislikes the idea that such a

criminal could have been using company property for his benefit."

"Would you say that he feels personally responsible?"

The questions continued for several minutes, though Fiona said little as they often ventured into "no comment" territory. The reporter eventually thanked her for her time and went on her way, saying that if she was interested in seeing herself on TV, her interview would likely be featured by sometime the following day.

As Fiona made to continue her search, she noticed that the interview had drawn a small crowd of onlookers. Some of them were discussing what they had heard, while others just seemed to want to be on TV. They parted easily enough as she made to leave, a man in a gray hoodie stepping aside to let her through.

"I see you."

Fiona froze, the voice tearing through her like a bolt from on high, seizing her muscles and stopping her heart.

She had heard it before. She had heard those same words, spoken by that same voice in exactly the same way.

When?

Where?

How?

She turned her head, but the man was gone. She spun around, desperately searching, but he was nowhere to be seen. In that moment, deep down, Fiona knew she would find nothing more. She would continue searching for the remainder of the day, as she had nothing better to do, but she knew with an absolute certainty that the one she had been looking for had just eluded her.

It wouldn't be until later, when she was preparing for a shower, that she would find the folded scrap of paper that had mysteriously appeared in her pocket.

Tomorrow evening. Five PM. Channel three.

C-O-N-T-R-A-C-T

Issa opened his eyes at the same time he usually did, even though his alarm hadn't been set for that morning. He felt uncharacteristically groggy and wondered at it for a few moments before he tried to sit up, prompting the deep ache that permeated his muscles to make itself known, causing him to collapse back onto the mattress.

"...Ow."

He hadn't felt like this since Zurie had first started his exercise routine. Until recently, a meal and a good night's sleep had been enough to make him feel fully restored, no matter what she had him do. Over the past couple of days though, he had been feeling progressively more fatigued.

I guess she meant it when she said she was going to step things up.

As though on cue, the covers next to Issa rustled as Zurie's head popped out from underneath them, blinking sleepily as her slitted pupils contracted, adjusting to the morning light.

"Wuzzat?"

"Gonna have to roll out of bed since I can't sit up."

"Oh." she appeared to doze off for a moment

before she shook her head slightly, "I'll get you something."

She crawled over him and nearly ran into the door before he heard her doing something in the kitchen.

I hope she doesn't break anything, being half-asleep like that.

He was mercifully spared the sound of breaking glass and before long she returned with some orange juice and a pair of pills that he recognized as painkillers from the medicine cabinet.

"It's not that bad—" he started to protest before he was cut off by her shoving the pills into his mouth and the juice into his hand. He drank obediently, after which she took the glass back to the kitchen and then returned to the bed, collapsing on top of it as though *she* were the one being put through the wringer.

"What's with you?"

She said something, but as her face was currently buried in the pillow, he wasn't able to understand her.

"What?" she groaned and rolled towards him.

"I said I'll need blood soon. All the excitement took more out of me than I thought."

"So take some. It's not like I have anything going on today." Issa replied, giving her a confused look.

Zurie traced a finger along his neck, lips parted slightly to reveal her fangs before she sighed and shook her head.

"I'd like to, but you're going to need your energy today. After you went to bed early yesterday, Rao called. I brought up that you were thinking about asking Vemris to train you and he said 'Sounds great, bring him over tomorrow around ten.' So... yeah."

"Oh. That means I've got..." he took another

glance at the clock, "a bit over an hour if we're walking. I'm not sure I'll be in a fit state for anything that soon."

"Just get up and start moving around a bit. It might not go away completely, but it should help you feel better. Remember, the primary thing we've been focusing on with you is recovery speed."

Issa sighed and forced himself to sit on the edge of the bed, grunting with the effort but noticing that it didn't hurt as badly as it had before.

Huh. Maybe there's something to this after all.

C-O-N-T-R-A-C-T

Rao Lassare was doing some stretches and light shadow-boxing as he limbered up for his spar with Vemris. They usually didn't do them this early in the day, but Issa would be coming over soon and Vemris was going to be preoccupied with assessing his condition and bringing him up to speed.

Most people who knew him in passing might assume that Rao would have jumped at the chance to have an easy day and, most days, this would have been right on the money. This day was different, though. Really, one might even have said that this Rao was different.

He was focused.

He was serious.

The reason was obvious to anyone who knew what had happened mere days before: Rao had experienced firsthand not only the difference his training so far had made, but also how much further he still needed to go. There had been a very real chance that he could have lost his life then, and there were few things that made for effective motivators like having one's mortality clarified for them in such a manner.

Across from Rao stood Vemris, rolling up his right sleeve using his disabled left arm, which hung in a sling. Apart from that and his bare feet, he appeared as he usually did. It was business as usual and Rao didn't think for a moment that today was going to be any easier.

The building they used for sparring was located in Rao's backyard. At first glance, it could've been mistaken for a shed, albeit much larger than average with sliding wood doors and an angular roof. On the inside, however, it had been furnished to look like a dojo of sorts with minimal furnishings and a polished wooden floor that carried numerous small scuffs and scratches from the activities that took place therein.

"Are you ready, Rao?" Vemris asked as he bent his knees and raised his good arm in front of him, palm open and fingers bent inwards.

"Yeah." Rao responded by adopting the basic stance that Vemris had taught him, slightly lower than his teacher's and more spread out to allow for greater stability, left fist extended in front of him with the right further back and close to his head.

"Do not hold back on account of my arm."

"I know."

As if I need you to tell me that. I know without a doubt that I don't stand a chance.

Rao began to shuffle forward and to the side, trying to get an angle on Vemris' weakened left.

That's the whole point of this: Contractors aren't

human. Whenever I go up against one, I'm fighting a losing battle right out of the gate. Vemris could take me apart with both hands tied behind his back if he had to.

Rao's fists tightened and his toes gipped the floor, allowing his foot to inch forward as he shifted his weight and did his best to focus his chi, preparing to enter Vemris' range.

I need to take full advantage of everything I can, even if it's fighting dirty! I'll go after his crippled arm right from the start!

"Shu!" Rao let out a quick burst of air as his left fist snapped towards Vemris' head in a sharp jab. The Contractor responded by batting it aside and retaliating with a quick strike of his own, but Rao had anticipated this and swayed back to avoid it. Taking advantage of his deep stance, he shifted his weight to his front leg and swung his body around, firing off a haymaker with his right arm directly at Vemris' injured forearm, which just so happened to be covering his solar plexus.

Whap

Vemris had rotated his shoulder, allowing him to catch Rao's fist in his right palm. Against a normal opponent, Rao might have been able to power through and still hit him, but Vermis' superior physique and chi control caused Rao's strike to stop dead.

Now! His arm's occupied!

"HA!" Rao pushed forward into Vemris' chest and rotated his hips, sending his right knee shooting towards his mentor's unprotected side.

Vemris flexed his fingers, dislodging Rao's fist and

causing it to slide upward and glance off of his elbow and over his head as he dropped into a horse stance and caught Rao's knee, leaving him in a precarious position.

"You're open."

"Oh, cra—"

POW

Vemris' palm slammed into Rao's abdomen, doubling him over and sending him flying into the door, derailing it, and out of the dojo with a crash. He tumbled across the ground and came to a stop in a position that Vemris would've called "undignified."

At least I was able to reinforce my gut before that landed, otherwise this would've been worse.

"Holy shit, Rao?"

...Goddamn it.

"Hey, Issa. You're early."

"I won't say your plan was wrong, Rao, but it was written all over your face. When your opponent has a blatant weak spot, they'll usually assume that you'll be aiming for it. Consider mixing in a few feints or going for another target altogether. Your chi control is improving, so that's—" Vemris cut himself off as he exited the dojo and saw Issa and Zurie, "Ah, good morning. I've been expecting you two. You in particular, Issa."

If anything good could be said about Issa seeing Rao get floored like that, it was the expression on his face when the man responsible turned to him and he realized what he had to look forward to.

"I blame you for this." he said to the petite girl at his side, who responded with an amused grin.

Yeah, this is gonna be good.

Chapter Twelve

Declaration

Issa swallowed nervously as he stood straight-backed and silent under Vemris' appraising gaze. The slightly more casual look, barefoot, sans vest, sleeves rolled up to his elbows and left arm in a sling, combined with the fact that he understood more about the man (and Contractors in general) should have made him more approachable, but the effect it had on Issa was the opposite; he was made all the more intimidating after he had caught a glimpse of what Rao's Contractor was truly capable of.

"I need you to relax, Issa." Vemris said as he slowly circled the younger man, "You're going to need to focus in order for me to accurately assess you."

"Right. Sorry." Issa took a slow, deep breath, willing himself to calm down.

It's fine. This is why I'm here. I can trust him. Worst case, Zurie's just over there.

"Better." though he was behind him, Issa heard the

approving nod in the Contractor's tone, "You said he's been under your care for a little over two weeks now, Zurie?"

"That's right." she confirmed from where she stood by the wall of the dojo alongside Rao, arms crossed as she observed the goings on, "I started his regimen almost immediately, though we've ramped things up a bit since the incident the other day."

Vemris hummed thoughtfully as Issa felt a hand grip his shoulder lightly before moving down his arm, then to his back, fingers lightly prodding. In a similar vein, the rest of his body was explored as Vemris continued to circle him, his clinical expression betraying nothing. He said little apart from occasionally asking Issa to raise an arm, tilt his head or other such things. After several minutes, he withdrew a few paces and stood in front of Issa, apparently having finished.

"Your physical condition is acceptable. If anything, you are further along than I would have hoped. Zurie clearly knows what she is doing. This means we will not need to waste time building the necessary muscle or flexibility for you to withstand my methods without undue risk of injury."

"He's gonna kick your ass, dude." Rao supplied.

"Thank you, Rao." Vemris deadpanned, "As I'm sure you've guessed, Issa, our first order of business is to get an idea of your capacity for chi, as that is a large factor when it comes to determining your overall potential. To be safe, it is a good idea to ensure that your physical abilities have reached a certain point before attempting to tap into it. In the event that one possesses an unusually large amount, a weak body might not be able to withstand it."

"Do you have any reason to think I have a lot?" Issa asked cautiously.

"I have no indication one way or the other. As such, it is better to be safe than sorry."

"Okay. So, how should I go about this?"

"The traditional method is for one to devote themselves to training their body and mind, engaging in meditations to unlock the power of their spirit, which is known to most as chi. This can take weeks, months, or even years depending on the talent of the individual in question."

"But we don't have time for that."

"Indeed. Even if we did, I would not want to risk wasting my attentions on a lost cause, which is why I favor an alternate method: I'm going to force my chi into your body in the hopes that it will react by bringing your own to the fore." he raised a hand, fingers extended inches from Issa's forehead, "We'll start with a more delicate approach and, should that fail, we'll move on to more...direct tactics."

"Is that what you did with Rao?"

"Nope!" Rao grinned, "I've got loads of potential, so my first beating was purely for the sake of honing my skills."

"You still got beaten up though."

"If you're ready, let's begin." Vemris pressed three fingers to the center of Issa's forehead and closed his eyes.

"So...what do I do?" Issa asked after several seconds of nothing.

"At some point over the course of the next sixty seconds, I will begin to send my chi into you. I will sustain this for ten seconds before stopping. After the minute is over, I will remove my hand and ask you if you felt anything. You will answer honestly."

Issa decided to copy Vemris and close his eyes, attempting to clear his mind.

It's a good idea, not telling me when he's going to do it. That way I can't trick myself into thinking I feel something when I don't. It might help if I knew what I was looking for though... I guess I'll just focus on his fingers? That's simple enough.

...There. Three points on my forehead. If I drew lines connecting them, it feels like it'd be a triangle. With another point in the middle.

Wait, what?

"Quit trying to mess with me, Rao."

"Huh? What are you talking about?"

Issa's eyes snapped open as Rao's voice came from the same place he had been before. Before him he saw that Vemris had opened his eyes as well and was wearing a satisfied smirk, three fingers still firmly planted on Issa's forehead.

"But you—there was another finger!" Issa insisted.

"You have my word, Issa, that there were only ever three fingers on your forehead. Did you feel anything else?"

Issa shook his head, still nonplussed.

"Well, that is more or less as I expected. The fact that you were able to feel the small amount of chi that I used shows that you have at least some potential, while the fact that this alone was not enough to trigger anything more shows that said talent is still within the realm of average, as far as those with any notable capacity goes."

"It's plan B then?"

"Indeed." Vemris rolled his right shoulder and adopted a one-armed stance, "On your guard, Mr. Aono; I'm afraid I'll have to get a bit rough."

Issa raised his fists with a growing feeling of dread, which he quickly stamped out. Even so, he couldn't help asking one more thing.

"Do I actually need to fight you? I mean, we both know I've got no chance and you just need to hit me with your chi, right? What if I just stand here and take it?"

"I'm a teacher, Issa, not a thug. Attacking a defenseless opponent is beneath me." Vemris said reproachfully, "Besides, think of this as killing two birds with one stone; you can never have too much practical experience."

Issa gave a resigned sigh, tightened his guard and began circling around Vemris' injured left side.

If I'm doing this, I may as well try my best. Wonder if I can at least lay a hand on him before he sends me through the wall?

Vemris didn't move. He didn't even turn to stop Issa from circling around him. Only his eyes followed the young Signer, cool and calculating. The message couldn't have been clearer.

Guess the first move is mine. Let's make it count!

Issa dug his toes into the floor once he was outside of Vemris' cone of vision and sprang forwards, sending his fist shooting towards the base of Vemris' skull. Predictably, he evaded, delivering a sharp, two-fingered jab to Issa's wrist as he did so.

"You were serious just now, weren't you?"

"You're a Contractor. I can't afford to play nice, teacher or not."

That remark earned Issa a smile and a second jab, harder than the first, which he avoided with a quick pair of backsteps before catching himself on his back leg and reversing direction, hoping to catch Vemris off-guard as he covered his head and charged forwards, attempting to tackle the man. Vemris responded by shifting his weight onto the balls of his feet, deepening his stance slightly and covering his injured arm with his good one just before Issa collided with him.

It felt like he had run into a pole. Vemris' feet barely slid on the floor at all, as though he had rooted himself to the spot.

"Come on, now; push with your legs."

Issa growled, feeling as though he were tensing every muscle in his body struggling to move the man just a fraction of an inch. He grunted as Vemris snapped his wrist, delivering another two-fingered jab to his midsection, then another and another, each one seeming to strike him a little harder than before.

"There exists a fine line between tenacity and stupidity, you know."

"Shut...up!" the condescending tone was starting to grate on Issa's nerves and he gritted his teeth in preparation for another hit. When it came, he felt as though a spike was being driven into his gut, "What else can I do?! I can't hit you, so it's either this or run!"

"If that's all you can think of, then perhaps you *should* run." with an apparent lack of effort, Vemris shoved Issa away from him and delivered a thrusting kick to his chest, sending him skidding away, barely staying on his feet, "Only suicidal fools fight losing battles, after all."

"Hey, Vem, don't you think you're being kinda hard on him?" Rao protested from the sidelines.

"Am I? Then maybe he should quit. What do you think, Issa?"

Issa glanced to the side, making eye contact with Zurie. Her expression was unconcerned as she stared back before giving him a small nod.

Alright then.

"You don't wanna know what I think right now."

"It seems I've touched a nerve. Good. Use that."

Vemris initiated the attack, closing the gap and delivering a flurry of the exact same jab he had been using the entire time, continuing to escalate the power of each one.

"Tell me Issa, does it seem as though I'm hitting you harder than before?"

"What kind of question is that?"

"It might interest you to know that my strikes have grown neither faster nor stronger. It has been the same prod each time. The only difference is the amount of chi I put into each one."

"You're showing off, in other words." Issa dashed forward and snapped off several jabs, trying to bait Vemris into countering.

This is all I can do. It's going to hurt, but I can take it. So go on. Do it. Do it!

"Come on." Issa found himself taunting, causing Vemris to narrow his eyes.

Issa's next punch was met with a two-fingered jab to his wrist that blasted his arm away, feeling as though a bullet had just ripped through it.

But this…is what I wanted!

Issa took the momentum created by his arm and twisted his body, shifting his foot forward to carry his weight as he brought his right arm around in a wild hook with all of his weight behind it.

There would be no coming back from this one. If it missed, he would be completely off-balance and Vemris was nowhere near kind enough not to capitalize on it.

But that didn't matter; he was too far along to stop. The only thing to do was commit to it all the way.

Issa experienced a brief moment of clarity, where everything seemed to slow down. His fist was loose, so he tightened it. His foot wasn't planted correctly, so he shifted it. There were still reserves of strength he wasn't using, so he gritted his teeth and willed his body to *move.*

His fist streaked through the air towards Vemris' face. It wasn't going to connect. Issa knew that. He was going to avoid or block it. There was no way he wouldn't.

…Why hadn't he moved?

What was he doing?

In the instant before his fist reached him, Issa thought he saw Vemris crack a smile.

Wham

The Contractor's head jerked to the side and his back leg shifted to prevent him from falling, at which point he let out a mild grunt and both men came to a halt, Issa's fist still pressed into his cheek.

"Hmm…I see." he gripped Issa's wrist and removed his hand, helping him regain his balance, "That will do. Remember how that felt. Instinctive chi usage feels different for each person, so I won't be able to help you there."

"Why didn't you dodge that?" Issa demanded, "I know you could've."

"Positive feedback. When you do as your teacher says, a reward helps the lesson stick and unless I am highly mistaken, you very much wanted to hit me right then."

"What's the verdict, Vem?" Rao walked over to Issa and brushed some dust off of his shirt where Vemris had kicked him, "That looked like a pretty solid shot."

"I'm more impressed with his sheer endurance than anything else; I got a little serious with those last few hits. The fact that he had the mental fortitude to continue with that plan, simplistic though it may have been, after I struck his arm is praiseworthy."

Vemris shook his head, seeming disappointed.

"It is unfortunate, then, that fortitude does not equate to talent. The fact that I had to go that far to get anything out of you means that, while you do indeed have the capacity necessary to use chi, it would be more accurate to say that you have the *minimum* capacity required." Vemris gave him an even stare, "Do you understand, Issa? You will still benefit from my teachings, but you will need to work hard and even then, you can only progress so far. It may sound harsh, but being anything other than truthful would be doing you a disservice. Knowing this, do you still wish to proceed?"

"If I say 'no,' will that make it all go away? Will me, Rao, Elsi, Zurie and you suddenly be safe?"

Issa shifted his gaze among those present. Rao looked away, Zurie's expression was unreadable and

Vemris tapped his chin thoughtfully.

"You know my answer then."

"Very well. I'll give you a day or two to recover and then we can begin in earnest. Regardless of capacity, I'll always recommend training your body, sharpening your mind and honing your skills."

"That won't be necessary."

"I beg your pardon?" Vemris raised an eyebrow.

"I don't need a day or two. Give me an hour and I'll be good to go."

"Come on man, don't be stupid!" Rao walked over and patted Issa on the back, "It's important to know your limits and stuff, otherwise you'll just get hurt."

Issa looked at his friend in confusion, unable to understand why he didn't believe him. Was it really that odd? Vemris' attacks had hurt, sure, but there wasn't anything that he couldn't work through.

After all, it was only pain. There wasn't actually anything wrong with his body. Couldn't Rao see that? Didn't he understand?

Does he think I can't take it? Is he treating me with kid gloves because I'm the "new guy?"

Too little, too late.

"Compared to that night in the alley, this is a joke." he said flatly, "I'm not trying to throw this in your face, but the fact is you were already out when I got there; there's no way you could know."

Rao pursed his lips and took a step back, clearly wounded by Issa's words.

"Then tell me."

"I was cut, stabbed, beaten and left on the ground in a pool of my own blood."

"...Oh."

"'Having had a brush with death, nothing else can compare.' That's a dangerous state of mind to have." Vemris cautioned.

"Zurie won't let me overdo it."

"I suppose not."

C-O-N-T-R-A-C-T

Due in no small part to sheer stubbornness, Issa spent the remainder of the afternoon at Rao's residence, alternating between being instructed by Vemris and drilled by Zurie when it was Rao's turn. He didn't consider himself to be the jealous type, but couldn't help feeling a hint of satisfaction upon learning that his exercise routine surpassed Rao's by a significant margin. Eventually, the two Contractors agreed that they had done enough for one day and, as Issa was about to say his goodbyes, the phone rang.

"Sorry, just a sec. Hello? Hey, Elsi, what's up?" Rao paused for a moment, "What, right now? Okay. No, don't bother, he's with me. Yeah, talk to you later." he hung up the phone and made for the front room, beckoning the others to follow him. He switched on the TV and flipping through channels.

"What gives?"

"Elsi said to turn on channel three 'like, *right now.*' Okay, there we go."

The local news station turned on to reveal an uncharacteristically excited-looking reporter anxiously watching a pair of policemen with a dog examining a manila envelope.

"For those of you just joining us, this mysterious envelope was discovered in our station's inbox earlier

this afternoon among the usual tips and scoops that the public submits for our consideration, though given the volume of these letters it is possible that it has been here since yesterday. We do not yet know what it contains and have brought in members of our local police force to ascertain whether it is safe to open."

"Why would we go to such lengths? Because if the note attached to the envelope is to be believed, it comes to us directly from the serial killer that has been terrorizing our city! I shall read it for you once more while we wait for the officers to complete their inspection."

"'The contents of this envelope are to be broadcasted on the channel three five o'clock news on Friday, March 23rd, 1990. Failure to do so will result in at least two unfortunate accidents. Sincerely, The Killer.' Well, I for one would have latched onto this story even without that threat, but it does seem to have encouraged the police to take this seriously."

The reporter turned around as one of the policemen began speaking, though his voice was not picked up by the mic.

"The officers have deemed the envelope save to open and, as it was delivered to our station specifically, they will allow us to be the first to examine its contents!"

The reporter took a moment to open the envelope.

"It appears to contain three sheets of paper. The first is a letter, written in what looks like the same hand as the initial note. I shall read it for you now:"

Dear Channel Three News,

Assuming that my instructions are being followed, and I shall know if they are not, this letter is currently

being read live on the five o'clock news on Friday, March 23rd. Allow me to take a moment to thank you for your cooperation. I am writing this letter to reveal to you and, through you, the city at-large, my next target.

Recently, law enforcement has decided to crack down on me, as it were. I do not blame them for this. After all, they are simply doing their jobs. One other group has also taken an interest in my doings, however. Namely, the private security team of the Moreno Group, though perhaps it would be more accurate to refer to them as Miguel Moreno's thugs.

They, unlike the police, are not playing by the rules. It is not their place to do as they are doing and Miguel Moreno needs to be reminded of this fact. I have no doubt that this message will make it to him one way or another, so I shall take this opportunity to speak to him directly:

The reporter moved to the next page.

Miguel Moreno, I hereby declare you to be my next target.

There is nothing you can do.

There is nowhere you can hide.

In the name of sportsmanship, I shall give you one week to prepare yourself in whatever way you see fit. Strengthen your security, bar your windows, send another hit squad to come find me. Do as you will.

One way or another, you shall not live to see March 31st.

Sincerely,

The Killer

P.S. – To ensure that there is no doubt as to my identity, I have included information regarding two

bodies that the police have yet to find. I encourage you to investigate.

The reporter scanned the remaining page and nodded to the policemen, who said something before taking the page and leaving.

"There is indeed information here regarding the location of two additional bodies. However, as per the request of the police, I shall refrain from disclosing that for the time being, so as to give them room to investigate properly. If anyone has any additional information, they are encouraged to call the tip line, the number for which should be on your screen now."

Rao turned off the TV and tossed the remote onto the couch.

"Well…shit."

"Which one of them do you think wrote that?" Issa pondered, "Shiku or Jensen?"

"Almost certainly Jensen." Vemris stated, "Or at least, the beast that has taken his place."

"So, what're we doing about this?" Rao prompted, appearing unnerved when nobody responded immediately, "We *are* doing something about this, right?"

"Why should we?" Zurie crossed her arms, "Whatever beef he has with Moron or whatever his name is, it doesn't have anything to do with us. If anything, we should be happy that he's found something else to occupy himself with; it gives us more time to prepare for when he decides it's time for round two."

"He's taunting us." Vemris frowned, "What possible reason could he have to make such a spectacle of himself? Additionally, there's the tone he used in the letter: 'Allow me to take a moment to thank you,' 'I am writing this letter to reveal to you and the city at-large,' 'not playing by the rules,' 'in the name of sportsmanship,' there's another layer to his message. He's saying 'you have one week to stop me or more people will die.'"

"He's mad," Issa concluded, "by both definitions. It's like you said before: he's not taking his defeat lying down. He wants to get back at us for it, so he's trying to make us come to him. To do things on his terms."

"Which we have no reason to do." Zurie re-iterated, "Vemris is still injured and I don't really feel like sticking my neck out because of some personal vendetta."

"But people are going to die!" Rao said incredulously, "Innocent people! Who have nothing to do with this! You can't think that he's just going to go for Moreno and leave everyone else alone! It'll be a slaughter!"

"And when that has anything to do with my Contract, I'll let you know." Zurie rebuffed, "I'm not saying I like it, but my duty is to my Signer. I'm not about to charge into a situation that *will*, not *could*, put him at risk."

"Nor would I presume to ask such a thing of you." Vemris concurred, "This problem is mine and Rao's to deal with. Elsi was never directly involved and the two of you only arrived at the very end; I have no doubt that their revenge is directed solely at the two of us."

There was the crux of the issue, as far as Issa was

concerned. Vemris was one thing. Issa liked the man well enough and was grateful for his help, but at the end of the day he didn't owe him anything. Besides, he could more than take care of himself.

But Rao? He was half of the reason Issa had summoned Zurie in the first place (and when the other half inevitably found out, she would insist on getting herself involved, danger be damned). He was more capable than Issa, as things currently stood, as well as having a better understanding of how the whole Signer/Contractor relationship worked, but none of that was going to save him if he went off half-cocked.

That moral compass of his is going to lead him straight into the lion's den. I do want to help, but how can I convince Zurie? I refuse to just be a tagalong and a liability here.

"Don't." Zurie had moved to stand in front of Issa and was shaking her head up at him.

"There's a counterpoint to all of this." Issa looked back at her with a steady gaze, "I think it needs to be considered before we decide one way or the other."

Zurie opened her mouth to protest before sighing and motioning for him to continue.

"Like you said before, Vemris is injured. What we need to remember is that the same goes for Jensen; Vemris gave as good as he got. Better, maybe. He's not just going to sleep that off."

Issa looked to Rao and Vemris and, seeing that he had their attention, continued.

"What's the biggest advantage that we have against those two? Numbers. There's five of us and two of them, plus we have two Contractors to their one. It's less a question of if Vemris and Zurie can handle Jensen and more a question of if Rao, Elsi and I can handle Shiku, especially with Rao being the only one who can fight on his level right now. It'd be really nice to have some additional manpower there, wouldn't it?"

"You're suggesting we join forces with the Moreno Group?"

"The way I see it, some trained professionals should give us the edge we need. Whatever Jensen might be, at the end of the day Shiku's just a guy."

"Hell yeah! See, Vem, Issa gets it." Rao gave his friend a thumbs-up.

"How, exactly, are we to get the Moreno Group to agree to this?" Vemris objected, "Think about this for a moment: their president gets a credible death threat and then a group of people that nobody knows suddenly offers to help protect him? Not only is that too good to be true, but it sounds like a trap."

"We'd have a hell of a time convincing them we're not allied with the killer," Issa agreed, "but don't you think it'd be worth it?"

"Only if it succeeds and we can guarantee media silence on the matter. Otherwise we'd end up facing a hail of bullets or a never-ending steam of publicity. Frankly, I'm not sure which would be worse."

"We could get the police in our corner." Rao suggested, "Tell them that we were the ones that gave them that tip."

"That would beg the question as to why we are so committed to personally opposing the killer. That we happened across the evidence we did is a plausible enough occurrence, but that is where any sane individual would let the matter drop."

"Questions we don't want to answer, in other words." Zurie summarized, "We need to be discreet."

"Okay, to hell with getting their permission. We'll just show up, help them out, then leave before anyone has the chance to ask questions." Issa gestured to the room at-large, "As long as we're not doing anything to get in their way, they'll have bigger things to worry about in the heat of the moment. We'll just have to disguise ourselves or something."

There were no immediate objections. In fact, it was nearly half a minute before anyone spoke.

"That might work." Vemris mused, "Act swiftly and decisively, then leave once the outcome becomes obvious. We will need to find out what the Moreno Group's plans are, at least in general, but as long as we can do that..."

"Sounds like Vemris is on-board." Issa turned to Zurie, "So?"

She looked as though she couldn't decide whether to be angry or not, eventually settling on a resigned sigh.

"Only if all of our preparations go well. Otherwise I'll keep you tied up in the apartment for the whole day if I have to."

"Deal."

Chapter Thirteen
Prodigy

"He said *WHAT?!*" Miguel Moreno's voice boomed through his office as the stocky man in front of him cowered in the face of his boss' fury, "Who does this rat think he is?! Who does he think *I* am?! He's killing our people left and right because *god* knows why and when I put a *goddamn hit out on him, he USES THE MEDIA TO GIVE ME THE FINGER AND TELLS ME I'M NEXT!!!* So tell me, as the head of my security detail, just *what the hell are you doing about this?!*"

Max watched dispassionately from his spot leaning against the wall as his father's head of security stammered out a list of things he had done, was currently doing and would soon be doing in order to maintain safety for him and the company and blah blah freaking *blah*. It was just words. Just meaningless air without any real oomph to it. The man cared more about maintaining his cushy position than he did

197

about following through on half of his promises or making sure they actually accomplished anything.

After all, as daddy dearest so often said, appearance could be just as important as fact. Max didn't necessarily disagree, but he felt that the old man had gotten too used to throwing his weight around and expecting everything to just fall in line. Now that this killer had defied a so-called direct attempt to bring him to heel, he was blowing his top in truly spectacular fashion.

Like hell that was direct. It's not direct unless you do it yourself. It would've been your security team that stopped the killer, not you. Maybe if you weren't so quick to take credit for everything, you wouldn't look like such a screwup right now?

Eventually Miguel grew tired of listening to his head of security kiss his ass and dismissed him, turning to look at that ever-so-special personal bodyguard of his, who had been standing as still and stone-faced as a statue the entire time.

"Kneel." he commanded, tapping his cane against the floor.

Wow, he's really *in a bad mood to go that far.* Max mused as Fiona complied with Miguel's order, taking a knee and bowing slightly, expression unchanged.

"Fiona." his father began, gripping his cane a bit more tightly, "Incompetent as you may be, I trust you can at least tell me if one of your kind is involved in all of this?"

That was right: her kind. Miguel had refused to explain to his son exactly what it was that made her so special as to warrant immediate hiring as his personal bodyguard or the laundry list of benefits that he granted to her, saying only that it would be as he had said and that Max was not to question him. Max had taken it upon himself to do a bit of digging or, rather, to order the head of HR to do some digging for him after being sworn to secrecy.

They found nothing.

Fiona had never applied to work for the Moreno Group. They had no driver's license, social security card, birth certificate, passport, DOD card, student ID, credit card, library card, casino card, freaking *anything* that might tell them who this seven-foot-tall freak of nature was.

Max could only be sure of three things: her name was Fiona, she worked for his father and, in spite of her passive personality, she was *not* someone to mess with.

It was the way she carried herself, Max had decided. She gave off a sort of...detached impression. As though nothing around her really mattered. Not in the way a nihilist or clinically depressed person would, but in the way someone might when they were absolutely assured that nothing in the world could possibly threaten them. As if the concept of fear just...didn't register.

It was unsettling when she would look at him with those yellow eyes of hers, like a hawk's. For a man so accustomed to being given looks varying between respect, fear, admiration or simple caution, to have someone stare at him so...clinically...was unsettling. It wasn't even a sort of passive interest like "oh, look, it's the boss' son, how cute," it was more like "he's still here, still not a threat, still not my concern."

"I believe so." Fiona replied, "I felt something a

few days ago and—"

"A few *days?!*" Miguel struck his bodyguard across the face with the head of his cane, causing it to snap off from the force of his blow, "When were you planning on telling me this you stupid, pathetic waste of power?!"

Fiona fixed Miguel with an even stare as she turned her head to face him properly again, her posture unchanged by the blow that would have sent most other people to the floor with a broken jaw. The blow that contained enough force to snap a reinforced fiberglass cane.

She looked mildly annoyed at worst.

"Just because one of her people is involved doesn't mean they're the killer, Dad." Max cut in before Miguel could start on another tirade.

"Maxxie, son, weren't you listening?" his father started with that patronizing tone that made Max want to punch him, "This worthless bitch just *said* the killer was one of hers! I have half a mind to—" he cut himself off as Max took a step away from the wall, straightening his back and squaring his shoulders to cut what he knew was a *very* imposing figure.

"I know brains aren't my strong suit, Dad. You've told me that often enough for me to get the picture." Max said as he watched the fat executive's brow furrow, his throat constricting as he dry-swallowed, "That's why I make sure to pay attention, just like you taught me. While I was paying attention, I don't think I ever heard Fiona say 'the killer is one of mine.' I just heard her say that one of her kind is *involved.*"

"Semantics, boy. Don't try and—"

"She also started to say something else before you interrupted her. Maybe you should take your own advice and listen for a change?"

"I don't like when you get mouthy, boy. Remember who keeps your future in line around here." Miguel scowled, "Well, Fiona? My son would like to hear what you have to say."

"Yes, sir. The energy I sensed was agitated; clearly involved in a struggle of some kind. If it did not belong to the killer, then it is possible that it was engaged with them."

Max clicked his tongue in annoyance. It figured that he would stand up for her only to be rewarded with more nonsense. All this talk of "her kind" and "sensing energy..." was this something they were doing on purpose? Deliberately keeping him in the dark? He wouldn't put something like that past his father if he thought Max might use the information against him.

In all fairness, he wasn't wrong. Miguel Moreno commanded obedience, but he didn't do much to inspire loyalty apart from signing paychecks and distributing small bonuses or benefits to those he really wanted to keep. Max would say what he wanted about the man (and there was quite a bit to say), but the effectiveness of his methods was self-evident.

"I see. Well then, Max, since you're so interested in this subject, I think I'll have you take a handful of members from my security force and do whatever you can to find out more about what the killer might be planning. We have to do our due diligence, after all. Find the bastard if you can; I'll more than forgive your attitude if you can manage that."

Fiona stood abruptly, an unusually focused look on her face.

"I will go too."

"No. You will not." Miguel put the kibosh on that plan immediately.

"I request that you reconsider."

"I said, 'no.' I'll hear no more of it."

Fiona's features tightened briefly and, for just a moment, her gaze met Max's. It was different than any look she had given him before.

"What, you don't think I can hack it?" Max scoffed, crossing his arms, "Don't you forget that I was the muscle before you showed up. Hell, I still am when the old man needs something more than ten feet away from him." he picked up the larger piece of the broken cane in both hands and, with a grunt, broke it in half, "Whatever it is you think I'm capable of, you're not giving me enough credit. Either of you."

He turned and walked towards the door.

"I haven't told you which security people to take with you!" Miguel protested.

"Whichever ones I want that are working today. I'll have Shirley show me the list." he replied flippantly and shut the door behind him, making his way across the needlessly large waiting room to where Miguel's personal secretary sat behind her desk, giving him a knowing look as she tapped away at her keyboard with practiced efficiency.

"List of available members of the security team for you, Mr. Moreno." she took the still-warm page from her printer and offered it to him the moment he was within arm's reach.

"Were we that loud?" he asked sheepishly as he took the page and began scanning it, marking the occasional name with a pen that was already waiting for him on the desk.

"No, but what else do you ever ask me for, apart from the occasional day off?" she joked.

"Sorry; I'll try to make my requests more varied and complicated from now on." he finished marking off the names he wanted once he had gotten to a total of eight, including himself, "I'll take these ones. I'd like them ready inside of an hour."

"Pull the van out front and I can make that thirty minutes. I know you've got keys."

"Thanks, Shirley."

C-O-N-T-R-A-C-T

Elsi Thompson took a deep breath and closed her eyes as she tossed one of three small rubber balls up and down in her hand, facing the wall of her room, which had been very carefully cleared of anything breakable. When she felt she was ready, she opened her eyes and hurled the ball as hard as she could in a random direction.

The objective of the exercise was simple: she was trying to learn how to control her freaky eye thing. In order to force herself to do that, she had decided to buy a three-pack of bouncy balls, throw them at her wall and try to catch them, which she would only be able to do consistently if she could track their motion, which she would only be able to do with her freaky eye thing.

The unfortunate side-effect of the exercise was that

she had a number of small bruises on her body from where the rubber missiles had hit her when she was still trying to figure things out.

Right wall, left wall, ceiling, desk, ceiling, corner, corner, corner, *there!*

Elsi's hand snapped out and grabbed the ball before it could fly over her shoulder, marveling at the minor movements of her hand muscles as she did so.

"Okay, that makes three. And..." she closed her eyes and willed herself to relax, to let the slowly rising headache fade away like a muscle cramp. Before long it was gone.

"...that makes three too. Nice."

After doing basically nothing but that for the entire weekend, only breaking to eat, sleep and shower, she had succeeded in completing the entire process of activation, tracking, catching and deactivation three times in a row. It was taking longer for her headaches to build up too, which was nice.

"Guess it really is like any other muscle: just keep using it and it'll get better, like Vemris said."

Rao had called her on Friday to let her know that Issa was being put through his paces by Vemris and to ask her if she wanted in. She had asked for advice and he had come back with that tidbit for her, saying that since Vemris didn't have anything like that, he couldn't really give her anything explicit.

She had taken the advice at face-value and decided to just bang her head against the proverbial wall until something broke. Thankfully, that something had been the wall. She had had her doubts when she had succeeded in activating her eyes on-purpose for the first time, only to realize that she still had no idea how to turn them off. Just keeping them shut helped in a pinch, but there was no way she'd be able to rely on that in a dangerous situation.

"Just getting better at using it isn't enough; I need to get faster too." she decided, reaching for a second ball and dropping it into her palm with the first, "Starting now, I've only got ten seconds to turn it on before I make the throw and fifteen seconds to turn it off after I make the catch. It's more important to be quick getting it turned on, after all."

"...Heh, I'm funny."

She closed her eyes again and mentally counted down from ten before hurling the two balls at the opposite wall. The difference was immediately apparent as she tried to track two high-speed objects simultaneously.

Back, left-right, desk-ceiling corner-cornercorner cornerdownupdeskdeskwallwallwallwallwallwallcorne rcorner—*THERE!*

Smack

"Ouch!"

She had thought she was on-target until the balls had *collided in midair* and shot off in opposite directions, causing her hands to knock into each other. She dutifully closed her eyes and started counting down from fifteen.

It was a good thing her mom was working most of that weekend, else she'd probably think her daughter was going crazy or something.

"Okay, it's harder. Two at once is definitely harder."

Elsi opened her eyes and smirked when she found that she had managed to turn them off within the time limit, so at least there was that. Three times in a row meeting the limit and she'd take a second off.

"Well, I didn't expect to get it right on the first try. Nothing to it but to do it, eh?"

She closed her eyes and began counting again.

C-O-N-T-R-A-C-T

"Rico and Williams, west gate. Willoughby and Dominguez, east gate. Nobody gets in or out until we're done here. Tucker and Simmons, we'll start in the middle and fan out. Question anyone you don't recognize. Long, you're watching the van."

The past three days of searching had yielded little in the way of useful information, but Max wasn't the sort to give up easily, for better or worse.

It's the 26th now. Just four more days. Three, really, since it'll be all hands on-deck if we don't find him before then.

The first place they had looked had been the warehouses where the killer had been holed-up until recently. Max hadn't really expected to find anything there, else the police would've already, but he had to start somewhere. After that they had gone down the list of every company-owned property in the city, which was quite a large amount.

Now they were searching an old parking structure that wasn't really used by the public anymore on account of it having been condemned. Of course, that made it quite popular for drug dealers, homeless people, horny teenagers…the usual sorts. Max had found more than one of his targets here before because, for some reason, they kept thinking that honor among thieves was worth more than a strap of twenties.

He, Tucker and Simmons made a beeline for the stairs, taking them to the second level of the structure, which had four above-ground levels and one sub-level.

"You two go up. I'll go down."

"Got it, boss."

They didn't question his decision to go alone into the sub-level, which was where the highest concentration of unsavory sorts was likely to be. They knew full well that he was essentially worth an entire team from just his reputation, let alone what he could do to anyone who was feeling special.

It wasn't always like that. In the early days, when he had started working for his dad at the age of sixteen, people thought he was just some dumb kid whose daddy was playing favorites. Max had laughed in the faces of the first people to suggest that, saying that they clearly didn't know his father.

Miguel Moreno wasn't that kind of man.

The truth was that Max had been born with a gift. He had grown quickly and always possessed a strong body, but what truly set him apart were his hands: They were massive, even in proportion to the rest of his body with strength to match. When he had crushed an apple with one hand at the age of twelve, it had become clear that he was anything but normal.

As he grew into his strength, his father became eager to capitalize on such a resource and gave him a job as a member of his security force. The other members, mostly in their 30s or 40s with experience as military, law enforcement, bouncers and such, didn't take kindly to a brat half their age with zero experience suddenly being on equal footing with them. In spite of their opinions, they were professional enough not to act on said opinions…

…for the most part.

A few decided it would be a good idea to haze the newbie off the clock and scare him into silence. When Max had knocked on his father's door dragging three unconscious grown men behind him, the glint in Miguel's eye had been nothing short of gleeful.

It was in this way that Max, though he was technically still in the same position as the other security personnel, became their de facto leader. In three years, he had become known in the business sector and feared in the underground. His mere presence became a reassuring barrier and an immediate cease and desist order.

He'd be lying if he said it didn't feel good.

Then Fiona had appeared out of nowhere and Max suddenly knew how his senior employees must have felt when he was first hired.

"If she's so big and bad, why not just send her to take care of all this? She *offered* for crying out loud!" he began talking to himself as he descended, threading his way methodically through the concrete pillars as he searched for anything that might be useful.

"He passed it off as 'due diligence,' but the truth is he's scared. The reason he didn't send his new bodyguard is because he's not sure she can hack it. He figured that he'd keep her close, since he's being targeted anyway, meaning the only reason he sent me out is to save face!" he snapped as he rounded a pillar and caused a half-dressed couple to run away shouting.

"If I can actually *do* something, great. If I can't, then I'm a fucking martyr! Me! His fucking *son!*" he kicked a chunk of something into a far wall, where it broke apart and sent a small cloud of dust into the air, illuminated by the dim bulbs that still worked. Behind it was some sort of graffiti, which Max found himself approaching.

"This thing...this whole thing...*is pissing me off!*"

Another bulb sparked to life as he neared the wall, revealing the graffiti to be a set of large, blocky words with a litany of smaller replies written using various styles and materials.

NAME YOUR DESIRE

As he absently scanned the wall, taking in the responses that ran the gamut from "money," "girls," "power" and "happiness" to more specific or sarcastic things, Max found himself remembering the things his father had said to him over the years.

"You aren't cut out for brain-related things; just do as I say."

"Come work for me, Maxxie, I've got something that's right up your alley."

"I don't pay you to think, boy! Stick to what you're good at and swing those fists!"

"Remember who keeps your future in line around here."

"Learn these lessons well, boy; they'll make your life much easier."

Max clenched his fists and glared at the words as though they had offended him.

"Oh, you can bet I've taken your lessons to heart, Dad, even the ones you didn't know you were teaching me. If you're going to throw me away, then

I'll clench these fists and *force* you to acknowledge me! I'll even do it playing by *your* rules, so you can't complain about it afterwards!" at some point, Max had placed his hands on the wall, staring up at it with a mad grimace, "Broken bones? Bloody knuckles? I'll pay that and more just to see you out of words and out of options! *That's what I want!*"

He breathed heavily, finding himself drained from the emotional outburst and thankful that he had decided to go alone, when he heard the sound of footsteps accompanied by someone slowly clapping their hands.

"Such burning passion in your words! I daresay I might be willing to make that deal, young man!"

CHAPTER FOURTEEN
PROPOSITION

"I think it bears repeating that this *really* feels like a bad idea."

"Yeah, not how I would've preferred to do it either, but Elsi was right when she called it 'the least bad idea.'"

"Just once I wish I could win an argument with her."

Issa made a commiserating noise as he privately thought that Zurie was aiming above her weight class with that one, instead focusing his energy on going over the plan one more time.

It was Wednesday the 28th, leaving only two days until Jensen's promised attack on Miguel Moreno. Whatever plan the Moreno Group was cooking up to fight him off, they had to at least have the broad strokes in place by then. As Vemris had pointed out, this was hardly the sort of situation they would leave until the last minute, meaning it was time to try and figure out what said plan was so they could plan around it.

The most efficient way to find out what the company was planning was simply getting one of the people in the know to tell them. Ordinarily, an idea like that would be insane, but Zurie's Suggestion not only made it possible, but laughably easy if they found the right person. The biggest problem they now faced was that the best place to find such a person would be at the Moreno Group's main building which, while still open to the public, was on high alert for anything out of the ordinary and absolutely crawling with security.

In an effort to avoid drawing unnecessary attention to themselves, Elsi suggested that Issa and Zurie should be the only ones to go.

"Ordinarily I'd say that Zurie and I shouldn't both go, since we've already got ties to this whole thing thanks to delivering that tip to the police, but her ability is kind of non-negotiable here. Same for Vemris, now that I think about it, since he got all that evidence for us in the first place."

Zurie had argued that Elsi was being overly careful and that they could be in and out more quickly with more people, with her resorting to Suggestion if anyone recognized them, but Vemris had shot her down.

"You rely too heavily on that ability. We need to conserve our energy and minimize our presence, which includes concealing ourselves from Jensen's ability to sense Contractor energy. As we have no way of knowing how skilled he is in this, we should assume he is on par with someone like me and that

anything other than a gentle Suggestion could alert him."

So it was that Issa found himself approaching the imposing skyscraper that housed the core of the Moreno Group, Zurie at his side and doing his best to look like he was supposed to be there. He had even worn a tie.

"Still the same plan, right?"

"Yeah."

"We could leave."

"No."

Zurie gave him some side-eye for his brusque responses, but didn't pursue the issue further. It wasn't as though he meant to be terse with her, but it was taking a good deal of self-control not to appear as nervous as he felt.

I'll apologize to her later, once this is all said and done with. Maybe she'll be hungry? Even if she isn't, she should probably have some blood either today or tomorrow, just in case. Not like I'll be much help, so it doesn't matter if I'm tired.

Any further thoughts were brought to an abrupt halt as the automatic doors slid open to admit them. As he stepped into the lobby, Issa was met with two opposing impressions. The open layout and welcoming décor provided a calming atmosphere, with such staples as a fountain, a few sculptures and a mixture of photos, framed news clippings and artwork on the walls.

As nice as this all was, there was an undeniable layer of tension. The security people spread throughout the area were armed and wore bulletproof vests, the voices they heard were hushed and clipped and in spite of having a fair number of people the lobby felt oddly…empty.

"Let's make this quick." Issa murmured as he walked steadily towards the reception counter, scanning the room.

The receptionist was pleasant enough once they had explained that they weren't journalists, simply a couple of students working on a project that wasn't due until the following week and who had no intentions of taking whatever they found to the paper, lest they claim the findings as their own. Issa produced his student ID as proof and that was all it took.

Unfortunately, the rest of their investigation didn't go quite as smoothly. The receptionist had recommended a few members of the security team and one or two office people she had seen in the lobby that might be willing to talk to them. They had followed her advice only to discover that, while these people were willing to answer basic questions for the most part, there was quite a lot that they simply didn't know.

The information they had so far obtained could be best summed up as "The number of active security members has been doubled and the higher-ups are scrambling to get a plan together on pain of suffering Miguel Moreno's displeasure. Seeing as how there hasn't been a mass firing, they've obviously come up with something but nobody on this level knows what exactly that is, probably to keep the possibility of a leak to a minimum."

"I really am sorry," the last of the security team members on their small list rubbed the back of his neck and gave a sympathetic grimace, "I've got a kid who wants to be a journalist, so I completely support what you're trying to do here, but the fact of the matter is that we just do what we're told. You'd have to talk to someone at least two or three levels higher than me in order to get the full picture."

"We completely understand. Honestly, we're just grateful that you were willing to take the time to talk with us, what with everything that's going on." Issa inclined his head and shook the man's hand when he offered it.

"No problem at all. You know, you've got a decent build and I like the cut of your jib. You want me to recommend you to my boss? We're not technically hiring right now but unofficial policy for the security team is to always keep an eye out for potential recruits. Benefits are good and the pay's not too bad either, especially if you're willing to keep an open schedule."

"I'll think about it. Do I just ask for you, Mr...?"

"Dominguez. Arlo Dominguez. You can ask for me or my boss if you happen to—" he cut himself off and looked at something behind Issa and Zurie, "Or you could introduce yourself right now, because there he is."

Issa followed his gaze and saw a large man dressed in black sporting sunglasses and a flat top speaking to another member of the security team. His jacket was unzipped, revealing a positively herculean physique.

"Non-standard uniform, huh?" Zurie observed, getting a chuckle from Dominguez.

"He gets certain concessions due to his position.

Believe me though: if he decides he likes you, that's your foot in the door right there."

"Maybe we should go say hi? Just in case?" Zurie suggested.

"Why not?" Issa concurred, not missing out on the gleam in her red eyes that told him she was thinking the same thing he was, "What's his name?"

"Maxwell Moreno, though he prefers 'Max.'" Dominguez grinned as his reveal garnered the response he had been looking for, having caused Issa to do a double-take, "Yes, Moreno as in the name on the building. If he's feeling talkative, you just lucked out."

Issa hurriedly thanked Dominguez and lengthened his strides to catch up with Zurie, who was already making a beeline straight for their potential goldmine.

"I'll pass that information along, sir."

"Good. Move along, Long."

"Excuse me, Mr. Moreno?" Issa spoke up when they were within several feet of him and he had dismissed the guard he was talking to, "Do you have a moment?"

"Depends who you are. If you're journalists, we've already given our statement and you're not getting anything else until this is all over."

"Actually, we were just talking to Mr. Dominguez over there and he recommended that I introduce myself." Issa quickly summarized that discussion and why he and Zurie were there, taking it as a good sign that Max hadn't immediately dismissed them and appeared to be listening, arms crossed.

"I think I get it. Yeah, sure, I'd be willing to give you a shot if Dominguez thinks you've got what it takes. You'd have to pass a couple tests, but they're not that hard."

"And our other reason?" Zurie pressed.

"You're outta luck. You've already been told as much as the press and that's all the info we're giving to the public until this is done. I'll confirm for you that there *is* a plan and it's pretty airtight as far as I can tell."

"You're sure you can't tell us anything else? Anything at all?" Zurie kept pushing and Issa got the impression that she had given that one a little something extra.

"I can tell you that the two of you match the description of a couple of kids that were asking questions in the warehouse district last week and that I don't plan on letting you leave until you answer a few questions of *mine*."

It took every ounce of discipline Issa possessed not to betray any sign of the sudden surge of adrenaline that flooded his system.

"Sorry to say, Mr. Moreno, but I think you have us mistaken for someone else. I can see you're busy though, so we'll get out of your hair."

"There's no reason to waste any more of your time on this, right?" Zurie added, maintaining eye contact with Max the entire time.

"That's quite enough of that, milady." a new voice said from behind them as a hand rested on Issa's shoulder and Zurie's head, "I fear your gifts, while impressive, shall avail you not."

A Contractor? Are you kidding? Since when? Issa's mind raced as he did his best to look politely confused.

"Why don't the two of you come with me?" Max

said as he looked over the top of his sunglasses, black eyes fixed on Issa, "Let's go for a ride. No sense in causing a scene, right?"

"If we go with you, you'll listen to what we have to say?"

"That's kind of the point of asking questions, isn't it? Let's go, Kasimir." Max replied as he turned Issa and Zurie around and ushered them towards the door, earning a bark of laughter from the presumed Contractor, who was revealed to be a man only slightly shorter than Max and nearly as broad with auburn hair pulled into a low ponytail and an eyepatch covering his right eye, his left being green. In spite of the situation, he gave the impression of being good-natured, even stopping to hold the door with a genuine-looking smile.

"This way please. Transportation and polite conversation await you. It would be in your best interests to partake, I assure you."

He's got us. Issa thought as he felt Zurie's hand tighten around his. *If Zurie's Suggestion doesn't work, there's no way out of this without having security all over us. We've got no choice but to do what they want for now.*

They entered the back of the van that was waiting, along with Kasimir, as Max took the driver's seat and began their trip.

"Well now," Kasimir clapped his hands, "where should we begin?"

C-O-N-T-R-A-C-T

Rao Lassare was experiencing conflicting feelings regarding his current situation. The group had agreed that while Issa and Zurie tried to get information from the Moreno Group, Vemris, Elsi and himself would work on narrowing down their list of possible hidey holes for Jensen and Shiku.

It was a good idea and it gave Rao something to do. So far so good.

Having no better place to start, they began at the top of the list and decided to work their way through the next-closest locations. The first few didn't teach them anything new but almost as soon as they had arrived at the most recent one, a shipyard, Vemris' demeanor took a sharp turn into serious territory and he said he could feel some residual energy that seemed to belong to Jensen.

Progress. Also typically considered a good thing.

It was around this time that Rao started to get excited. He had found himself almost *hoping* that they would find either Jensen or Shiku so that he could make up for his last two failures when it came to defending Elsi. He had done alright during his fight with Shiku right up until the end, but there was still no excuse for getting blindsided on their date like that. He wanted to prove himself.

That was the main source of his internal conflict: Rao was hoping for his group to run into a dangerous situation so he would have a chance to help get them out of it. He knew this was an immature, irresponsible line of thinking, but his bruised ego demanded that he do something to heal it.

After all, what was Vemris' training for if not situations like this one?

Then the other shoe dropped and Rao very nearly had to scrape his jaw off the ground.

Right in front of them, sitting on an overturned bucket of some sort without a care in the world, was Jensen Kuro. He didn't even look surprised, as though he had been *waiting* for them or, more specifically, for Vemris.

"Hello." he raised a hand in a half-wave, seeming almost relieved, "I was wondering if I'd left enough of a trail; I didn't want to risk someone else finding me first."

"It was sufficient." Vemris inclined his head, seeming equally unsurprised.

"Wait," Elsi looked from one man to the other, "are you saying you *knew* we were walking into a trap? Because that's what it sounds like."

"This isn't a trap." Vemris shook his head, his gaze not leaving Jensen, who still sat on his bucket, "He genuinely wanted to talk, though I can't fathom why."

"You are aware of *his* plans for this Friday?" Jensen queried.

"Not in detail, but yes."

"I'm hoping you'll stop me."

"What?" Rao was having a difficult time processing what was happening, "I knew you were crazy, but why would you *want* us to stop you? It's your plan, isn't it?"

"No, it's *his*." Jensen tapped the side of his head with a finger, "I honestly want no part of it, but it's long since passed the point where I can overpower him completely. To that end, we made a deal: I stop fighting him and he keeps his slaughtering to a minimum during this…publicity stunt."

"You can't stop this alternate personality of yours from doing whatever he wants, so you're trying to reign him in instead by voluntarily letting him have control?" Elsi sounded skeptical, "I'm not an expert in psychology, but that sounds like a slippery slope that ends with you losing control altogether."

"That's exactly why, isn't it?" Vemris' fists clenched at his sides, "You're trying to end this before it gets to that point."

"As I said: I'm hoping you'll stop me, though I doubt it, unfortunately. You had a difficult time keeping up while I was still holding him back, so without that…"

"I won't have to worry about Rao getting caught in the crossfire this time." Vemris shot his Signer a look over his shoulder, "Will I?"

As much as Rao wanted to tell him to shove it and that he would be behind him all the way, he knew he was a liability in a fight between Contractors. He sighed and forced himself to shake his head.

"No. I'll take Elsi and get out of here."

"I can tell you where Shiku is, if you want." Jensen offered, "If you're anything like I remember, you'll have a hard time sitting still while Vemris does all the fighting."

Rao's immediate instinct was to say yes before Vemris could stop him, but then something struck him about the *way* he had said it.

"What do you mean, 'anything like you remember?' The only time we've met was last week and we didn't exactly have time to get to know each other. You're talking about where you're originally from, aren't you? You and Vemris?"

"That's right, though I'm afraid I don't have time to tell you any stories at the moment." Jensen said as he rested his hands on his knees and stood up.

"Go ahead and deal with Shiku." Vemris said, much to Rao's surprise, "You and Elsi together should be more than capable. Besides," he shot Rao a smirk as he began rolling up his sleeves, "he's absolutely correct about you."

"Follow the docks until you reach that ship with the blue stripe, then enter the building across from it. He'll be there." Jensen pointed.

"Come on." Rao grabbed Elsi's hand and tugged her along, since she seemed to be struggling to decide between her own safety and watching the two Contractors fight, "Let's go pull our weight."

"Right."

C-O-N-T-R-A-C-T

"ANYONE WHO'S HERE, GET THE HELL OUT OR SUFFER SERIOUS PAIN!" Max's voice boomed through the concrete walls of the old parking structure. After a few moments of no response, he gave a satisfied grunt and turned his attention back to Issa, "Present company excepted, of course."

"You heard our explanation on the way here, so you should know we're on your side, or at least not against you." Issa put his hands in his pockets to hide the involuntary twitching of his fingers, "I'm sure you don't take kindly to us sticking our noses in your business, but we've got as much reason to want to stop these guys as you do."

"I won't argue that." Max conceded, "You helped me confirm a couple of suspicions I had about our current most-wanted and you haven't done any actual damage as far as I can tell, which is the only reason you're still conscious."

"We have something you want, in other words." Zurie snarled.

"That's right:" Max nodded, pointing at Zurie, "You."

"...What?"

"It's actually really simple: I'm after a numbers advantage. You've confirmed for me that the killer, or at least the man *behind* the killer, is a Contractor. I might be relatively new to all this, but I do know that the best way to beat a Contractor is with another Contractor. Stands to reason two would be better than one, yeah?"

"Sounds to me like you don't have a lot of faith in your partner." Issa scoffed.

"It's more that I'm going to do whatever I can to strengthen my position relative to my dad's. He's got a Contractor of his own, see, but if I had two under my control then I could take advantage of all the chaos the killer causes to corner *him* after we take the psycho down."

"The reason for all this is *daddy issues?*" Issa could hardly believe what he was hearing, "You do realize that people could die? *Have already* died? And you're more concerned about one-upping your old man then actually dealing with the situation!"

"They're roughly equal to me, actually." Max motioned with one massive hand, "Can't have some guy off the street stealing my win, can I? Anyway," he clapped his hands once and rubbed them together, "details: You'll be spending some time with a few select members of the security team, who will have orders to shoot you if you or your Contractor try to escape. She, meanwhile, will be doing exactly as I say until this is all over and done with. After that, I'll have what I want and you'll be free to go."

"Or you could save yourself a lot of trouble and let us go *now*." Zurie put enough force into that last word that Issa felt the hairs on the back of his neck stand up and from where she was looking, it seemed to be entirely focused on Kasimir.

...Who stood there looking mildly amused.

"I was not boasting when I said that your ability would avail you not against me, milady." he explained, "There is no force in this or *any* world that can bend the will of one who possesses the Ultimate Spirit."

"An Aspect Holder?!" Zurie gasped.

"A what?" Issa asked, concerned at her reaction.

"Everyone has something they're good at, right? Some part of them that just...shines a little bit brighter? That's truer for some people than others, sometimes to the point where that aspect outshines *everyone* else. If they can learn to harness it, they can display abilities beyond what's ordinarily possible, even for a Contractor."

"Not good, in other words."

"No, definitely not."

"You done with your tricks?" Max smirked, "Ready to come along quietly?"

"I'll admit you've got us in a pretty tight spot," Issa took a deep, slow breath, trying to visualize his body the way Vemris had taught him, "but there's one option you've overlooked."

"What's that?"

Wham

With a speed that Max had clearly not anticipated, Issa crossed the distance between them and delivered a chi-infused uppercut directly into the large man's abdomen, digging upwards into his ribcage.

"We use force and *make* you let us go."

Issa felt the muscle around his fist spasm and for a moment he thought that he had succeeded in knocking the wind out of Max like he had intended, until he realized that his opponent was chuckling.

"That's not a bad punch. Lemme show you a good one."

WHAM

Issa felt as though he had been hit in the gut with a sledgehammer. The world around him split in two and there was the sensation of motion and gravity before his back collided with a concrete pillar and he bounced off, coming to rest on all fours as his body simultaneously tried to cough and gasp for air.

One punch. That was all from just one punch! If I hadn't been able to react in time to focus my chi into my gut, there's no telling what kind of damage that might've done!

Issa forced himself to exhale slightly and then took a series of shallow breaths to get his wind back, looking up at a grinning Max.

"You're tougher than you look; I can't remember the last time someone got back up after a punch like that. What do you say we revisit that job offer?"

"I'm gonna need a little more convincing." Issa spat as he rose to his feet and raised his guard.

Focus on what I know: He's strong and tough, but the fact that I can react tells me that I'm still faster.

"Zurie, I can hold him off. Can you handle Kasimir?"

"No need for that, young man: I'm quite content where I am." Kasimir waved from where he was leaning against a nearby wall, arms crossed with a frustrated-looking Zurie standing a few feet away from him, "As long as she does not interfere, neither shall I. Let this battle be between our Signers, yes? Besides, I'd sooner not harm a lady."

"If I get injured, they can't use me for their plan." Zurie gritted her teeth, "As much as I hate to admit it, if my Suggestion doesn't work then I don't have much of a chance against an Aspect Holder, at least not without knowing how his abilities work."

"Which works out quite well for me, I must say!" Kasimir laughed.

"…Right." Issa cracked his neck as he processed the new circumstances, "Guess it's up to me then."

"He doesn't use chi!" Zurie called as Issa prepared to close with Max again.

So that monstrous strength is all him? Talk about unfair. At least that means I don't need to worry about him getting any stronger!

Issa dashed forwards, focusing his chi into his fists and his left foot.

I need to hit harder, but I don't have enough chi to keep up my defense and offense at the same time. That means I can't get hit again!

As he predicted, Max swung his fist to intercept Issa before he could get within striking distance, whereupon Issa kicked the ground with his left foot and dodged at a higher speed than Max had yet seen, causing him to miss and leave his side open.

"HAH!!!" Issa slammed his fists into Max's ribs simultaneously, one high and one low before leaping away to avoid a retaliatory backhand.

"Better. Keep that up and this could be fun." Max idly patted the spot where Issa had struck him, "You'll have to hit a bit deeper if you're looking to do any real damage though."

That's not good. The only way I can hit any harder than that is by focusing all of my chi into just one of my fists, which won't leave me anything to dodge or guard with. Body shots aren't cutting it either; I need to go for his head.

Issa tightened his focus as much as he could, willing for his body to respond to him, to give him just a little bit more.

If I lose here, there's no way that Rao and Elsi won't come looking for me, dragging Vemris along for the ride. If Zurie's compelled to obey Max, then there's no way all of them get away safely. If the only way to keep them from getting hurt is by getting hurt myself, well...

...I've made that sacrifice once before.

Issa charged forwards, prepared for whatever Max had in store for him as long as he could land a single hit with his full strength behind it.

Zurie had strengthened his body.

Vemris had sharpened his skills.

Rao and Elsi had reinforced his resolve.

All that could not, *would* not be for nothing.

"RAAAH!!!"

POW

Issa's fist connected with the side of Max's head in a massive hook that snapped his neck to the side, a look of shock on his face as he—

Issa couldn't see what happened after that because

of the large hand that gripped his head and hoisted him off of the ground as though he were a doll.

"Whatever you did to take that hit before, you're gonna wanna do it for your head."

This was all the warning Issa received before his skull collided violently with a concrete support pillar, a loud crack echoing through the air as a ringing filled his ears and his vision was filled with bright lights and swimming stars.

Was he still in the air? Was he on the ground? He was floating and clinging onto consciousness thanks to the hasty reinforcement he had been able to give his head, but the rest of his body felt like lead.

He couldn't hear.

He couldn't see.

He couldn't feel anything but a throbbing ache, like the worst headache he had ever had pulsing throughout his entire body.

"Issa!"

"Zurrr..." he slurred, recognizing the voice.

Hands. There were hands on his head, but they were small and cool to the touch. His vision was slowly returning, but all he could see were blotches of white, red and pale skin.

There was the feeling of breath on his neck.

"Take..." he struggled to speak, "Take what...you need."

"No." she whispered in his ear, "This time it's your turn."

Issa's foggy mind could only wonder at Zurie's words as he felt her fangs pierce his neck and warmth began to flood through his body.

CHAPTER FIFTEEN
GHOUL AND GHOST

I was never a very successful Contractor. I didn't get that many Contract opportunities and the ones I *did* get tended not to go very well. I tried to stay positive, but after a while I couldn't help feeling a little depressed.

It's kind of embarrassing to admit, but for someone with an ability like mine, I'm not that strong of a person. You've got me beat when it comes to inner strength, hands down. Hell, you've probably got most people beat when it comes to that.

...Maybe that's part of what caught my attention?

It was an accident; did you know that? I wasn't going to be in active rotation again for another few days, so I was just killing time doing some people-watching. Flipping through proverbial channels on the interdimensional TV set, seeing what was on. Maybe I'd get an idea where to drop a lure or two, but I probably wouldn't.

When your numbers aren't that good, you can't just use resources like that whenever you want; you've got a limit and I'd just about hit mine, meaning that if I wasn't careful about where I dropped my Contracts, all I'd have to choose from would be other people's rejected ones.

Honestly, I still don't know why I decided to give one to you. You were just another face that I happened to see. Just another "oh, look, another dud, time to move on."

But I didn't. Maybe it was something about you? Maybe it was my instincts speaking to me? Maybe I was just so completely *done* with everything that I couldn't see the point?

So I spent the day watching you. I saw how you went about your life, not excelling but not failing. Not smiling but not complaining. A couple friends but not many. Some worries, but none that were too big. You were...content. There wasn't anything especially that you wanted, at least from what I could tell.

It made me wonder, in some small, cruel corner of my mind, just what would happen if something were to interrupt your routine of adequacy? If you were given the chance to have anything you wanted, how much would it change you? How easily would you throw away the life you had, not knowing how good it was?

How little would it take for you to give up the thing that I wanted the most?

Then I gave you one. I put it somewhere I knew only you would find it and presented it in a way that I thought would pique your curiosity. I watched as you tried to decide whether or not it was real and nearly threw it away. I had to intervene a little when that happened; it would've been a boring way for it to end.

Your will was stronger than I expected. If you hadn't been so on-the-fence about it, then I probably wouldn't have been able to stop you from getting rid of it from so far away. As it was, it took a considerable amount of my own energy just to do that much.

I saw when you decided to give it a try and I thought "here it is; here's the moment," but then you did something I'd never seen anyone do after coming that far:

You couldn't think of anything you wanted. Nothing. No "I want to be rich" or "I want power" or "I want that girl to like me." Nothing. You tried too. I know you tried, but you were just smart enough and just cautious enough that you saw the whole picture and tried to weigh any potential gain against what it was likely to cost you.

At that point I nearly gave up. The only chance I had with someone like you, with a life like yours, was that you would be dumb or impulsive enough to just fill the Contract out and not think about the consequences.

…I didn't plan on what happened next. For what it's worth, I *am* sorry. When I used the last bit of spare strength I had to make you take the Contract with you on your walk, I didn't realize how it would end.

You died, Issa. Or at least, you were going to. Getting your blood all over that Contract gave me just enough of a loophole that I could cross over into your world and save you. It worked out that there was plenty of spare blood nearby for me to replenish my energy beforehand.

There was one thing that you never thought to ask, whether that was because you were out of it or because you didn't realize how bad your injuries were, it just didn't occur to you:

How do you think I healed you? And, not to belittle your efforts, but why do you think your physical training has been progressing so quickly? The reason that you're almost never sore no matter what I put you through?

It's the same answer for all three. It's the same reason why I can't teach you like Vemris does: All of my power comes from my blood, so the only thing I could do was put some of it into you.

It wasn't enough to turn you, obviously, though that initial dose *was* pretty substantial. It had to be in order to let you heal quickly enough that you wouldn't just bleed out.

During the time I've spent getting to know you, combined with the intuitive understanding I've gotten from your blood, I've started to get a vague sort of idea about what your Desire might've been. What it might *still* be. That, among other reasons, was why I took your training routine beyond what it needed to be just to keep you producing blood at a decent rate.

Ever since we started getting serious about it, I've been putting small amounts of my blood, no more than a drop or two, into your food. By itself, that amount doesn't do much, but taken over an extended period of time it's allowed you to start recovering more quickly, which lets you train harder and get stronger more quickly, which lets your body handle more, etc. etc.

Eventually, you'd be strong enough that you'd be able to make a choice. We aren't there yet, not even close, but you need my power *now* in order to stay on the path to fulfilling your Desire. That's why I'm taking the risk of giving you the same size dose I gave you on that first night.

I...honestly don't know what's going to happen. There are a bunch of ways this might go and only one of them is what we need right now. That's why I'm telling you all this. You'll absorb my thoughts and feelings along with my blood.

You deserve to know. After all this, with how this might turn out, you at least deserve to know the truth. If we make it out of this and you don't want me around anymore...I'll understand.

...I'm sorry.

C-O-N-T-R-A-C-T

My head hurts.

This was the first clear thought that crossed Issa's mind as he felt the heat spread throughout his body, spiking for a moment wherever he felt pain. When the sensation passed, the pain was gone.

The air smelled different. Clearer? Sharper? It was hard to tell with the thoughts that weren't his rushing through his head like a cassette tape on fast-forward.

The concrete felt ultra-defined against his skin as he propped himself up with his hands, every crack, pore and imperfection standing out in high-relief.

He could hear the small intake of breath close

behind him as he stood, feeling as though his body had become strangely light.

He opened his eyes slowly and saw Max staring at him curiously, sunglasses having been broken by Issa's last attack. He had wondered how he could see with them in such dim lighting, but it wasn't as dim as he remembered.

"Issa?"

He turned slightly to see Zurie giving him an anxious look. Her eyes widened as he looked at her, seeing her in a new light as his mind worked on processing the new information she had given it.

"Hey." his mouth felt strange as it formed the simple word.

"How do you feel?"

Issa considered that for a moment as he raised a hand to his neck where it felt a little stiff and cracked it experimentally.

"Better, I think. Strange, but better."

"You probably have questions."

"None that can't wait until after we're home."

"But I—"

"What? Were you planning on going somewhere?"

She blinked rapidly before shaking her head.

"No problems then." he made to turn back to Max before something stopped him, "Actually, there is one thing: Do I look any different?"

Zurie apparently found this being his one question rather amusing, if her sudden case of the giggles was anything to go by.

"A bit." she managed to respond, "Your hair is a bit lighter, your teeth are a bit sharper and our eyes match."

"Is it permanent?"

"No. I made you into a ghoul temporarily. It'll last until you've burned through the blood I gave you."

"So what you're saying is I just need to keep beating on him until he stays down." Max cut in, "Works for me; I could use the exercise."

Issa turned back to his opponent and started rolling up his sleeves.

"This isn't going to be the same as before. I guess it'd be too much to ask you to let us go?"

"Not happening." Max said as he removed his jacket, tossing it to Kasimir, "I'm not about to turn down the first decent fight I've had in forever. Besides: you broke my shades."

The two began to close the distance and Issa tried to gauge the best approach.

Should I risk hitting him full-force when I don't know what this body's capable of? He's not trying to kill me, after all.

No, I can't think like that. I have no way of knowing how long this'll last, so I can't afford to take any longer than necessary. Besides, if anyone can take it, it's this guy!

Issa shot towards Max with a sudden burst of speed and buried his fist in his opponent's midsection, launching the surprised man away from him. Max leaned forward as his boots caught the ground and he skidded to a stop, preventing himself from falling over.

"Hoo…" Max rested a hand over the spot where Issa had struck him, "Wasn't expecting that nice of a punch. Keep 'em coming."

"Stop trying to talk big; I know that hurt you." Issa

decided to try one last time, "Give it up and I won't have any reason to keep fighting you."

"You've got it backwards." the grinning man said, "Even if you don't have a reason to fight, I *do!*"

He charged at the ghoul, swinging a massive fist that smashed against Issa's guard with incredible force, causing him to feel a snapping sensation coming from his forearm followed by a wave of heat and pain. He snarled and swiped at his opponent's ribs, only for Max to backstep away.

"Huh. That broke a bit easier than I thought. Maybe I should dial it back a bit?" he taunted.

"Maybe," Issa held up his arm as the sensation of heat flowed through it so that Max could see the bone resetting itself, "but it's like you said: the trick is getting me to stay down and unlike me, your injuries stick around."

It doesn't lessen the pain any, but I can get used to that. As long as I keep pouring it on, he has to go down eventually.

Issa closed the gap and sent a flurry of strikes into Max's torso, only for him to be interrupted by a left hook to the head that sent him to the floor, where he had to roll to avoid a follow-up.

Even with my increased strength, anything less than full power doesn't even make him flinch! Looks like I have to play his game after all.

Issa sprang at Max and punched him in the head, earning him a counter that cracked his ribs. He slammed an uppercut into his gut, only to receive a retaliatory strike to the chest. The exchanges went on, over and over as Issa felt himself slipping into a haze of pain that threatened to render him unconscious as his body was repeatedly broken, remade and broken again.

Head. Chest. Ribs. Shoulder. Head. Head. Gut. Ribs. Chest.

He forced himself to focus on his next target, saying them in his head as a way to keep himself going. Eventually he lost the ability to guard himself effectively and started taking more and more direct hits, focusing only on landing as many of his own as he could. The impacts formed a rhythm that he and his opponent both found themselves slipping into.

One. Two. One. Two. One. Two. One. Two. One. Two. One. Two. One. Two. One. Two. One. Two. One. Two. One. One. Two. One. One. Two. One. One—

What?

Issa noticed when the rhythm changed and suddenly he was landing two blows for each one of Max's. He hadn't let up on his power, though it had been a while since he was coherent enough to use any of his chi. In fact, ever since he had gotten back up, it had felt like he couldn't access it anymore. As if the power thrumming through his blood was blocking it somehow.

He really is an incredible guy. How many times have I hit him and he's still standing? Still fighting back? How long has it even been? A few minutes? A few hours? I can't have that much of Zurie's blood left, can I? My arms are starting to feel heavy...

He needed to end it.

They needed to leave.

Thud

Then the rhythm stopped as Max fell to one knee,

his boot having slipped on the wet concrete just as Issa was sending a hook at his body that was now on a collision-course with his temple.

No!

"…Why'd you stop?" Max said past his swollen mouth as flecks of blood and spit dribbled down his chin.

"Do you give?"

"What?"

"If I kept going, that would've been a really bad hit. If you give up right now and swear that you won't follow us, we can both walk away from this and forget it ever happened. If you refuse…then one of us isn't leaving here the same as he was when he got here."

"…You're serious." Max stared at him, "What's stopping me from promising to leave you alone and then sending more guys after you?"

"You could've had a bunch of guys on us back at your company, but instead you brought us here to talk to us alone. You could've knocked me out and taken me hostage as soon as we got here, but instead you took the time to explain yourself and try to get me to come along willingly. You could've killed me during the first part of our fight if you wanted to after it became clear that I didn't want anything to do with you, but you didn't. In fact, you warned me about a bad hit. Why do that?"

Max didn't respond, prompting Issa to continue.

"I think you've got your own way of doing things. Whether that's because of some code, a sense of honor, part of your Contract or whatever else doesn't really matter. If that's not good enough for you, then think of it as me making things square between us for your warning earlier."

"You're an idiot."

"Probably. Now I'm asking one last time: Do you give?" Issa cocked his arm back, prepared for whatever decision Max might make.

"Okay. Fine."

"Say it."

"You win. I give up and I won't come after you or send anyone else after you."

"Or Zurie."

"Or her."

The two Signers regarded each other for a moment before Issa nodded.

"Alright. That's good enough for me. Zurie, let's get out of here."

"Are you sure you wouldn't like a ride?" Kasimir offered as he walked over to Max and pulled him to his feet, "Even if it's just back to the company building?"

He gave an amused chuckle at Issa and Max's incredulous looks.

"Your quarrel with my Signer is ended and he has promised peace. What rule is there that says we cannot be civil with one another? Yesterday's enemy is today's friend, after all!"

"It's not yesterday yet." Max grumbled as beeping emanated from the jacket slung over Kasimir's shoulder, "What the hell?"

He fished out a pager and looked at it, scratching his head in exasperation.

"Can either of you read this thing? I don't have my reference sheet."

"I use them sometimes for work, so maybe." Issa replied.

"Do it and we'll give you a ride to wherever." he tossed the device over.

310176 90173-060

"It says 'Fiona gone-Dad.'" Issa translated as he gave the pager back.

"How the fuck would I know where she went? Fucking senile old—" Max griped as he pulled his jacket back on, grimacing with discomfort from the multitude of bruises appearing on his body, "Just get in the damn van, I don't care anymore."

C-O-N-T-R-A-C-T

Vemris Masia was being sorely tested. He had never expected a serious fight with Jensen to be easy, but he was at least familiar with how his old friend fought.

Not so the bloodthirsty ghost that had again taken his place mere moments after their fight began. Where Jensen was sharp and precise, the ghost was brutal and overpowering. Where Jensen favored discretionary usage of his power, the ghost threw it around at every opportunity, obviously not caring whether anyone else came along.

He'd most likely welcome that.

"What happened to you?!" Vemris shouted in an attempt to gain a moment to think and recover, "You were past this! You overcame the beast!"

"I resent that." Jensen's face emerged from the dust, sporting a feral grin that looked so very wrong on him, "But if it's the analogy you want to use, chaining a beast up and throwing it in a cage isn't the same as overcoming it; all you've done is give it time to get hungrier. Sooner or later, someone's going to let it out."

"Is that what happened?" Vemris pressed, "Does this have something to do with your Contract?"

"I'm getting bored." the ghost raised Jensen's left arm as his dark chi enveloped it, forming an oversized claw, "Hope you can listen and fight at the same time!"

He charged and slammed the claw into the ground where Vemris had just been, carving deep furrows into the concrete. Vemris responded by stomping his foot down, filling the furrows with ice that spiked upwards only to be avoided by the crazed Contractor.

"Shiku was crazy when Jensen found him. Proper crazy."

A claw swipe followed by a back kick that Vemris deflected with his ice gauntlets as he sent his other arm forward in a punch, extruding an icicle from his fist as he did so in an attempt to stab his target.

"'There's voices in my head making me kill these people' crazy."

The ghost leapt back to dodge the stab, prompting Vemris to fire the icicle at his head while he was in midair. He tilted his head to avoid it, but earned a cut on his cheek that only made his grin wider.

"Every now and then he'd have a moment of clarity where he'd realize what he'd done."

Vemris hastily threw up a wall of ice as his enemy kicked off of an anchored ship and shot towards him, claw extended. He broke through the wall as if it wasn't there, but it had blocked his vision for long enough that Vemris had been able to shift his position and ready a counterattack, icy palm colliding with Jensen's face, breaking his nose and sending him careening into a pile of crates.

"Meg theb stob." the ghost rose and flash-stepped away to avoid Vemris' follow-up attack, realigning his nose with a grunt and giving a quick snort to clear the blood out of it, "That's what he wanted."

He closed the gap once more and began launching a flurry of swipes and strikes, forcing Vemris back and adopting a mocking voice.

"Make them stop! I'll give you anything you want if you just take them away! Please!" he landed a heavy kick on Vemris' chest, sending him crashing into a storage container with a loud clang.

"He actually said that. 'I'll give you anything.' What sort of Contractor could turn down an offer like that?" the ghost stayed where he was, shaking his head in mock disbelief as Vemris regained his air, "Of course, Jensen always had a fairly literal mindset when it comes to these sorts of things. Shiku asked him to 'take them away' so that's exactly what he did. Took the crazy straight out of his head and popped it into his own! Talk about rattling the cage!" he cackled.

"That's it then." Vemris said, "Jensen's mind became unstable enough that you could influence him again and you've been using Shiku to bring you victims ever since, else you'll take his soul. Does that sound about right?"

"I was always going to take it eventually, once I'd had my fun. Speaking of which, I think it's about time you started giving it all you've got. Unless you want me to kill you, of course."

"Last I checked we were fairly evenly matched. You won't overwhelm me so easily with such low-level flash steps."

"Yes, that was never my best technique." the ghost admitted, "I don't have the right mentality for it, you see. I much prefer slashing and smashing my target into hamburger! To that end…"

He raised Jensen's right arm, fingers spread as a ball of dark energy coalesced in his palm, seeming to grow denser darker until it was nearly pitch black, at which point he gripped it tightly. The energy was forced through the opening in his fist, lengthening and reshaping itself until it resolved into a single-edged sword forged from a dark gray material with a black blade and a hollow, diamond-shaped guard.

"…I think it's about time to reintroduce you to *this* old friend!"

Vemris' eyes widened in shock as he saw the once-familiar blade. He knew that Jensen had always been a swordsman. It stood to reason that he would be more powerful with an appropriate weapon, but there was one thing that he simply couldn't comprehend.

"How do you have that?!" he demanded, "We don't retain any of our possessions when we die and neither you nor Jensen ever had the ability to form solid objects out of nothing! The most you could do was form that claw!"

"Jensen told you, didn't he? He's not fighting anymore! I've got full access to my power and I was always better at manipulating energy than he was. I'll say it again, Masia: You need to quit messing around and show me the real deal!"

"I suppose you're right." Vemris sighed, "It's too

bad really: The look of this place is about to change."

The air around Vemris froze as, for the first time in a long time, he felt the familiar prickling sensation at the back of his skull and the itching in the tips of his ears. His mind felt clear, as though it had been stuffed with cotton that muffled his thoughts. He moved his chi as easily as his fingers, marveling at how anyone could ever live their lives in such a hindering state.

It was such a pitiable thing, he thought to himself as he raised a hand to the side of his head, tracing his pointed ears and one of the horns that grew from the back of his head, running along the sides like a crown.

He was about to attract a lot of attention.

He would need to run away quickly once the battle was over.

He would need to ensure that nobody had any idea what had caused the scene he was about to create.

Yet, in spite of all this, he couldn't deny that it was good to be back.

"That's it. That's the look." the ghost had twisted Jensen's face into a demonic mask of violence, "Those eyes of yours; they're the reason."

"The reason for what, pray tell?" Vemris asked as a coating of ice rapidly expanded along the ground in all directions, sharp icicles emerging randomly, all pointed away from him.

"The reason why, out of everyone I've fought," the ghost shot forward at full speed, heedless of the danger before him, "you're one of the ones I wanted to kill the most!"

THOOM

The ground between the two fighters exploded with a noise like a thunderclap, sending them flying in opposite directions amidst chunks of concrete and shards of ice. Vemris caught himself with the aid of his ice and a nearby shipping crate, scanning the cloud of dust for what might have caused the sudden impact.

"I found you before it was over this time." a low female voice spoke from the center of the crater as a tall figure rose up and slowly began to climb out, "That's good."

As the dust settled, Vemris saw that it was indeed a woman, but not one he recognized. She was dressed in a loose-fitting black outfit with red trim on the zip-up top with a matching thin red scarf around her neck. Her pants were tucked into militaristic-looking boots and dark gloves concealed her hands.

Without a doubt however, her most striking feature was her imposing stature. It had been difficult to tell how tall she was from within the dust, but now Vemris could see that she towered over anyone he had ever met. If there had been any doubt that she was a Contractor from her looks alone, the fact that she had just caused an impact like that and stood up as though it were nothing confirmed it.

"Who are—" Vemris began before he was interrupted by an exclamation from the ghost, who was gaping at the newcomer in shock.

"How can you be here?! How can *both* of you be here?! No! NO!!!" was that *fear* on Jensen's face?

"I won't let you!" the ghost sprang towards the newcomer, intending to run her through with his sword before she could do anything else, "I WON'T LET YOU RUIN EVERYTHING AGAIN!!!"

Chapter Sixteen

Before

"This isn't right! It isn't right, it isn't right *itisn'trightitisn'tright!*" tri-clawed slashes rent the air as Shiku's attacks became wilder and more desperate, "You weren't like this before! The boy only held his own because I was down to one arm and all the girl could do was watch!"

"HA!!!" Rao took advantage of an opening to drive Shiku back with a chi-infused double-palm to the chest, "He does have a point though, Elsi: Since when were you this awesome?"

"I'm giving you a pass on that one since we're in the middle of something." Elsi replied as she slowly circled their opponent at a distance, not taking her eyes off him for an instant, "You don't think you're the only one who's been working on something, do you?"

"You only joined us for chi training that one time!"

"Can't use it; don't have the talent. I've got my own

thing going. I'd love to explain it to you later but for now just know that I can see every little thing this guy does and the longer we draw this out, the better I'll get at reading him." she sent Rao a telling wink.

She's bluffing. Whatever her ability is, she hasn't had a lot of time to train it. Odds are her time limit is her biggest weakness right now. She's playing it cool to try and psych Shiku out so he does something reckless and gives us an opening. He's crazy as it is, so that's a gamble, but I'll admit I'd be having a hard time without her help.

It was true: While Elsi had done little in the way of direct fighting apart from throwing the occasional piece of debris to keep Shiku from focusing entirely on Rao, she had spotted several key moments that had led to him avoiding some particularly nasty attacks. It was almost as though she could tell what he and Shiku were going to do before they did it.

Oh well. If that's the plan, we may as well go all-in with it.

"If you'd rather wait a bit, I'd be fine with that." Rao taunted, "I'm sure Vemris will be finishing things up pretty quickly, then you can deal with him instead of us. You remember how that went last time, don't you?"

"AAAAHHHHH!!!" Shiku charged at Rao and attempted to carve out his windpipe, which earned him a shot to the liver. Rao would've liked to follow up, but Shiku lashed out with his other claw, forcing a retreat.

That armor's as much of a pain in the ass as ever and I can't tell how much damage I'm doing because of his mask! Then there's those claws...

It wasn't that Rao's usage of chi didn't afford him defensive benefits in addition to offensive ones, but that the effectiveness of these benefits was drastically reduced against anything that wasn't blunt-force or chi-related. He simply wasn't skilled or powerful enough to resist piercing or cutting.

In other words, without using any chi himself, Shiku was able to effectively resist Rao's offense and overcome his defense. To say that Rao found this irritating would be an understatement.

"Use your super strength or whatever and break his damn arm!"

"Not how it works!" Rao responded to Elsi's advice as he closed with Shiku for another exchange, "And he's flailing around too much for me to get a clean hit in!"

"So get a dirty hit in!"

"He's wearing a codpiece!"

"Not what I meant!"

THOOM

The combatants were shocked into stillness as the air in the building vibrated from the intensity of whatever had caused the thunderous noise.

Crunch

"AAUGH!!!"

All except for Elsi, who had taken immediate advantage of the distraction to dash behind Shiku, grab his left arm and wrench backwards while driving her opposite elbow into his shoulder joint. The one Vemris had previously dislocated.

"Rao!"

No further instructions were needed. Rao seized Shiku's right wrist, yanked, pivoted and drove his chi-infused palm into the murderer's taut elbow, breaking it and sending Shiku to the floor, writhing in pain.

"Grab his legs!" Elsi ordered, "I'll find something to tie him up with! *Do not* let him go!"

Rao seized an ankle in each hand and did his best to keep Shiku's legs extended and spread apart so he couldn't kick him or otherwise cause trouble.

"What do you think that noise was?"

"Lucky." Elsi responded as she continued her search, "Whatever it was, it probably came from that pair of wish-granting supermen."

"You can call them 'Contractors,' you know."

"I just won us this fight; I'll call 'em whatever I want!"

Elsi found a length of cable that they wrapped repeatedly around Shiku's legs until they ran out, at which point they tried to tie a knot but mostly failed, deciding they would just have to keep an eye on him.

"Is it weird that I kinda feel bad about this?"

"He was trying to kill us, Rao."

"I know, I know. It just seems a bit…brutal."

"I'm not saying I like it either, but we did what we had to. Be grateful that we didn't have to break his legs too." Elsi replied as she knelt down next to Shiku and began fiddling with his armor.

"What are you doing?"

"I'm taking his stuff. Or are you saying we should leave the dangerous madman armed and armored?"

"I guess not. Leave his mask on though; he might try to bite you."

"No point." Shiku murmured.

"What's that?" Elsi raised an eyebrow as she divested his ruined arms of his claws, "Have you decided to behave yourself?"

"My...Contract. I have to give him whatever he wants. He wants victims. If I can't give him victims, then he'll kill me instead. Whether you leave me here or take me to prison, it doesn't matter. He'll still get me."

"Not after Vemris kicks his ass." Rao pointed out.

Shiku remained silent.

C-O-N-T-R-A-C-T

Clang

The ghost's desperate lunge had driven his sword straight towards the tall stranger's midriff, only for it to be stopped dead with the accompanying ring of metal on metal. The tall woman remained expressionless as Jensen's face contorted into a myriad of expressions that Vemris had never seen it make before as he threw his full weight into his sword, determined to pierce the newcomer.

Some manner of armor? It would have to be exceptional to repel an attack like that so completely. Could that be the purpose of her loose clothing? To conceal it?

The stranger's left hand swept around to grip her opponent's sword by the blade. The ghost attempted to pull it away, but her grip prevented all movement. Her dark gloves made it difficult to tell, but Vemris was positive that, even with all of the wrenching and twisting, there was no blood.

Even when he was alive, that blade was exceptional. This version is a construct composed entirely of his chi; no ordinary defense could hope to resist it. Even I, a master of chi manipulation, could not hope to duplicate this feat.

"I demand to know your identity!" Vemris shouted with as much authority as he could muster, raising an ice-covered arm for emphasis.

The newcomer turned her head and regarded him with steady, yellow eyes.

"Hello, Vemris."

"You know me?"

"I did." she replied as the ghost continued his attempts to reclaim his sword, "Do I still?"

How do I respond? Was she an ally or an enemy? The ghost seems to fear her…so I shall place my bets on that.

"As I was, so I remain." he responded, "Though it would seem some of my memories do not."

"That is good. It means I can count on your assistance." the woman gave him a small nod and returned her gaze to the ghost, "I am Fiona. I wish to have Jensen returned. Please prevent his escape."

"Escape? You think I'm going to run?" the ghost growled as the dark chi around his left arm flared up, the claw expanding as he drew it back, "Now of all times, when I've finally managed to take full control?!" he swung the claw at Fiona's head, causing her to release her grip on his sword in order to avoid the blow, "Now that I think about it, your timing couldn't be better!" he grinned madly as he charged, blade swinging wildly, "I'll kill you right here! Both of you! Then there won't be anyone left who can inspire him to fight back!"

"That might be correct…mostly." Fiona stepped into one of his slashes, catching it on her forearm with no apparent damage other than to her sleeve as she deflected it to one side, throwing the ghost off-balance long enough for her to step in and send a fist shooting towards his chest.

WHAM

The impact was louder than Vemris had anticipated and there was no doubt that if the ghost hadn't managed to guard with his left arm in time, the damage would have been significant. As it was, he was sent flying through the air and into a pile of debris.

"You aren't the same as you used to be. You're confident because of that." Fiona reached up underneath her outer layer of clothing and grasped something, "What you don't realize is that I'm not the same either. Once you do…" she withdrew her hand, producing what appeared to be a rectangular bar of metal with one side sharpened into a blade, connected to a rounded handle that looked like brass, "…you will most likely run."

As Vemris looked at her weapon, the sound of metal scraping against stone appeared unbidden in his mind. A half-remembered scene of steady footsteps and a trail of sparks.

Even as the ghost flash-stepped behind Fiona, bearing down on her with his claw, Vemris felt no inclination to intervene.

Some part of him knew that her words were no mere bluff.

Fiona sidestepped the claw of chi and retaliated with an overhand swing of her weapon that was reminiscent of how one might swing a hammer or an axe. It was far too slow to catch one as fast as Jensen, but when the blow struck the ground, its efficacy was demonstrated in brutal fashion.

KROOM

Dirt and concrete sprayed from the ground as though a bomb had gone off. Shards of ice flew from the portion that was still frozen from earlier, requiring Vemris to shield his face, only one thought present in his mind:

What insanity is this?!

The amount of raw power Fiona possessed was immense. Even so, it was within the bounds of what Vemris knew to be possible for a Contractor. He could set that aside.

The probability that such an attack would have mortally wounded Jensen if it had struck him was high. Still, it was likely that Fiona had already known that he would avoid it and had instead damaged the ground in order to keep him from capitalizing on the opening. He could set *that* aside.

What truly shocked Vemris was the complete and utter disregard for any degree of subtlety. Fiona pressed her attack with absolute abandon, inflicting incredible amounts of destruction to her surroundings that there would be absolutely *no* way of covering up. At least his ice could've been broken up and thrown into the water.

She truly doesn't care about anything beyond her current objective, does she? She's like a machine.

"Such viciousness, Fiona!" the ghost jeered, "Are you trying to kill us?"

Fiona gave the brass handle of her weapon a quarter-turn, causing it to triple in length with an audible click. She gripped the end of the elongated handle and held the weapon, now resembling a bardiche, behind her. As she approached the ghost, the blade dragged on the ground, leaving a trail of sparks and producing that same sound of metal grinding against stone.

Sparks. The grinding of metal against stone. An implacable approach that could only come from something inhuman.

"No, not now!" Vemris desperately tried to keep his attention on the matter at-hand, but just like his previous confrontation with the ghost, his mind was being overtaken by the sudden surge of memories.

Two pairs of eyes, yellow and red, stared at him. Two faces with the exact same lack of expression.

They had come to ask him another question. It had become something of a habit for them lately, whenever they couldn't find their answer in a book.

Fiona swung her polearm in a wide arc, carving a swath of destruction wherever it passed. The range of her attacks was making it difficult for the ghost to get close. He was becoming visibly frustrated; he was going to try something soon. Vemris needed to be ready!

The two were rarely seen outside of each other's company anymore. He would usually scoff at the sorts of rumors that were floating around, dismissing them as mindless gossip.

But he could see the effect the automaton was having on Jensen. Insofar as the man expressed such things, he seemed...happy.

"You aren't getting away!" Vemris lashed out with his chi, extruding a series of spear-like icicles from the ground and forcing the ghost to alter his course or be skewered. Before he could attempt another escape, Fiona was upon him once again.

Too close. Master your thoughts, Masia! What use is your vaunted mind if you cannot control it?! Demonstrate your superiority!

"My apologies!" he shouted, "You may fight without restraint, Fiona! I swear that I will not let him die!"

It only lasted a fraction of a second, but Vemris saw Fiona's gaze flicker to him, eyes widening slightly before she returned to attention to her opponent, the viciousness of her attacks redoubled.

She'll fight with all she has now; without fear of killing the one she is determined to save. The onus for that is on me and by fulfilling this responsibility, I shall even the scales between us. Even if it was not her intent, she saved me from having to take the life of an old friend. A debt such as that cannot be allowed to stand.

"Foul specter! Affliction of my friend's mind! Blight on his soul!" Vemris growled, his voice gradually rising as he channeled more and more of his energy, "In both this life and the last, you have slighted me! You have caused pain and suffering to those under my watch and now you think to avoid retribution?! You have incurred the wrath of Vemris Masia! Your defeat shall be swift and final!"

C-O-N-T-R-A-C-T

"What the fuck is going on over there?!"

"You've been saying stuff like that for the past minute and the view from back here is still really bad." Issa griped, "Maybe be a bit more specific? I don't have X-ray vision you know."

"You're some kinda vampire; I dunno *what* you have." Max retorted from the front of the van, "Someone's raising all kinds of hell over at the old dockyard. Loud noises, clouds of debris, that sort of thing."

"The dockyard? Wasn't that one of the areas that the others were going to check?" Issa looked to Zurie for confirmation.

"Yes. I've been feeling elevated amounts of Contractor energy coming from there for a bit now."

"As have I." Kasimir concurred from the driver's seat.

"What? Why didn't you say anything?!" Issa demanded.

"I'm with him! What gives?" Max added.

"Because if we said anything, you'd insist on heading straight there when there's nothing you could contribute except for a liability." Zurie said.

"Quite so. I've been taking the scenic route until now." Kasimir explained, "By this point, the battle will likely have concluded by the time we arrive. I would suggest stationing a blockade of sorts to deter any curious individuals, however."

"What do you think I'm doing?!" Max practically tore open the glove compartment and fumbled with his pager reference sheet, "I swear to god, Dominguez, if you're on a smoke break..."

Issa, meanwhile, was rather cross with Zurie.

"I could've helped! Especially now!" he tugged at his shirt, showing his unblemished skin, "Look! I'm already completely healed!"

"Fucking good for you." Max grunted.

"You feel invincible, but you're not." Zurie lowered

her voice, "Do you think I gave you my blood on a whim? You're in a very dangerous position right now, Issa, even if you don't feel like it. I didn't exactly have time to measure how much I was giving you and you've been burning through it at an incredible rate *just to keep yourself alive*. When I say you're going to crash once this wears off...it's an understatement. So do us both a favor and try to keep it going until we're not around these two anymore."

She's right. I'm doing it again. This is the same type of behavior that nearly got me killed before. I'm no good to anyone unless I get a grip.

Issa took a deep, deliberate breath and let it out in a half-sigh.

"Alright. We'll do this your way."

"Right. Good." Zurie appeared taken aback by his change of heart, "You aren't going to make a break for it once we get close or something, are you?"

"Why would I do that?"

She regarded him carefully, like she wasn't sure what to make of him.

"Something wrong?"

"No. I don't think so." she shook her head, "You're a weirdo, but that's not exactly news."

"The interdimensional wish-granting vampire says that *after* having met my friends?"

"Them I can understand. *You*, though? I'm still trying to figure you out."

C-O-N-T-R-A-C-T

This body is troublesome.

This was the thought that crossed Fiona's mind as

she continued to swing Guillotine in wide arcs, trying to drive Jensen against a wall where Vemris' ice would be more effective. A dull ache was beginning to develop in her muscles, though it was easy enough to ignore. Of greater concern was the difficulty she seemed to be having in getting enough air.

Things were simpler before.

Which before? The before that was only a matter of days ago or the before that she had begun to remember upon hearing his voice speak those words?

Everything made so much more sense now. Why she had felt drawn to this world, why sensing his energy had impacted her so heavily, why hearing his voice had sparked a chain reaction in her mind and why she had abandoned her post at Miguel Moreno's side as soon as she had sensed him again, providing only the briefest of excuses.

"'I see you.' Why did you say those words to me?"

"What?" Jensen snarled as he avoided another of her strikes and attempted to rush her, only to have his blade deflected by Guillotine's haft.

"When you planted that note on me, that was what you said. Why did you choose those words?" Fiona capitalized on his off-balance position by charging forward, pinning his body to a slab of ice with the haft of her weapon.

"What are you on about? Why does there have to be a reason?" he struggled to break free, but her strength combined with Vemris' ice hindered his efforts, "They were just words! Random and meaningless!"

"Not to me. Not to us."

"I sometimes wonder if I am real."

"Why? Because of what you are?"

"Others who are like me seem to be overlooked, as though they were invisible. When people learn my nature, it seems it becomes difficult for them to see me."

"That is unusual…"

"What are you doing?"

"Looking."

"And?"

"I see you."

"Even if you didn't realize it, there was a part of you that was trying to reach out to me." the ice began to crack, "The old you is still there, Jensen. I see you."

"RAAAGH!!!"

Kroom

Jensen had directed the chi from his left arm into the wall behind him, causing it to shatter and collapse on top of them. Fiona leapt into the debris, having expected this. He had done something similar when he had been overcome by this part of himself before.

"Why are you treating Jensen as if he has become someone else?"

"Fiona, can't you see? Whatever that thing is, it's not Jensen anymore."

"How did you determine this? By my observations, he is still very much the same person. This is just…a part of him we don't usually see."

"How can you presume to know better than us? No matter how she tries to dress you up, you're only a—"

"Ngghh…how…" Jensen twisted and wrenched, but was unable to escape Fiona's hold, "He's done something! Broken our deal! Betrayed me somehow!"

"I know you." Fiona stared down at him,

"Whichever part of you is dominant at the moment, you're still the same person. You think the same way. You're a pragmatist."

"You shouldn't constantly charge in blindly like that."

"Why not?"

"You could suffer unnecessary injuries."

"I do not feel pain."

"That just means that you won't know when you're badly hurt. You should choose your battles."

"How?"

"If you can win without significant injuries, then fight. If you can't, then run."

"...I will try."

"Don't compare him to me!" Jensen tried to kick her, but he couldn't muster enough force to do significant damage, "He's *weak!* He's a coward!"

"Why would you say that?"

"Because it's TRUE!" Jensen stopped his thrashing and glared into Fiona's eyes, "He ran away! He chose defeat! *He let us DIE!* And you know what? He did it because of *you.*"

A familiar ceiling. A familiar bed. Unfamiliar footsteps pacing the room. Her body feels sluggish. Her movements are stilted and jerky.

"Try not to move; you're badly damaged."

"Where is Jensen?"

"...He's not here."

"When will he be back?"

The reply is cut off by a violent fit of wet-sounding coughs.

"What's the matter, nothing to say?"

"Thank you for telling me."

"...What?"

"None of us knew what happened to you. The others assumed you were dead, but I insisted on proof. After a long time of searching and finding nothing, I had no choice but to accept it."

"Then what? You moved on and lived happily ever after?"

"I killed myself."

There was a change in Jensen's face then. His expression wavered between a hate-filled battle mask and shocked grief.

"You what?"

"It might be more accurate to say that I let myself die. With Mother gone, my condition was deteriorating. I saw no reason to seek further aid."

"Heh. Heheh. Hahaha*hahahaha!*" Jensen dissolved into mirthless laughter, "Hear that, you idiot?! Do you?! You wasted our death even more than I thought! Such a cruel joke! I'm almost impressed!"

"You seem to think that I died because I could not see you anymore."

"Didn't you?"

Fiona shook her head.

"I died because it was the only way I might see you again."

Jensen's laughter ceased.

"I didn't fully understand Mother's research, but the basic concept stuck in my head: Those with strong wills sometimes gave off strange readings shortly after death. These readings were similar in nature to those given off by Contractors. She hypothesized that this could be related to the 'souls' that they coveted."

"How does this relate to me?"

"Out of everyone I'd known, I doubt I could name

many with a stronger will, a stronger *soul,* than you. It seemed likely that you would have become a Contractor instead of simply 'passing on.' This only left the question of whether or not I could do the same."

"And you just...went for it?"

"It happened slowly; Mother's craftsmanship was undeniably superb. During the final week, I was only able to move my eyes and mouth. Vemris kept me company when he was able. He offered his counsel when my resolve wavered, though I was already beyond saving."

"Still with me?"

"Ye...s."

Speaking was becoming laborious. Her eyes no longer moved smoothly. Had one of them stopped working?

"Vem...ris."

"Yes?"

"Do...I...have..."

She saw him raise a hand, clasped between his own. Was that hers? She couldn't feel it.

"From an intellectual standpoint, I would have to say 'no.'" he said, *"After all, that would mean that mere humans have the ability to truly play god. Such things are reserved for...but I digress."* he gave her a self-deprecating smile, *"But when I look into your eyes now...when I take the time to see all the little things behind them...how can I not say 'yes?'"*

Fiona smiled slightly.

"I suppose I received my answer."

"Yes." Jensen's gaze softened, "I suppose you did." the corner of his mouth twitched, "I know I always said...but I could never be sure. I regretted that. Dying without knowing."

He tried to move his hand. Fiona allowed him to free it.

"I had a wager, I think. With Rao." his hand approached her slowly, "Loser gets punched in the face. Typical."

As he touched her cheek, a look of wonder passed over his face.

"You're warm." his lips quivered, "You're warm." his eyes glistened, "You're…"

Jensen couldn't speak anymore, but as Fiona pulled him to her, she didn't mind.

There would be time to talk later.

Chapter Seventeen

After

"I don't think I've seen you up here before."

"I've come here a couple times, but that was before we met. I don't do it often." Issa replied as Zurie sat next to him, legs dangling off the edge of the apartment's roof.

"What's the occasion, then?"

"Everything just...looks a little different. I felt like spending a moment taking it in."

"It's a side-effect of the transformation. You should go back to normal once it wears off. Your hair's already darkening back up a bit." she lifted a few strands, inspecting them curiously.

"That's part of it, but I think this is something that's been going on since before today. At first, it was so subtle that I didn't notice it, then there were other things I needed to be concerned with, but now that I don't have anything else to focus on...I can't ignore it anymore. I just...I don't think I can look at the world the same way anymore."

Zurie didn't say anything, but Issa felt her gaze on him.

"This whole thing started because I felt like there was more to the world than just what I could see. It used to just be a sort of hobby, you know? I'd poke around forums and watch Weird World Wednesday and I'd think 'look at that; isn't that neat?' Then all this started and it just kept getting more and more real."

"First, I met you and nearly died. Er, not in that order." he amended, "Then I found out that there were a bunch of other people involved with the Contractors, Rao being one of them. Of all people, right? And I'd never have known. I saw the guy practically every day. We hung out. I never suspected a thing."

"Not like I blame him or anything, but if an open book like *him* can hide something like that, well…it was definitely less surprising to find out about someone like Shiku or Max; doesn't take much to figure them out. You know I still don't know what Rao's Contract is for? Never seem to get the opportunity to ask."

He was rambling. He knew he was, but for some reason once he started talking, he couldn't stop.

"Then, just as I was starting to get used to everything, we got ambitious with a school project and went straight into the fire. Missed the frying pan altogether. As soon as I understood what was going on, I knew that we were out of our depth; the best thing to do would've been to get as far away from all that as possible, like you said."

"I couldn't do that though. Not if Rao already had a

target on his back and there was no way Elsi was leaving it alone. We buckled down and did everything we could to get ready while the situation just kept spiraling out of control. Suddenly we couldn't just wait anymore; we had a *deadline*. We had a plan too. A good one even, not that it really mattered in the end. It still came down to just doing everything I could to *get there* in time to help. It was the alley and the warehouse all over again."

"You *did* help though." Zurie pointed out, "If we hadn't brought Max and Kasimir, Vemris' plan wouldn't have been possible and we'd have a lot of explaining to do. Having them involved means that a lot of this will get swept under the rug, which is much better for us in the end."

"I'm still not sure I like it." Issa said as he watched the sky change colors while the sun set behind some buildings, "I can't put my finger on it, but it seemed like they were in a hurry to get rid of us."

Not for the first time, he thought back to a mere few hours ago, trying to figure out what was making him feel so uneasy.

C-O-N-T-R-A-C-T

The van containing Issa, Zurie, Max and Kasimir ended up arriving shortly before the roadblock that Max had called for, though when he checked his pager he found a confirmation message.

"Holy shit…"

Issa was about to remind Max yet again that they didn't have a good visual from the back of the van, but as soon as the vehicle stopped and the back doors were opened, it became immediately apparent.

A large portion of the dockyard was in ruins. Walls had collapsed, crates had been demolished and large pieces of the thick concrete ground were simply *gone*, replaced with impact craters and savage-looking gashes. Sprinkle in several sizeable chunks of ice and you had most of the ingredients necessary to create a localized warzone.

"Issa, Zurie. You made it. Good." It was only once he spoke that Issa noticed Vemris and the two other apparent combatants, which were a docile-looking Jensen and a towering woman that he had never seen before. All three of them looked to be varying degrees of scuffed up, with Jensen appearing the most beaten.

"Did you win?" Issa asked warily, noting the horns and pointed ears that Vemris was now sporting.

"More or less." Vemris replied, giving Issa a once-over of his own, "You seem to have been in something of a scuffle yourself."

"We worked it out."

"Who are they?" Vemris jerked his head towards Max and Kasimir, who were approaching the tall woman as though they knew her.

"Max Moreno and his Contractor, Kasimir." Issa watched as Vemris processed this new information, giving a small nod after several seconds.

"That could work to our advantage. You have my thanks."

"Where are Rao and Elsi?" Issa followed Vemris as he made his way over to where the other four were talking.

"They went to deal with Shiku. I can't imagine them failing with the condition he's in, but I'll be checking on them shortly."

"I'll go now; point me in their direction."

"No. You should hear the plan."

"It had better be a damned *good* plan." Max crossed his arms, having overheard Vemris' last statement, "This place looks like a fucking *bomb* went off!"

"Exactly." all eyes were on the horned Contractor as he began to explain, "The story will be that Shiku's plan for attacking the Moreno Group was to infiltrate the building and plant a bomb. However, as he is not a demolitions expert, he made a mistake and it went off early, which drew Max here. Upon arrival, he heroically cornered Shiku and defeated him. You can spin the rest any way you like."

"Who in their right mind would believe all of *this* came from a bomb?" Issa protested.

"Once we've finished modifying the scene it will be more believable. I can get rid of the ice and with enough muscle we can take care of the rest quickly enough. You will help, Fiona?" he addressed the tall woman, who glanced sideways at Jensen.

"I won't leave." he said, "I'll go with Vemris to check on Rao and then I'll come right back."

"Then I will help." Fiona agreed.

"I'll go with you guys." Issa took a step in the direction that Vemris and Jensen were facing, before being stopped by a shake of Vemris' head.

"No. You need to leave. I'll be sending Rao and Elsi away as soon as I can confirm their health."

"What? No! I'm—"

"A lot of people are going to be here soon asking a lot of questions." Vemris cut him off, "When I make my escape, it will be quickly. You cannot keep up."

"We can offer transportation." Kasimir spoke up, "I am sure there will be vehicles available once the blockade arrives."

"You two can use the van we came in." Max adjusted his jacket, "I won't be leaving for a while; gotta come up with a good story. I'll send your friends home in a separate vehicle once they're back here. Call 'em on the phone later or something. Kasimir, get them to Dominguez; he should be here by now. Make nobody gets any ideas."

"As you will." Kasimir gave a grinning salute then beckoned to Issa and Zurie, "Come along now."

As badly as Issa wanted to object, he knew that he wouldn't accomplish anything by defying Vemris or Kasimir, let alone *both*. What was worse, he knew Zurie wanted to leave too.

"Fine. You win." he conceded, "But I'll want to hear more about what happened later."

"Likewise." Vemris said as he waved over his shoulder, Jensen at his side.

Kasimir had parked their van close to the scene of the battle, so instead of walking back to the dockyard's entrance, he instructed Issa and Zurie to get back in the van and he drove them to the blockade, which was now fully present. Black vehicles of various types were idling in a staggered line, men and women milling around placing cones, erecting barriers and speaking into their radios.

As they drew closer, Kasimir slowed to a stop and told them to stay where they were as he parked the van and rolled down his window.

"Hello, Mr. Dominguez. Having a pleasant

afternoon, I hope?"

"Oh, the new guy. Where's the boss?"

"Back a ways; there's a matter that requires his personal attention. I'm here to request your services as a courier of sorts."

"What's the package?"

"I believe you've met. Take them wherever they wish to go and then return here. Your discretion in this matter is appreciated."

"Sure, sure. Better than standing around here anyway."

Kasimir exited the van and the man Issa had met earlier that very day entered and peered back at him and Zurie.

"Well, hello again. Looks like you've had that interview, eh? How'd it go?" he asked as a couple of cars shifted to make an opening for the van.

"The word 'thorough' comes to mind."

Issa's response earned a laugh from Dominguez as he shifted the van into gear and got them moving.

"You're still conscious. That's something." he chatted once Issa had finished giving him directions to a convenience store that was about half a mile from his apartment, "A fair few of us weren't after the boss' Q&A session."

"That's *normal* for you guys?"

"Personal security detail is by invitation only. Even the interview has a strict NDA associated with it. Now you know why."

"I'm guessing this isn't entirely legal."

"Probably not." Dominguez chuckled, "It's not a bad job though, honestly; I meant what I said before."

"I'm guessing that you might be a bit higher up

than you led us to believe though."

"In practice, I'm something like the boss' number two. I've been around for a minute and he knows he can trust me to get things done when he can't be there himself. On paper I'm just another member of the team, though."

"Sounds like you should ask for a raise."

"Another couple days like this one and I might."

The rest of the trip was spent mostly in silence until they reached the convenience store, whereupon Dominguez let them out and bid them goodbye. Issa and Zurie waited until the van was out of sight before heading directly back to the apartment.

C-O-N-T-R-A-C-T

"I dunno." Issa sighed, "It just seemed like Vemris was in a bit *too* much of a hurry to get rid of us. Get rid of *me*, more like; he hardly looked at you, now that I think about it."

"He's probably figured out what I am, if he hadn't already. There're only so many explanations for your temporary look. He might've actually been doing us a favor by making sure as few people saw us as possible."

"You don't sound sure."

"It's also possible that he doesn't like vampires and just wanted us gone. You don't have them in this world, so it might not be obvious to you, but we tend to be unpopular a lot of the time."

"I guess it'd be naïve to think they're all like you?"

"A bit."

"Too bad."

"If I didn't know any better, I'd say you were trying to be sweet." she gave him a playful shove with her shoulder, "Come on, let's get some food in you. I need you good and replenished for tomorrow; I worked up an appetite today."

"Right, right." Issa got to his feet and started heading back in, "I think I'll have a shower first; I might want to turn in early tonight. I'll have to work in a couple of phone calls while I'm at it; Rao and Elsi are probably home by now."

C-O-N-T-R-A-C-T

"Zenith protect me from reckless fools!" Vemris cursed as he stormed out of the warehouse, nearly knocking the metallic door off its hinges in his fury, "*One* reckless fool in particular!"

He made his way to the railing overlooking the water, withdrawing a cigarette from his pocket and lighting it with a spark of chi from his fingers. It was a handy trick he had long since mastered, but hadn't used in a very long time. It seemed like repeated trips down memory lane were starting to bring back old habits. He was half-finished with his cigarette when he heard footsteps behind him.

"I didn't know you smoked." Jensen remarked as he approached, tying off a simple knot on a small cloth bag that looked to have been fashioned out of his gray hoodie, leaving him in a dark undershirt.

"You were already gone when I started."

"I see." he made to clean his sword before thinking twice and dematerializing it instead, "I suppose we have much to catch up on."

"Which would be much easier had you not just drastically limited our time."

"It was the only way."

"You breached the Contract!" Vemris shouted, the remainder of his cigarette freezing in his grasp, "As soon as someone notices, you'll be branded a rogue! You *must* know what that means! You could have renegotiated! You could have found another way to end it!"

"It might not be official, but I have another contract that I value more. I'll do what I must to honor it."

"Is it worth having a target on your back?"

"Yes." he held Vemris' gaze for a long moment before the latter gave a tired sigh and shook his head, gesturing for his friend to follow him.

"I'll get rid of the remaining ice while you deliver your package. I'm leaving as soon as I'm done and you're coming with me. Use the intervening time to explain things to Fiona."

"Where will you take me?"

"Somewhere we can talk like we used to. I'd have liked to plan ahead, but that's no longer possible."

C-O-N-T-R-A-C-T

Max cleared his throat as the elevator transported him and Fiona to his father's office. The unpleasant sting of bile stuck in his throat and he wanted a drink of water, but he wasn't going to carry around that bag any longer than he needed to.

It wasn't as though he was a stranger to grisly sights, but when the black-haired guy had walked up to him without a word, showed him what was in the bag and then handed it over, he had thrown up in his mouth a bit. People just didn't *do* that sort of thing anymore.

The fact that the plan required him to take credit for it wasn't improving his mood any either, but the knowledge that it should at least give the old bastard a good scare was helpful.

"Are you unwell?" Fiona gave him a sideways glance.

"Be lying if I said I was great."

"I am capable of handling this if you want."

"No. We'll do it like we discussed."

Fiona nodded and resumed standing at attention as the elevator doors opened into Miguel's waiting room. It was after hours, so Shirley was gone and the lights were dim, causing the windows to cast shadows onto the floor. Miguel himself would ordinarily have been gone too, but with what he thought was still coming, he was burning the midnight oil.

Briefly, Max considered postponing the plan a couple days. Let the old man stew for a bit and bite his nails as he waited for the hammer to fall, only for nothing to happen. It might be worth it to see him look like such a moron.

No. Maybe on a different day, but Max had had his fill. He opened the door without knocking.

"Maxxie!" Miguel exclaimed as he spun around, "For the love of god, *knock* first; you nearly gave me a heart attack! First you up and vanish, then I can't find Fiona anywhere, then half my security team suits up and leaves! If I wasn't so sure you had something to do with it, I'd have called the police!"

"It's a good thing you didn't. They'd have made

things…complicated."

"Oh?" Miguel squinted as Max approached his desk, getting a better look at him, "Looks like someone gave you a run for your money, boy."

"I found him." Max said plainly.

"Him? Him who?" Miguel's eyebrows rose, "Don't give me false hope, Maxxie; say it clear."

Max responded by tossing the cloth bag onto Miguel's desk, where it landed with a thud and rolled slightly.

"What's this?" Miguel asked rhetorically as he undid the knot before recoiling as the severed head of Shiku Anshin stared up at him, "Fuck, Maxxie! You ripped his damned *head* off?!"

"That was me." Fiona lied, "He was dead by the time I arrived and we would have attracted attention carrying the body."

"…Perhaps you had better start from the beginning." Miguel steepled his fingers and looked at the pair intently.

"It was luck, mostly." Max began, "I got a tip he might be around the old dockyards. Nothing concrete, but it was all I had at the time so I figured, why not? I was driving around the perimeter, looking for a reason to dig deeper when a fucking bomb went off. Blew half of Dock C's plaza to shit. Turns out the bastard was planning on blowing us up, but he didn't know what he was doing."

"Right, of course he'd be an amateur." Miguel muttered, "A professional wouldn't have made a big deal about it on the news; he'd have just done it and collected his money."

"Exactly." loathe as he was to agree with him,

Max's father was making things easier right then, "Of course, after seeing that, I headed straight over and called for a roadblock. That's where the security team went. While they were on their way, I caught up to him. *Crazy* bastard. Had claws just like the police reports said he would. If I hadn't been expecting it, he might've gotten me. Nearly did, actually."

Max showed Miguel a row of tears in his jacket that Vemris had made Jensen put there to help sell the story.

"Then you offed him?" Miguel prompted.

"Didn't want to, but he didn't leave me with much choice. It wasn't by coincidence that he was able to kill those people, dad."

"No. I guess it wouldn't be." Miguel seemed to accept this before shifting his attention to Fiona, "And where were you during all this? Did my son contact you?"

"No, Mr. Moreno." Fiona replied, "I felt the same sort of energy that I had noticed before and left immediately to maximize my chances of finding it before it disappeared again. I happened upon your son just as the would-be bomber's own Contractor did."

"So he *did* have one." Miguel nodded before doing a double-take and beginning to sputter some sort of explanation to Max before he was cut off.

"I know already, dad. Watching the two of them, it became pretty obvious they weren't normal. I made Fiona explain it to me on the way back."

"Couldn't be avoided, I suppose." Miguel looked as though he had bitten into something sour, "You fought, then? You and the other Contractor?"

"Yes, sir." Fiona confirmed, "In other circumstances, he might have gotten away, but he was unwilling to abandon his Signer. Your son's battle kept him from fleeing and allowed me to overcome him."

"Where is he, then?"

"Gone. Once his Signer was dead, there was no reason for him to remain. The Contract was nullified."

"Mercenary school of thought. If your boss dies, you aren't getting paid, so there's no reason to stick around."

"Essentially, sir."

"By that point, it was pretty much over." Max took over, "Security team showed up and secured the area, I collected the package, threw the rest in a van, gave the team their orders and got out of there before the police showed up."

"Right, this isn't the sort of story you tell to the cops." Miguel rubbed his chin, "Go get yourself cleaned up, boy. I'll cook something up by the time they come knocking."

C-O-N-T-R-A-C-T

"Here you are. If you gentlemen require anything else, please flip this switch. It will alert me and I shall come at once. You will not be bothered otherwise."

"Many thanks."

"Not at all, sir." the well-dressed waiter inclined his head as he exited the small private room, shutting the door and leaving Vemris and Jensen alone with a pair of glasses, a bucket of ice and a bottle of whiskey which Vemris wasted no time in opening, pouring a generous measure for both himself and Jensen.

"This is a fair amount." Jensen indicated the bottle.

"Depending on how much you feel like listening, I may need it."

They drank in silence for a couple minutes and Vemris recalled times when they had done this exact thing, albeit without the need for a private, soundproofed room that only a select clientele even knew about. It was the sort of place that didn't print prices on their menus.

Vemris was not overly wealthy, though Rao's family certainly paid him well for his services as the boy's tutor. Neither was he seen as such an important individual that he would have access to such a place. However, having grown up amongst the wealthy and influential, this Rao knew various tidbits of useful information.

"I should start with an apology." Vemris sighed as he set his glass down on the wooden table, "It was not my wish to separate you and Fiona so soon after you were reunited."

Jensen shrugged and took another sip of his whiskey. Vemris took this as a signal to continue.

"There is much I would discuss with you, but first and foremost we must decide how to keep you safe. The time until an Enforcer is dispatched may be measured in days or hours."

"I won't use my power." Jensen stated as though that was the entire solution, "No Contracts and no use of Contractor Energy. How would they find me?"

"That depends on who they send, which would depend on how they choose to interpret the situation. In the beginning, all the information they have will be that your Contract was terminated by means of Signer death and you failed to return. The question they must answer is whether your signer died by your hands or not. If they decide he did, then they'll send someone they believe can defeat you. If not, then they'll send someone more diplomatic to determine why you chose to linger."

"In that case, I would tell the truth, barring the fact that I took his life."

"That would create its own set of problems, though you would likely not be terminated for it. There being three of us from the same realm who all knew each other in life being summoned to this same place, then recovering our memories on top of everything else? It's unheard of. It would be bound to attract troublesome attention."

"I could always run. I doubt anyone could catch me without using Contractor Energy. At that point, I'd know exactly where they were and so would every other Contractor in the city."

"Even you can only run for so long. No, I think hiding would be your best option. Your saving grace is that you've spent the majority of your time in complete isolation; hardly anyone knows your face and even fewer know your name. You would need to lay low, possibly for a long while, but if they can't find you for long enough, they might label you as dead."

"Is there truly no chance that I could be exonerated? I'll stand trial if I must."

"I understand your reasons for doing what you did, Jensen, and I respect them." Vemris said after draining his glass and moving to refill it, "However, the fact of the matter is that Shiku was not in breach of Contract at the time. He claimed that Rao and Elsi were offerings to you, as per your Terms. Although they bested him, the fact remains that he presented them to you as victims in ostensibly the same manner that he had done up until that point. You and I both know that he was trying to save himself, but as that cannot be proven, it won't help your case. At the end of the day, *you* were in breach of Contract, not Shiku. It would take an *extraordinary* set of circumstances for you to overcome that."

"Then we should assume that I'll have to evade or deal with whichever enforcer they dispatch. Who do you think it might be?"

"It could be anyone." Vemris considered the question for a while, "If I had to come up with a shortlist, I'd say the most likely candidates would be Anderson, Walt, Dicht, Krieger or Wynn."

"I spar with Wynn."

"Are you close?"

Jensen made a noncommittal gesture with his hand.

"Take her off the list then. Honestly, my suggestion *would* be for you to escape to the other side of the world, but there's no chance of you leaving while Fiona's still here, is there?"

"Never again."

Well, that settled that. No sense in arguing with him when he had that look; not unless he was willing to knock him out and tie him up.

And there had been quite enough of that for one day.

"Well, what have you been up to since you got a

second chance at life? Apart from contracting yourself to a deranged psychopath?"

"You're sure about that?"

"Yes. Our latest update shows that Contractor Kuro's Contract has been terminated, but we have not received payment and he has exceeded the standard return deviation set by his previous Contracts."

"Hmm...my records show that he generally returns immediately. This is by no means a requirement, as you know. Do we have any evidence to suggest he has decided to form another Contract while still on-world?"

"No. His resource allotment has remained unchanged since his departure and remote usage has not been authorized for him."

"Does he have any blank Contracts still floating around?"

"Not that we can see, Ma'am."

"I see. If he returns within the allotted time, he is to be detained for questioning and released if he can clear reasonable suspicion. If he does not...send Rose and Mager to retrieve him."

"Both of them, Ma'am? Don't you think that's a little...excessive?"

"If this goes according to standard procedure, then perhaps."

"Is there some reason we should believe that it won't?"

"Possibly."

"...Ma'am?"

"I show you leniency because it amuses me, but it is not a requirement for you to understand my judgments; only to abide by them."

"As you say."

As she watched the man exit the room, the Overseer smiled to herself.

Things were about to become interesting.